5.25

# THE GINGER HORSE

Redways Preparatory School, two miles east of the little village of Wainsford, is a reasonably successful school. Although the headmaster's treatment of both staff and boys is too formal and unbending to make it an entirely happy one . . . The Head, his assistant masters, and their womenfolk live in a world of petty jealousies and gossip. But this is nothing compared to the intrigue which develops when a murder is committed in their midst . . .

J. F. STRAKER

◆

# THE GINGER HORSE

*Complete and Unabridged*

**LINFORD**
*Leicester*

First published in Great Britain

First Linford Edition
published 2008

British Library CIP Data

Straker, J. F. (John Foster)
  The ginger horse.—Large print ed.—
Linford mystery library
  1. Preparatory schools—England—Fiction
  2. Murder—Investigation—Fiction
  3. Detective and mystery stories
  4. Large type books
  I. Title
  823.9′14 [F]

ISBN 978–1–84782–448–6

Published by
F. A. Thorpe (Publishing)
Anstey, Leicestershire
Set by Words & Graphics Ltd.
Anstey, Leicestershire
Printed and bound in Great Britain by
T. J. International Ltd., Padstow, Cornwall

This book is printed on acid-free paper

# 1

## Prelude to Tragedy

'Now that that delicious repast is over,' said Colin Russell, helping himself to sugar, 'I can appreciate Diana's wish to clear off for the weekend *before* the evening meal. Diana likes her creature comforts; in her modest way I think she's a bit of a voluptuary. What do you suppose she's cooking for herself tonight? Chicken soup, perhaps . . . followed by fried Dover sole with shrimp sauce . . . roast duck . . . strawberries and cream . . . asparagus tips . . . a ripe Stilton.' He sighed. 'No perhaps not. Not on that Bunsen-burner of hers. But it sounds nice, doesn't it?'

'It sounds fine,' Chris Moull agreed. He was a slight young man with a round, freckled face and close-cropped hair that stood stiffly erect in front. 'But she'd be a gourmand, not a voluptuary, if she got

1

through all that at one sitting.'

'She would also be sick,' said Smelton. 'Pass the sugar, please.'

Anne Connaught had been doubtful of the propriety of Colin's description of Diana Farling as a 'voluptuary'; for her the word conjured up visions of languorous females generously proportioned and inadequately clad. But since Chris Moull was smiling and had even used the word himself she supposed it must be all right. Chris would not countenance a doubtful reference to his beloved Diana.

'It's not fair to grumble about the food,' she said. 'Friday is the cook's night out. You can't expect Doris to dish up a banquet on her own.'

'I don't,' Colin said. 'But I like my fish cooked, not raw. And, talking of Doris, wasn't she rather over-dressed for the part tonight? I mean — well, the pink dress . . . and all that jewellery . . . '

'Probably meeting her boyfriend. You're very critical this evening, aren't you?'

'Me? Good Heavens, no. I'm all in favour of personal adornment — it's part of my creed. I just thought . . . '

2

Chris grinned. 'You'd look rather fetching in a pearl necklace,' he said. 'Particularly with your green sports jacket, the one with the plunging neckline. And drop earrings, of course.'

'A horse-collar would be more suitable than a necklace,' Anne suggested, laughing. 'He has that type of neck.'

Colin grunted as he put down his coffee-cup, and wrinkled his nose in disgust. 'Ugh! I don't think much of that witches' brew. They might at least teach the girl how to make coffee.'

'It's much the same as usual,' said Anne, 'and I've never heard you complain about it before.'

'I may not complain, but that doesn't mean I approve of it. One has to fill one's belly with something.'

'Well, you shouldn't fill yours with coffee. It's bad for your ulcer.'

Colin winced. He was rather ashamed of his duodenum. He considered that in developing an ulcer so early in its existence (Colin was only twenty-four) it had let him down badly. 'Seriously, though, I do envy Diana her cottage,' he

3

said, hastily changing the topic. 'It must be heavenly, come Friday evening, to get away from the boys, and the school, and . . . and all this.'

He flicked the soiled table-cloth with the back of his hand and then waved an arm expansively to indicate the whole of the common room. The expression on his face made Anne want to laugh, but she restrained herself. Colin did not like to be laughed at. He was a hefty young man, short of neck and broad of shoulder, whose sense of humour was somewhat maladjusted. His opinions were sacrosanct. One might disagree with them, but one might not laugh at them.

'Feeling the strain rather early, aren't you?' said Chris. 'You've only been here a month, old boy.'

Philip Smelton, the senior master at Redways, had taken little part in this conversation. He was forty-five and looked older. Chin and forehead receded sharply, and the watery blue eyes and untidy wisps of ginger hair on crown and upper lip gave him a melancholy appearance.

'What's wrong with the common-room?' he demanded now. 'By the time you've reached my age, my lad, you'll be lucky if you haven't lived in many a damned sight worse.'

Colin shook his head in disbelief. The room was low-ceilinged and dark, the windows fronted by a high brick wall. The furniture was old and shabby, the carpet threadbare, the distempered walls spotted with damp. To Colin, fresh from the comforts of home, there was nothing right with it. He was about to say so when James Latimer, the headmaster's son, opened the door and surveyed the four seated at table.

'Any of my friends here tonight?' James asked hopefully. He was a tall, good-looking man of twenty-eight with dark, bushy hair and the prominent nose and eyebrows of his father, but lacking his father's stiffness of character and build.

'Friends? You actually have friends?' Colin looked amazed. 'They must have an abnormally low I.Q., poor things.'

James ignored this. 'I want someone to take my prep with the Fourth tomorrow morning. I'm away for the night — shan't be back until after breakfast. Hello, Anne. What are you doing here?'

'Sitting in for the matrons. They've both gone to the flicks.'

'I wish I'd known. I'd have joined the *hoi polloi* for dinner. The family board was a little chilly this evening, something or somebody appears to have upset the old man.' His glance roved round the table. 'Well, now — how about this prep?'

'Sorry. I'm taking the Fifth,' said Smelton.

'And I'm happy to say that I too cannot oblige,' said Colin. 'I'm taking the Third.'

They all looked at Chris Moull. But Chris was sipping his coffee and frowning at the table-cloth, apparently unaware of what was expected of him.

'How about you, Chris?' asked James, after a long pause.

'Sorry. Can't be done,' said the other curtly, between sips.

He offered no explanation — presumably, thought Anne, because he hadn't got one. The First and Second Forms were excused prep.

'I'll take it, James,' she volunteered, as the silence became embarrassing. 'I only have to sit with them, don't I?'

'That's all. And many thanks, Anne. It's good to know that your love for me is not entirely dead. Remind me to take you out to dinner one evening.'

'Remind me to knock his ruddy block off one evening,' Colin said angrily, when James had gone. 'He's got a nerve! Why do you pander to the fellow like that, Anne?'

'It makes for peace and quiet,' said the girl.

Conversation died after that. Chris Moull's former good humour seemed to have departed with James Latimer, and he retired into his thoughts — which, judging by the scowl on his face, were unpleasant. Smelton too was preoccupied. He had stayed for dinner at the school because he had requested an interview with the headmaster. Now, with the interview only a few minutes away, he was still uncertain how to frame his demands.

The other two had much to say to each

7

other, but they could not say it in public. They were glad when first Chris and then Smelton left the common room.

'James's unwelcome entry seemed to put a blight on the party,' said Colin, taking advantage of the opportunity to embrace his companion. They were not engaged, since she wished it that way; but neither had any doubts but that they would eventually marry. 'I always said he was a blighter.'

'I wonder why Chris refused to take his prep,' Anne said thoughtfully. 'He's usually so willing to oblige, and he can't have anything else to do.'

'Chris can't stick the fellow. Told me so.'

'But why not?'

'Because he's got sense — that's why. Or perhaps James has been making passes at his girlfriend now that you've given him the cold shoulder.'

The girl considered this. 'You never see them together,' she said doubtfully.

'No. Well, maybe it's the other way round. Perhaps Diana *used* to be James's girlfriend, and he dropped her when you came on the scene.'

'That's even less likely. If I know Diana she isn't the girl to allow any man she covets to escape so easily. She may look stately and aloof, but inside she's pretty intense, I imagine.'

'Hidden fires, eh?'

'Yes. *And* she's got a tongue. Obviously she's not in love with Chris, although he's so blind he can't see it. But I don't think that has anything to do with James.'

'Well, I wish the long-legged ape would lay off you,' Colin growled. 'I'm going to poke him on the snout one of these days.'

'Don't be silly, darling. After all, I did encourage him. There wasn't any you last term, and it was fun having someone to take me out and make a fuss of me. It certainly wasn't fun spending every evening alone with grandfather. Of course, when you came on the scene I saw the error of my ways. But you can't expect a conceited man like James to retire gracefully. He probably doesn't believe it possible that I can prefer another man to him.'

He kissed her. 'He'll get around to it

eventually,' he said, pleased at his conquest. 'Well, how long have we got? When do you have to go home? We're not often left alone here, so we may as well make the most of it.'

'That's because the matrons aren't usually allowed out together,' said the girl. 'But I'll have to go as soon as they return. Grandfather hasn't had his supper yet.'

'Poor old J.C. He'll be getting peckish, won't he? And what will you do about his breakfast tomorrow now that you're taking James's prep?'

'I'll leave it ready for him. I'm hoping he won't insist on his morning swim; he seems to have got some form of laryngitis, and has lost his voice. As usual, he won't see a doctor, so I don't know how bad it is.' She laughed. 'He tried to bawl me out this morning when I told him I needed more money for housekeeping. You should have seen the look on his face when he opened his mouth and only a faint whisper emerged.'

Colin grinned. 'Yes, I can imagine that would hit J.C. right where it hurts him most. He's a great one for bawling people out.'

Some time later feet thumped purposefully along the corridor. The two young people on the settee drew apart as the door opened and Philip Smelton, still struggling into his overcoat, hurried into the room. He strode across to the fireplace, grabbed a book from the mantelpiece, and without a word or a nod went out again, slamming the door behind him.

'What's biting him?' Anne wondered aloud, as the footsteps died away.

'The interview with our revered headmaster cannot have gone according to plan,' said Colin. 'Not according to Smelton's plan, that is. I wonder what it was in aid of.'

★   ★   ★

The headmaster's study at Redways was less dingy than the common room. It was also more spacious. The chairs, although worn, were upholstered in leather; the furniture was massive and good. But it

11

was not a comfortable room, nor did it possess the friendliness of its inferior in the social scale. There were paint and distemper in the common room, dark stain in the study. The glass-fronted shelves which lined one wall were filled with impressive-looking tomes which gave the impression of being seldom looked at and never read; there were no gaudy dust-jackets, no paper-backed novels. The sole concession to luxury was warmth. A fire burned cheerfully in the old-fashioned grate, for the October evening was chilly and Joseph Latimer was a thin man and a cold one.

At a knock on the study door Mr Latimer put down his pen impatiently, looked for a moment at the last paragraph he had written, and then swung round in his swivel-chair to warm his hands at the fire.

'Sit down, Smelton,' he said as his visitor entered. 'I hope you won't keep me long, for I have an ungodly amount of correspondence to wade through before I go to bed tonight.'

Smelton sat down. Much cogitation

had failed to suggest a diplomatic opening gambit, and he did not attempt one. 'I was hoping you could see your way to raising my salary,' he said tonelessly, without greeting or preamble.

The headmaster frowned.

'That's out of the question, I'm afraid. I am already paying you a higher salary than I have ever paid to a member of my staff before. I'm sorry if you consider it inadequate, but I certainly cannot increase it.'

Smelton nodded gloomily. This was what he had expected.

'I'm not saying it's inadequate for the job, Mr Latimer. But it's inadequate for me. I'm getting into a financial mess.'

Latimer's frown deepened. He did not particularly like Smelton, but he respected his ability. Apart from the man's occasional outbursts of violent rage, he was an excellent schoolmaster; and excellent schoolmasters were hard to come by.

'Can't you cut down your expenses?' he suggested. 'I do not wish to interfere in your domestic economy, but — well, is a car really necessary, for instance?'

Smelton knew it was not. Neither the car nor so many other of the extravagances on which Dorothy insisted. But he would not admit this to Latimer. Anger rose in him — anger against his wife for her stupid subservience to social prestige, against Latimer for exposing the weakness of his case.

'I think so,' he said coldly. 'It is over two miles from here to my house. I don't intend to tackle those hills twice daily on a push-bike.'

'It could be motor-assisted,' said Latimer.

Smelton checked the angry retort. Quarrelling would get him nowhere, and real trouble lay ahead unless he accomplished something quickly. 'It's the rent on the house that's crippling me,' he said. 'Together with the rates it comes to over a hundred and sixty a year. I've tried to find something cheaper, but there just isn't anything suitable to be had.'

It depends on what you call suitable, Latimer felt like saying. Only it would be no use. He had known the Smeltons for eight years and was under no delusions as to the cause of his senior master's financial difficulties. If Smelton were ever to become solvent it was his wife he would have to get rid of, not his house or his car.

He offered the other a cigarette and refrained from comment.

'Some time ago you mentioned the possibility of converting the ground floor at Abbey Lodge into a flat for us,' said Smelton, flipping the dead match into the fire. 'Any chance of that yet?'

'None whatever.' Latimer spoke curtly, irritated as he always was by any reference to Abbey Lodge or its occupant. John Connaught was at the root of most of his present worries. 'Not until J.C. dies.'

'A pity.' Smelton hesitated, uncertain how to persuade the other to satisfy his curiosity further. Until the previous April most of the staff had been housed at Abbey Lodge, and now there were only J.C. and his granddaughter living there. Why? Maybe the old boy *had* been a master at Redways for donkey's years, but that did not entitle him to monopolize accommodation that belonged to the school and was so urgently needed. 'I know it is none of my business, Mr Latimer; but it seems a shocking waste of space. Can't you turn the old man out — or at least take over part of the house?'

'No.' It was Latimer who was angry now. As Smelton had said, it was a shocking waste. With the school so crowded, that in itself was galling enough. Still more galling was the knowledge that he could do nothing to remedy the position. 'My father left him the tenancy of the house until his death. I thought that was common knowledge.'

The other shook his head.

'There's a lot of life in him yet, I imagine, despite being all skin and bones,' he said gloomily. All his hopes had been set on that flat. 'He can't be much over seventy.'

'He's sixty-nine.'

'But why did he turn the staff out? He didn't object to them before. I know he won some enormous sum in a football pool last March, and obviously he no longer needed the money you were paying him for their lodging. But he must have known it would make things difficult for you, and after all those years as a master here you'd think he would have some regard for the school.'

'Maybe he has. But not for me. He holds me responsible for the fact that my father left him only the tenancy of Abbey Lodge and a small pension instead of the partnership he had expected. Well, he has some justification for that. J.C. and I never liked each other — it would have been a most unhappy partnership.' Latimer's voice was bitter. 'He would not even have had the Lodge if I could have prevented it. But my father thought he knew better than I — and this is the result. In order to accommodate the staff here I have had to reduce the number of boys — which is one very good reason why I cannot raise your salary.'

You hate him, don't you, thought Smelton, eyeing the other curiously; he had never before heard the normally detached Latimer speak so bitterly. You may be a pillar of society and the headmaster of a well-known preparatory school, but I wouldn't care to be in J.C.'s shoes if you bumped into him one dark night when no one else was around. And more power to your elbow, I'd say. Blast the old devil! He's the nigger in the woodpile all right — for me as well as for you. As it is —

'I'm sorry, Smelton, but there is really no point in discussing the matter further.' The headmaster spoke briskly, his voice once more dry and indifferent. 'You see how things are. Unless you care to reconsider the proposition I put to you last term there is nothing I can do to help, I'm afraid.'

'You mean — about some of the staff lodging at our place?'

'Yes. It would help you financially, and it would give us more room here. We could come to some arrangement about transport, no doubt.'

'I'll talk to Dorothy,' Smelton said. 'She wasn't keen the last time I mentioned it.'

That was an understatement, he thought, as he drove home. Dorothy had been furious that he should even have dared to suggest it. 'So we are to take in lodgers now, are we?' she had said scornfully. 'Why, I'd never dare to look my friends in the face again! Lodgers, indeed! You'll be asking me to go out charring next, or to take in washing. No, Philip. You can tell your Mr Latimer from me that there will be no lodgers in *this* house.'

Recalling this conversation, his foot came down hard on the accelerator, and the car shot forward. Then, realizing that speed might feed his fury but would not abate it, he drove the rest of the way at a more restrained pace, turning over in his mind what he should say to Dorothy.

A light was on in the hall, but although it was not yet nine o'clock the rest of the house was in darkness. She will have gone to bed, he thought bitterly, the same as she always does when there's only me for company. She's not even sufficiently interested to want to know how I got on with Latimer, despite it's entirely because of her I had to go cap in hand to him tonight. Well, slipping off to bed won't help her *this* time. We'll settle this thing once and for all, even if I have to wake her up to do it.

He poured himself a generous whisky, pushed his wife's large white cat from out of his armchair, and sat down to consider what he should say. Dorothy usually got the better of him when it came to words. He must say his piece quickly and firmly, giving her no chance to interrupt.

After a while the whisky mellowed him, and his thoughts drifted back to the first years of their marriage. Her many extravagances had then seemed amusing and even rather endearing: they had laughed at them together, he had even boasted of them with pride to his friends and colleagues. They had set Dorothy apart from the ordinary run of women, for she had considerable taste and her extravagances were never petty. But as the years passed and his capital dwindled he had become alarmed; amusement had turned to nagging worry, and he had tried to impress on her the need for economy. But it seemed that he had left it too late. She had grown used to reckless spending, and her response was trifling and ineffective; small cuts in the housekeeping bills, mostly at the expense of things he particularly liked — so that when he asked for them she could righteously remind him of the need to economize.

It was then that the rows started in earnest.

Dorothy had an exasperating habit of putting him in the wrong, of making thrift appear as meanness; and when he started to reprove her she somehow managed to turn the tables. There had been occasions when he had jibbed at the frequency and lavishness of her entertaining, and she had accused him of grudging her her friends; and when he had protested that he meant nothing of the sort, that she might have all the friends she wanted provided she spent less money on their entertainment, she had called him inhospitable, had accused him of expecting her to be inhospitable also. It usually ended in his begging her pardon, and later wondering why he had been fool enough to do so.

It had been like that up to a few months ago, when ruin stared him so

21

fully in the face that peace at home had become secondary to peace of mind. He began to dread going home; not only because of the quarrels and the atmosphere of stale love that filled the house, but also because of his fear of what new piece of foolish extravagance Dorothy might have indulged in during his absence.

The truth was, of course, that Dorothy was incapable of appreciating how serious the situation had become. Bank statements meant nothing to Dorothy. And it was partly his fault. He had indulged her at the beginning and for too long, so that when indulgence ceased it appeared to her as meanness and the waning of love. Always in the past she had had what she wanted, and always he had accused her of extravagance; and if they could go on like that for nine years it was clear to Dorothy's unbusinesslike mind that they could go on like that for ever.

When eventually he went upstairs much of his anger had left him. He still resented the dilemma to which she had brought them, and his resentment needed little fuel to cause it to burst into flame; but the position was now too serious for petty squabbling. If he were to get anywhere with Dorothy he must be reasonable — and reasonable to her way of thinking, not to his. If she tried to aggravate him he must remain calm. When he lost his temper she immediately established a mastery over him.

As he switched on the light she said sharply, 'Don't! It hurts my eyes. Use the standard lamp if you must have a light to undress by.'

'I'm not coming to bed yet,' he said, obeying her. 'I want to talk to you.'

His wife groaned. 'What — again? What is it this time? The same old thing?'

Her cheeks gleamed under the cold cream. Yet despite the lack of make-up and the sullen expression her face was still beautiful. He said, inwardly cursing the financial stress that had driven them so far apart, 'Latimer refused to raise my salary.'

'Why should he?' She sounded indifferent. 'He's a mean devil, anyway. Every one says so.'

'He thinks we ought to economize,' he said. 'Get rid of the car, for instance.'

He waited patiently until the expected outburst evoked by this statement subsided. He had some sympathy with her wrath: it was, as she said, no business of Latimer's how they spent their money — and he nodded agreement, placating her, hoping that when fury had been spent on this red herring she would accept more calmly what he had to say next.

And when he began to tell her about John Connaught, of his feud with Latimer and his reason for ousting the staff from Abbey Lodge, she listened quietly. Dorothy was not interested in the school itself, but she liked to hear all the local gossip. Noting her interest, he said, with a faint hope of success and trying to make his voice sound unconcerned, 'I was wondering whether we should offer to help them out by having one or two of the staff to sleep here next term. Latimer would jump at the offer, I know; and he'd pay us what he used to pay J.C.'

Dorothy was not deceived.

'So he's been on at you again, has he? I might have guessed. Well, I told you before — I'm not having lodgers *here*. That's final. This is neither a boarding-house nor a school annex — it's my home, Philip, and I mean to keep it that way.'

'But what's the harm?' he pleaded. 'Every one would know we were doing it to oblige the school. No stigma in that, is there? They wouldn't be in your way; there'd be no meals to cook — they would only sleep here. And you know how badly we need the money.'

'No, Philip. No and no and no. Don't ever dare to mention it again.'

Her flat refusal was too much for his self-control.

'You don't care, I suppose, that we are practically bankrupt?' he stormed. 'You think you can go on writing cheques *ad lib*. and that the bank will honour them. Well, I warn you, Dorothy — the next cheque you write will bounce, and bounce high. That's how bad it is. There'll be no money for gin or new clothes. The hire-purchase people will be taking back the furniture and the T.V. and the 'fridge and all the other gadgets they have so kindly supplied and which you haven't yet paid for. We'll have to sell the car and clear out of the house; and if J.C. hasn't conveniently pegged out and made the flat available you will probably be living in a tent in the school grounds. And if any of your fine friends care to visit you there they'll be welcome.'

As his anger grew so hers diminished. She yawned.

'Don't be melodramatic, Philip. It doesn't impress me in the least. And what is all this about J.C.'s flat?'

Impatiently he told her, too angry now to notice her interest or to profit from it. The flat was problematical, dependent on Latimer's whim and J.C.'s death. It promised no early relief from worry.

'The old man isn't as tough as he likes to make out,' Dorothy said thoughtfully. 'Anne says so, anyway, and she ought to know. And bathing in the river all the year round can't do him much good at his age. What's the flat like?'

'I don't know. I've never been inside the place.'

'It would probably be far too small for us,' she said. 'And I don't think I'd like to be shut in by all those trees. Too gloomy.'

'Gloomy or not, if J.C. died tomorrow we'd be out of this place in two ticks,' replied her husband. 'But he won't. We've got to find some other solution.'

'But not tonight, Philip. I'm tired, and it's time you were in bed.'

He made a last appeal.

'Dorothy, listen. Stop behaving like a damned ostrich and face facts for once. I tell you, we're in the soup. Small economies won't help now — it's got to be something really drastic. If we are to keep afloat we've got to chuck overboard all but the barest necessities. We've got to count every penny, we've got to — '

With a bored sigh she turned on her side, her face away from him, and pulled the bedclothes over her head. The gesture infuriated him more than any words could have done. Inarticulate with rage and frustration, he stamped across the room, switched on all the lights in a

27

childish gesture of defiance, and slammed the door behind him as he went out.

★ ★ ★

Beyond the school playing fields the ground dropped steeply down the tree-lined slopes of the Wain valley to the river below. Here, at a point some two hundred yards above its junction with the Tan, the Wain was spanned by an ancient wooden bridge — out of bounds to the boys, for its timbers were rotten and in some places missing altogether. Anne always hated going home after dark; the bridge terrified her. She was glad to have Colin with her that evening.

As they plodded up the slope on the far side of the bridge to reach the main Tanbury road a car approached noisily from the direction of Wainford. They stood to watch it pass.

'That's Smelton's old bus,' said Colin. 'Where on earth is he haring off to at this time of night?'

'Probably had a row with Dorothy,' said Anne. 'It's supposed to be a regular occurrence. I expect he's about to drown his sorrows in drink.'

'He'll drown them in the river if he carries on at that lick; the bend after the bridge is pretty tricky. What's his wife like?'

'Terribly smart and very attractive,' said Anne, as they crossed the road and turned down the track that led through the woods to Abbey Lodge. 'People say she's selfish and bad-tempered, but I like her. She's gay and vital — such a change from the local frumps one normally meets. I believe she's very well connected, and knows lots of interesting people and gets asked everywhere. She entertains a lot herself, too.'

'Not on an usher's salary she doesn't,' said Colin. 'She must have money of her own.' He was silent for a moment, and then added, 'People will be saying that about you one of these days, I suppose. I'm not sure whether I like the idea or not. I can't get used to the fact that you are an heiress, darling.'

'I don't mind it. In fact, I like it,' Anne confessed. 'It's a comforting thought.'

'Maybe. But I wish we could get married soon, so that you will be dependent on me for a few years at least. I wouldn't feel so bad about it after that — I hope. Maybe I'd even get around to liking it.'

They paused at the Lodge gates. Through the trees they could see, silhouetted against the light that shone out from the hall, two figures — one tall, one short — standing in the open doorway.

'The old man has a visitor,' said Colin. 'Is he coming or going?'

The closing of the front door and the sound of footsteps on gravel answered his question. Instinctively Anne drew back into the shadow of the trees, pulling Colin with her.

'Who is it?' he asked, surprised at her action.

'I don't know. Shush!'

The visitor was at the gate — a tall figure wheeling a bicycle, his fawn raincoat a pale blur against the dark sky. Then he was gone, cycling down the track away from the school.

Colin whistled softly. 'James Latimer, eh? Did you know it was him? Was that why you didn't want to be seen?'

'Yes. At least, I thought it might be James.'

'Why? I didn't know he and J.C. were buddies.'

'They're not. But James has already been to see him twice this week.' She sighed. 'I wish I knew why.'

'There's dirty work afoot if James is involved,' said Colin. 'And I thought he was away for the night. Leaving it a bit late, isn't he? However, don't let's waste time discussing James. He leaves a nasty taste in the mouth.'

He made to open the gate. But Anne stopped him.

'I think we *ought* to discuss him, Colin,' she said. 'Him — and the money.'

'Why?'

'Well — and don't blame me for this, darling, it isn't my fault — if I marry you before Grandfather dies it's almost certain he won't leave me a penny.'

'You mean he doesn't like me?' asked Colin, astonished that anyone could feel that way about him.

'Not exactly. He hardly knows you, does he? But he wants me to marry James.'

'James? Marry James? Good Lord, what a horrible thought!'

'Yes, isn't it? Of course I've no intention of doing anything of the sort — you know that. But it does make things rather awkward.'

'I'll say it does! What on earth put that idea into his head? What's James got that I haven't?'

'Nothing — at present,' said the girl. 'But one day James will be headmaster of Redways, and you know how keen Grandfather was to have a share in the school. He didn't get it when old Jacob Latimer died — now he hopes to get it through me. If I marry James he reckons that one day, when Joseph dies or retires, I will provide him with a sort of second-hand interest in the place.'

'Optimistic, isn't he? He'll probably peg out long before Joseph. Does James know about this?'

'Grandfather hasn't actually asked him to marry me, if that's what you mean. But he has thrown out plenty of hints — encouraged James to take me out, that sort of thing. He even told him he was going to leave me his money, just in case James didn't find me attractive enough without it.'

'The dirty old so-and-so!' Colin was genuinely horrified. 'So that's why James thought he was on a good wicket with you. And that, I suppose,' he said, with sudden insight, 'is the reason for these nocturnal visits of his. He and that wicked old grandfather of yours — oh, hell! Why on earth didn't you tell me about this before?'

'I didn't want to hurt you. I just kept you out of Grandfather's way so that he wouldn't discover how we feel about each other. But you can see now why an early marriage has its drawbacks. I'm not mercenary, darling, but I just hate the thought of losing all that money. I'm tired of being poor, I want to travel and enjoy life. Of course, if it comes to a choice between you and the money, then it's you every time. But I was hoping I'd be able to have both.'

'It's tricky,' said Colin. 'Damned tricky. The old man is liable to live for years yet. And even if I were prepared to wait that long — which I'm not — you can't stall him off indefinitely about James.'

'I could try. However, it's up to you, darling. If you want a wife with no prospects say so. I'll marry you whenever you like.'

'But it isn't as easy as that,' he protested. 'I can't ask you to chuck away a fortune just to marry me.'

'I'd rather do that than marry James,' she said, squeezing his arm. 'But we don't have to decide tonight, do we? After all, we haven't known each other long, we can afford to wait a little while. And who knows? Something may turn up to put it right.'

He kissed her goodnight, although some of his normal ardour was lacking.

'The only thing that could do us any good would be for either James or J.C. to peg out suddenly,' he said gloomily. 'Preferably both. And that isn't likely to happen unless someone has the kindness to assist them.'

# 2

## A Man is Missing

Redways Preparatory School for boys stood on a hill in the angle formed by the river Tan and its tributary the Wain, south of the Tanbury road and two miles east of the little village of Wainsford. It was a two-storey building in the form of an E, and had been built by Jacob Latimer, father of Joseph (the eldest sons of the Latimers were invariably named after biblical characters whose names began with J), to accommodate some sixty boarders. There were no day-boys at the school in Jacob's time; but John Connaught's action in ousting the staff from Abbey Lodge, where three of them at least had always been housed, had forced Joseph Latimer to reduce the number of boarders. In an effort to mitigate to some extent the financial loss resulting from this reduction, he had, against his

35

inclination, admitted as day-boys to the school the sons of a few local residents.

Mrs Latimer, as thin and angular as her husband, was seldom in evidence as a person, however much her work behind the scenes contributed to the smooth running of the school. She was a timid woman with no conversation, and she left the interviewing of parents to her husband. Mr Latimer complained bitterly on occasions of her lack of spirit and her habit of effacing herself when visitors called, failing to realize that it was his domineering manner and Victorian notions of a woman's place in the home which had effectively killed what little spirit his wife might once have possessed.

It was a reasonably successful school, although the headmaster's treatment of both staff and boys was too formal and unbending to make it an entirely happy one. To these unfortunate characteristics had lately been added financial concern and a sense of bitter frustration that made him irritable and unreasonable. Old John Connaught, secure in his retirement at

Abbey Lodge, would have been maliciously content had he known how complete was his triumph over his enemy.

★   ★   ★

At just after half-past seven that Saturday morning Colin Russell, hurrying down the main corridor to take the Third Form prep, encountered a breathless and perspiring Anne.

'You're late,' he said, unnecessarily and with mock severity.

'I know. I ran all the way. I clean forgot I had promised to take James's prep for him. Anyway, you're late yourself.'

'Admitted. I have many faults, but early rising, thank heavens, is not one of them.' The gloom that had encompassed him at their parting on the previous evening seemed to have vanished. 'Which reminds me — do I get breakfast in bed when we are married?'

'Only if you cook it yourself.'

The Third Form classroom was at the far end of the middle arm of the E, and from it Colin could see the trees which

37

surrounded Abbey Lodge. Between the Lodge and the school the mist that had earlier obscured the Wain valley was beginning to clear, although it still lay like a dirty white shroud over the Tan and the swampy ground beyond. It looked like the start of a fine day, thought Colin; which, since he was not on duty and not due to take a game in the afternoon, was a satisfying thought.

He had been some time in the room before he noticed that one of the desks was unoccupied.

'Where's Cuttle?' he asked the form at large.

The form at large answered him. But, since Cuttle was a day-boy and the rest were boarders, their knowledge was no greater than Colin's. The general opinion, that Tony Cuttle was sick, was therefore accepted.

A duffel-coated figure emerged from a patch of mist and came striding across the playing-field. Even before he could see his face Colin recognized him as Chris Moull; no one but Chris would be wearing a beret. He was just wondering what could have driven Chris so early from his bed when he became aware that in the Fifth Form, one room removed from the Third, all was not as quiet as it should be. There was talk and some laughter.

Since no noise ever emanated from a class over which Philip Smelton presided, Colin went to investigate. Silence was instant as he opened the door, heads bent hastily to their tasks. There was no sign of Smelton.

'Has Mr Smelton been in yet?' he asked.

A chorus of 'No, sir,' answered him.

'Well, get on with your prep and don't let me hear any more noise,' he said sternly.

As he left the room Joseph Latimer came hurrying down the main corridor. 'Is Smelton in there?' the headmaster asked.

'No, sir. He should be, but I gather he hasn't turned up yet. I was going to get Moull to take them.'

'Is James taking the Fourth?'

Colin looked his surprise. Didn't the

old man know his son was away? 'Miss Connaught is taking his prep for him,' he said, and left it at that.

Latimer clucked in annoyance. 'One of them will have to take prayers this morning,' he said. 'I have to go to the hospital. Young Cuttle was knocked down by a car on his way to school.'

'I noticed he wasn't in prep,' said Colin. 'Is he badly hurt?'

'I understand not. But I would prefer that the school should at present remain in ignorance of the accident. I will tell them myself when I have more information.'

Colin supposed that 'the school' referred only to the boys, and talk at the staff table during breakfast was at first devoted to speculation on Tony Cuttle's injuries.

'I hope Smelton hasn't had an accident also,' said Colin. 'Last seen he was going like stink in the direction of Tanbury. That was around nine-forty last night.'

'We should have heard before now if he had,' said Anne. 'I expect he overslept this morning.'

'The poor man may be ill,' Miss Webber, the senior matron, suggested. She was a neat little woman, of no beauty and unadorned by beauty's aids, but with a constant cheerfulness and ready sympathy not yet dulled by years of attendance on the wants and ailments of small boys. 'He hasn't been looking at all well lately.'

'I hope he isn't sick and I hope he hasn't had an accident,' said Colin. 'With the old man at the hospital and James returning God knows when we're going to be short-handed this morning.' He looked across at Moull. 'All set for a really heavy spasm, Chris? Your early-morning walk indicates an abundance of energy. Where did you go?'

'Past the Lodge and round by the river.'

'Phew! Quite a stroll. What got you up so early? Something on your mind?'

'Something on his stomach, more likely,' said Anne. 'Those pancakes last night would have sunk a battleship. Only an appetite like Chris's could have coped with them.'

But he hasn't much of an appetite this

morning, she reflected, watching him. The young man's round and freckled face had lost its usual grin; he had refused the porridge and was making heavy weather of a boiled egg. He seemed nervy and on edge; and when Miss Dove, the under matron, accidentally jogged his arm, causing tea to spill on his grey flannel trousers, he snapped his annoyance in a manner most unlike him.

Diana again, Anne decided. That girl doesn't half lead the poor boy a dance.

When Smelton had not appeared by the end of breakfast Colin decided to telephone to his house. Anne went out to the hall with him. 'I must ring Grandfather,' she said. 'The woman can't come this morning, so I've left a cold lunch ready for him in the larder. He'll never think to look.'

'Wasn't he up when you left?'

'Oh, yes. But he'd gone off for his swim and hadn't come back. He was in a filthy temper, too. He accused me of trying to 'manage' him when I told him he ought to stay in bed on account of his throat.'

'Pig-headed old devil,' said Colin.

'How's his voice? Has he got it back yet?'

'No. I think that's what made him so bad-tempered.'

Anne stood by Colin while he telephoned the Smeltons', her curiosity growing as she listened. When Colin put down the receiver he looked puzzled.

'Mrs Smelton says she hasn't seen him this morning.'

'Eh? What on earth did she mean by that?'

'I can't imagine. I asked her, but she just hung up.'

'It's an odd way for a woman to talk about her husband,' said Anne. 'As though you'd asked her whether the milkman had called. I know she is given to staying in bed of a morning — that's why Mr Smelton so often has breakfast here. But if she meant he had left the house before she woke up — well, why isn't he here?'

'Search me. But it's my guess that he didn't go home after we saw him last night. His wife sounded extremely huffy.'

'He doesn't strike me as a night-bird — but you never can tell with men. Now let me ring Grandfather.'

There was no reply from the Lodge. 'He must be in the garden,' said Anne. 'I'll try again later.'

Neither of them heard Smelton's car, but as they turned away from the telephone he came in through the front door. When he saw them he took off his hat and began to apologize for having missed his prep. 'Clean forgot I was taking it this morning,' he said, not very convincingly.

They looked at him curiously. He seemed in poor shape. He had not shaved, his suit was badly rumpled, and his hair looked as though he had poured water over it and then smoothed it down with his hands. 'Maybe his wife told him to go jump in the river and he obeyed her,' Colin said later to Anne.

'He *must* have spent the night out,' she declared. 'He would never come straight from home in that condition.'

'He's been up to something he didn't oughter, too,' said Colin. 'Unless he had an extremely guilty conscience he would never have bothered to apologize to humble folk like you and me, ducks.'

Colin's main reaction to the senior master's arrival was relief that he would not now have to take morning prayers himself. That was something he had not yet been and hoped he might never be called upon to do. He was not afraid of small boys *en masse* on the playing-field or in the classroom, where disorder could be quelled and discipline restored by a stentorian roar or a sharp rap on the knuckles with a ruler. But the thought of taking prayers terrified him. What could he do if the sudden hush that descended upon the assembled school at the entrance of the headmaster or Smelton did not descend for him? An Army-type bellow or a well-aimed hymn-book *might* have the desired effect, but neither remedy seemed in harmony with the occasion.

When Anne tried to telephone her grandfather again after morning school there was still no reply. 'I shall have to go home after lunch and make sure he's all right,' she said to Colin. 'Thank goodness I'm free this afternoon.'

'So am I. I'll come with you. We might go in to Tanbury for tea and the flicks afterwards.'

Although the staff had their evening meal in the common room, for lunch they sat with the Latimers at the top table in the dining hall. With fifty-odd boys eating and chattering around them general conversation was not easy, and normally they conversed only with their immediate neighbours. But that day most of them were silent, for Mr Latimer had returned from the hospital and they were anxious to hear the latest news about Tony Cuttle's injuries. These, said Mr Latimer, were not serious. There were no broken bones and remarkably few bruises. The boy was suffering mainly from shock and slight concussion, and should be back at school within a week or ten days.

'How did it happen?' asked James. He had appeared in time for the first lesson, although neither Anne nor Colin had seen him return.

'I have not heard Cuttle's version, of course,' said his father; he never referred or spoke to boys by their first names, a practice common among the staff and frowned on by him, 'but I had a talk with the driver of the car. He told me that he had just crossed the bridge — there was a thick mist along that stretch of road, and he was going very slowly — when the boy appeared from nowhere and ran into the side of his car.' He frowned. 'If the man was going as slowly as he tried to make out it seems to me that he should have seen the boy in plenty of time. Cuttle must have been on the road; he didn't dash out from a house, or anything like that. And although there certainly was a mist down by the river I did not myself find the visibility poor when I drove in to the hospital.'

'But that was later,' said Anne. 'It was very thick down by the wooden bridge when I came across this morning.' She turned to Moull. 'You went along the river, Chris. What was it like there?'

'Pretty thick,' said Chris. 'But it lifts quickly.'

A thought occurred to Anne. 'You didn't see J.C. taking his morning dip, I suppose?'

47

The young man shook his head.

Smelton had not spoken during the meal. Anne had seen the headmaster looking with undisguised disapproval at his unshaven chin, but Smelton seemed to be either unaware of or indifferent to the disapproval. I suppose he will go home and tidy up after lunch, she thought, but he certainly does look a mess. I should have thought he would hate the boys to see him in that condition.

She mentioned this to Colin as they walked across to Abbey Lodge after lunch. The sun was shining, and they stood for a few minutes on the wooden bridge watching the water as it frothed and sparkled over the succession of tiny waterfalls.

'He's an odd chap,' said Colin. 'I can't make him out. Tell me — if his wife is as attractive as you say she is, why can't he get on with her?'

'He makes out that she's extravagant. But Dorothy says she is no more extravagant now than when they got married. It's just a bee in his bonnet, she says.'

'I hope that doesn't happen to us.'

'It won't.' She caught his arm. 'Come on. I'm worried about Grandfather.'

'I don't see why. He looks pretty tough to me. Those skinny chaps often are.'

'It's not his health — it's what he may be up to that worries me. The only other time he got really mad at me he cleared off for two whole days.'

'Good Lord! Why?'

'It was all so silly,' the girl said, panting a little as they neared the top of the rise. 'It happened last Easter, a few days after the end of term. I came into the breakfast room one morning and found him reading a letter. He immediately slipped it into his pocket, but not before I had seen there was a blue stamp on the envelope. I knew it must be from abroad — so, quite innocently, I asked him who it was from. You wouldn't think there was any harm in that, would you?'

Colin assured her that he would not.

'Neither did I. But Grandfather flew into a rage and accused me of spying on him, and glowered at me all through breakfast. I thought that was the end of it;

but unfortunately — and quite by accident — I found him reading the letter again. That really tore it.'

'That was when he cleared off?'

'Yes. He came back later in the morning while I was out shopping, packed himself a bag, and disappeared until the following evening.' She laughed. 'I don't know where he went, but he was in extremely good spirits when he returned. I've never seen him so cheerful.'

'Perhaps he's got a girlfriend,' Colin suggested. They had crossed the main road and were on the track through the woods. 'In which case bang goes your inheritance. Was he equally mad at you this morning?'

'He seemed to be. I think it was not being able to bawl me out that irritated him. All he could manage was a feeble croak. I was upstairs making his bed when he went off for his swim, and there he was, standing in the garden in his dressing-gown and shaking his fist at the house. So childish. And he is always back for his breakfast by seven-fifteen. I'm sure he stayed out later on purpose to annoy me.'

'We'll soon see,' said Colin.

There was no sign of the old man when they reached the house. Neither his breakfast nor the lunch that Anne had left for him in the larder had been touched.

'Looks like you may be right,' said Colin, as they went upstairs.

J.C.'s room was as Anne had left it that morning. On a chair beside the bed were his clothes, underclothes neatly folded, jacket hanging on the back. On the dressing-table, methodically arrayed, were money and other articles from his pockets.

'His trousers seem to be missing,' said Colin.

'He was wearing them under his dressing-gown.' The girl's voice was troubled. She went quickly to the wardrobe and rummaged among the hanging suits. Then she turned, fear in her eyes. 'His dressing-gown isn't here. He must still be down by the river.'

He caught her arm. 'We'd better get down there,' he said, her fear communicating itself to him.

The river was some two hundred yards

from the house, and they ran all the way; through the neat garden, across the fields to the trees — with Anne stumbling occasionally on the uneven, rutted ground, but never pausing — until they came to the river-bank and the small sunlit clearing that John Connaught had made his private bathing point.

Anne's fingers bit deep into her companion's tweed-clad arm. J.C.'s towel and dressing-gown lay on the grass, their bright colours somehow grimly foreboding. A slipper lay near them, a second slipper had been tossed some feet away. And on the brink of the river, one leg turned inside out, were the old man's trousers.

But there was no sign of J.C. himself.

The girl burst into tears. Colin put his arms round her, trying to comfort her. But as he gazed over her head at the smoothly flowing river, its waters unruffled by bobbing head or floating body, his stomach felt sick and his eyes were troubled.

# 3

## A Man is Found

J.C. was still missing the following afternoon.

'I keep hoping he may be alive,' Anne said. She looked pale and tired after a sleepless night, but was no longer tearful. 'I'm not pretending I was devoted to him, and I don't think he had much affection for me; but at least he was my grandfather and the only relative I had. Without him there'll be no one.' She sighed. 'I know that's a selfish thought, but I can't help it. It's frightening to be so completely alone.'

'You've got me,' said Colin. 'And how about your father? Isn't he still alive?'

Anne shook her head. 'He may be. But it's twelve years since he walked out on Mummy and me, and he's never bothered about either of us since. I don't know where he is or what happened to him. I don't suppose he even knows that

Mummy's dead.'

They were together with Chris Moull in the common room. James Latimer had taken the boys for their Sunday afternoon walk, and for a little while the school was quiet. This was a time normally devoted by the non-duty staff to reading the Sunday papers and to dozing. But that afternoon none of the three had any inclination to read or doze. The missing John Connaught filled their minds to the exclusion of all else.

'The police haven't found him yet,' said Chris, uncertain whether this was consolation or not.

'No. And his keys weren't in his trousers' pockets. They weren't on the dressing-table either,' said Anne. Chris had been told of the previous occasion on which J.C. had disappeared, and she saw no need to explain her train of thought. 'So where are they if he hasn't got them? It's true that none of his clothes appears to be missing; but I can't be absolutely sure of that, can I?'

'His money was there, Anne.' Colin did not wish her to build too surely on what seemed to him to be a very shaky foundation. 'And what about his things down by the river?'

'He might have left them like that to frighten me,' the girl said stubbornly. 'When you were on your walk yesterday morning, Chris, you didn't hear a cry or anything, did you?'

Chris shook his head. Colin thought he looked embarrassed, and wondered why. He was about to protest against Anne's refusal to accept the facts when the door opened and Diana Farling came in.

Diana was Mr Latimer's secretary. She was a tall, well-built girl with close-cropped red hair and an almost regal beauty. She crossed the room with studied grace and laid a hand, on which glittered a large imitation emerald, on Anne's shoulder. They had teased her about that ring, accusing her of ostenta-tion. Diana had said that her finger was swollen and she could not get it off, but they had not believed her. Her fondness for jewellery was well known.

'I'm terribly sorry, Anne,' she said quietly.

55

'What are you doing here, Diana?' asked Colin, surprised. 'I thought you were spending the weekend at the cottage.'

'I am. But Chris told me the news on the phone, and I cycled over. I thought there might be something I could do to help. They haven't found J.C. yet, have they?'

Colin shook his head. Diana accepted a cigarette and a light from Chris and sat down, crossing her shapely legs. 'You won't want to stay on at the Lodge, Anne, will you?' she said. 'You can move in with me if you don't mind a squeeze.'

'It's sweet of you, Diana — but Mrs Latimer said I could have the sickroom for the present. I slept there last night. I'm sorry about your spoilt weekend, though. There's nothing you can do — nothing any of us can do, unfortunately — and it seems such a shame to have cycled all that way for nothing.'

'I don't mind. It's only four miles, and the exercise does me good. I'm getting fat. I'll go back after tea.'

'Why not stay now you're here?' asked

Colin. 'It would save you the ride tomorrow morning.'

'No, I must go back. I haven't tidied up or anything. When I heard the news I just hopped on the bike and came.'

James returned with the boys, and once more the school came to life. But none of the four had duties to perform, and they sat long over tea. Diana did most of the talking. She was sympathetic towards Anne, but cheerful and matter-of-fact. 'At least you won't have to worry about money,' she said. 'Believe me, that's a happy thought for a single girl. It's a happy thought for a married one too,' she added, with a sly glance at Colin. '*And* for her husband.'

Colin frowned. It was a tactless remark, he thought.

It was nearly dark when Diana rose to go. Chris Moull stood up also. 'I'll come with you,' he said.

'No, Chris, I'm not going to drag you out at this hour. You'd miss your dinner, for one thing.'

'But I'd like to come,' he protested.

Diana smiled at him. 'It's sweet of you

to offer, Chris, but I'm not going to let you. When I get back I have things to do which won't get done if you are there. And don't worry about my cycling home alone in the dark. I'm used to it.'

Chris looked puzzled and a little shattered, but he did not argue further. After Diana had left he went up to his room.

'Poor Chris,' said Anne. 'I wonder whether Diana realized just how much he wanted to go with her.'

They went across to the Lodge after lunch the next day. Anne wanted to collect some clothes, and would not go alone. As they walked up the path to the house she said suddenly, 'There are men down by the river, Colin. I can hear them.'

'I think they're dragging the river,' he said gently.

She shuddered, and hurried indoors. Colin stayed with her while she packed the few things she needed, and afterwards accompanied her on a tour of the house. In each room she paused, her eyes travelling slowly and somewhat mistily over its contents — 'to make sure everything is all right,' she told him. Colin nodded, although he did not believe her. She had a further and more intimate reason, he suspected.

In the sitting room she paused longer than usual, staring hard at J.C.'s desk. Then she turned to him excitedly, her eyes shining.

'He's *not* dead, Colin! He can't be!'

'How on earth can you tell that?' he expostulated.

'Because he's been to his desk, that's why. That chair — I pushed it into the knee-hole before I left, and now look where it is. *Someone* must have moved it.'

'A burglar,' he suggested weakly.

'With all the doors and windows locked? Don't be silly, darling.' She went over to the desk and opened it. 'See? It's all neat and tidy. A burglar wouldn't leave it like that.'

'Didn't your grandfather keep it locked?'

'Usually, yes. He must have forgotten. I expect he was in a hurry to get away before I came home and found him here. That would have ruined his scheme.'

'Damn it, Anne — I can't believe J.C. would go to such lengths to frighten you just because of what happened Saturday morning,' Colin said earnestly. 'If he did it's — well, it's downright wicked.'

'You don't know Grandfather,' said Anne. 'Come on, let's go down to the river and tell those men they're wasting their time.'

They went out into the garden — and stopped. Across the fields from the river a group of men was approaching the house. Two of them carried a stretcher, and on it . . .

'Oh, no!' cried the girl. 'No, it can't be!'

Colin took her arm and led her back into the house. 'You wait there, darling,' he said. 'I'll go and meet them.'

They lifted the rough blanket for him to look. Colin gulped, nodded, and turned away.

'He was caught in the weeds,' said one of the men. 'Must have been carried down there by the current.'

'You mean — that was how he died?'

'No, sir. He'd be dead long before that.

Cramp, most likely — or maybe a heart attack.'

They picked up the stretcher. 'You're not taking him to the Lodge, are you?' asked Colin, alarmed.

'No, sir. We brought him up this way because it's nearer to the road. But if we might use the telephone — '

'It's in the hall,' said Colin. 'Help yourselves.'

He went into the sitting room to comfort the weeping Anne.

\* \* \*

The inquest on John Connaught was held the following Wednesday. Mr Latimer formally identified the body, and the police described how and where it had been found. According to the medical evidence, death was due to drowning, with no indication as to how the accident might have occurred.

Anne was the only other witness. She told the court how her grandfather had been accustomed to take an early-morning bathe daily throughout the year, and how she had seen him set off in the direction of the river at seven o'clock on the previous Saturday. That, she said, was the last time she had seen him.

'Was the deceased a strong swimmer?' asked the coroner.

Anne said she thought he was reasonably strong for his age. 'During the holidays I often went down to watch him bathe, and he never seemed to be in any difficulties. But I was wondering — '

'Yes?' prompted the coroner, as she paused.

'He had a bad throat the day before. It was so bad he could only whisper, and I was wondering whether that might have affected him when he was in the water. Made him feel faint, perhaps.'

The coroner nodded. 'Didn't his doctor advise him against bathing?' he asked.

'He refused to see a doctor. I told him he ought not to bathe, but he was very — ' she had been going to say 'pig-headed,' but stopped herself; it seemed a callous and light-hearted word to use under the circumstances — 'he was rather obstinate. It had become almost a point of honour with him not to miss a morning, you see.'

The coroner thought this over.

'I understand that Mrs Connaught died last January. Would you say that the deceased had become resigned to his wife's death?'

Anne looked round the court. There were many there, she thought, who could answer that question better than she. She had not seen her grandmother since childhood, but from all accounts the old lady had been a bit of a tartar. And J.C. was not the grieving kind.

'He *seemed* quite resigned,' she said guardedly.

'I have a reason for putting that question,' the coroner told her. 'When found, the deceased was still wearing his wristwatch. Now, that might be due to forgetfulness — I have done it myself, unfortunately — but do you think that in this case there might have been another reason? Could it not be that your grandfather, in a fit of depression caused by his wife's death at the beginning of the year — a depression accentuated, per- haps, by his low state of health — decided to take his own life? I am not suggesting that this is what actually happened — I merely mention it as a possibility. It would explain why in bathing that morning he disregarded your advice and, presumably, his own common-sense. And under such circumstances he would be unlikely to concern himself with the removal of his watch.'

Anne was shocked. To imagine J.C. committing suicide was preposterous, almost indecent. With his newly acquired wealth, the power it had given him to annoy Joseph Latimer, and his plans for her own marriage to James, he had much to live for. As for disregarding her advice — why, that was typical of J.C.

'He would never do such a thing,' she said firmly. 'Never.'

The coroner left it at that. It had obviously been an alternative which he had considered it his duty to put forward but to which he personally gave little credence.

A verdict of accidental death by drowning was duly recorded.

Joseph Latimer wasted no tears over

the death of his old enemy. He also lost no time in making his plans known. 'I don't know how you feel about going back to the Lodge,' he said to Anne, shortly after the inquest, 'but I suggest you move into the small sickroom for the rest of this term. It won't be needed unless we are unfortunate enough to get an epidemic.'

Ann thanked him and accepted the offer.

'The Lodge never belonged to your grandfather,' the headmaster went on. 'He had only a life tenancy, and it now reverts to the school. I could, of course, move some of the staff over there, but I would prefer not to. Not this term. I intend to convert the ground floor into a flat for the Smeltons — they find that house of theirs very expensive to run — and the top floor can be done up to accommodate the male members of the staff.' He was talking now more for his own benefit than for hers. This was a moment to which he had long looked forward. 'It is essential to get the work started immediately if the Lodge is to be ready in time for next term. That is why I would prefer you to stay over here.'

Anne said again that she would prefer it too, but she felt some repugnance at this haste to carve up her grandfather's home. She had not had much affection for the old man — he had been selfish and malicious, and she knew that he had sent for her to live with him only because, after his wife's death, he needed a housekeeper. It had not been through any concern for her welfare — but at least Mr Latimer might have tried to conceal his satisfaction at J.C.'s death. Particularly when talking to the dead man's grand-daughter.

When she recounted this conversation at dinner that evening the headmaster's attitude caused no surprise. 'He's a fish, is our Joseph,' said Diana. 'You mustn't expect sympathy from a fish.'

'I didn't. I just thought he need not have gloated so openly.'

'I haven't seen him gloating,' Diana said thoughtfully. 'It must have been rather beastly.'

'What annoys me is Smelton having a

flat there,' said Colin. 'It would have suited . . . ' He paused awkwardly; his engagement to Anne was still supposed to be a secret. 'Smelton's a wily old bird, if you ask me. He's got in on the ground floor in more senses than one.'

'His wife may have something to say about that.' Diana had no liking for Dorothy Smelton. 'Don't give up hope.'

She laughed — rather maliciously, Anne thought — at the obvious embarrassment her remark caused.

Later that evening, when the others had gone to bed and Anne was alone in the common room waiting to say goodnight to Colin on his return from going round the dormitories, James Latimer came in. He sat himself astride a wooden chair, his arms resting on the back, his long legs stretched out before him.

'Sorry about J.C., Anne,' he said. 'Unlike my father I got on well with the old man. I know it's a bit late in the day to express my condolences, but you're a difficult person to corner. That fellow Russell dogs you like a shadow.' He smiled what he considered to be an all-conquering smile, showing a large expanse of white even teeth. Anne had been subjected to it before, and guessed something of what was coming. 'Well, next term your shadow won't be quite so permanent, thank goodness. He and Chris will be parked over at the Lodge. That may be my opportunity to cash in, eh?'

'Don't be silly, James,' she said, hoping to halt him before he became difficult. Death is always frightening to the young, and the inquest had depressed her. She felt in no mood for coping with an amorous James Latimer. 'It won't make any difference, you know that.'

'A pity.' He got up and stood over her, looking like a younger but more genial edition of his father. 'I had an idea that J.C. rather hoped you and I would make a go of it.'

'I can't imagine why you should think that,' lied Anne.

'Perhaps not. But I do. Mind you, I'm not proposing — we'd need to get together a bit more before it came to that.' He bent lower, smiling down at her. 'How about making a start with dinner at the George tomorrow night?'

Anne slid sideways and stood up. 'No, thank you. Not tomorrow or any other night,' she said.

He caught her arm, pulling her towards him. Unaccountably Anne felt scared. 'I can be damned obstinate,' he said, still smiling. 'I don't give up easily.'

'I can be obstinate too,' she retorted. Freeing herself, she ran from the room.

She found Colin on the landing. He wanted to go down and have it out with James, but Anne stopped him. 'It's partly my fault,' she said. 'I shouldn't have encouraged him last term. Now he can't understand how I manage to resist him.'

'Why not tell him we're engaged, then? That would put a stopper on his Don Juan act.'

'It might not. You don't know James as well as I do. And I shouldn't be surprised if this re-awakening of his interest in me is connected with Grandfather's death.'

'What difference does that make?'

'James has an eye to the main chance.

It's rumoured that I'm something of an heiress,' Anne reminded him.

The rumour was well founded. John Connaught had left her the bulk of his fortune. 'It has not yet been possible to ascertain the exact amount,' the solicitor told her, 'but after death duties and other bequests have been paid your share should be in the neighbourhood of twenty-five thousand pounds. Perhaps a little more.'

'And very nice too,' was Colin Russell's comment. He seemed to have overcome his reluctance to marrying a girl with money. 'On that you should be able to support me in the style to which I have not yet become accustomed, but which I am not averse to trying.'

There were two minor bequests, both surprising. 'Two thousand pounds,' ran the will, 'to be paid to Philip Raynes Smelton or whosoever shall be senior master at Redways Preparatory School in his place; the money to be administered by him in conjunction with the rest of the teaching staff for the benefit of the boys at the school.' But the real surprise lay in the proviso. Neither the headmaster nor his family were to benefit from the money or to be consulted in the spending of it.

The second bequest was even more startling. 'Three thousand pounds to Diana Euphemia Farling provided she be still unmarried at the time of my death.'

The boys' legacy caused fury in the meagre bosom of Mr Latimer. He had no objection to money being spent on the school, but that his enemy should be able to mock him even after death was almost unbearable.

'What do we do with the cash, Smelton?' asked Colin, after he and other members of the staff had discussed, with accuracy and not a little glee, the possible effects of his bequest on their headmaster. 'How about refurnishing the common-room so that the little dears will have somewhere cosy to sit when they come to pour out their troubles to us?'

Smelton frowned. 'It's no joking matter,' he said. 'In fact, it's a hell of a responsibility. We'll need to think it over most carefully.'

'Why?' asked Anne.

'Because it's not going to be easy. Not if we stick to the terms of the will, as I suppose we must. Practically everything that benefits the school must also benefit the Latimers.'

'You could build a new swimming-pool,' Diana suggested. She was a keen swimmer. 'Joseph can't abide cold water, and it is about time that wretched little duckpond was scrapped.'

'Latimer would still benefit. It would enhance the value of the school, make it more attractive to parents.'

'How about a tuckshop?' asked Chris. He had brightened up since the inquest. Anne wondered whether that was because Diana had been noticeably sweeter to him. 'We could give the stuff away free.'

'No need to decide in a hurry,' Smelton said. He too had become more cheerful. The rest of the staff attributed this to the prospective flat. 'And if it's going to fill old sourgrapes with the milk of human kindness, then I no longer grudge him it,' Colin Russell had declared.

Diana Farling's legacy also caused much comment, the general opinion (not voiced when Chris Moull was within hearing) being that Diana must have put in some behind-the scenes vamping on J.C. before, with the rest of the staff, she had been turned out of the Lodge. But the girl herself seemed startled, almost shocked and annoyed, at her good fortune, and fiercely resented any allusion to it.

'I'm sure Diana would never have encouraged J.C. in *any* way,' said Miss Webber, who, although scandal was as meat and drink to her, made a point of refraining from unkind remarks. They had much of the boomerang in them, she had found. 'But there is no denying she is extremely good-looking, and he must have liked having her about the house. Any man would. Particularly if he had a wife as bad-tempered as — ' She stopped, flushing, and looked at Anne apologetically. 'Sorry, my dear. I keep forgetting she was your grandmother.'

'Don't mind me,' said the girl. 'I never saw her after I was about six years old. But I think you're wrong, Webby. J.C. wasn't like that. If he was, why did he turn her out of the house last Easter with the others?'

'He could hardly single her out to stay,' Smelton said. 'That would have been most injudicious. Personally I think Miss Webber may be right.'

'Well, I don't,' said Anne. 'Last term he never once suggested that I should ask her over, and there would have been nothing injudicious in that.'

It was a pity they could not discuss it with Diana herself, Anne thought. But Diana, like Smelton, would allow no intrusion on her privacy. She was friendly and easy to talk to on impersonal matters, but she was rather the cat that walked alone.

'But why else should he leave her all that money?' asked Miss Webber. She could have made suggestions, some of them highly scandalous; but since it was against her policy to voice them she hoped someone else would voice them for her.

'I don't know,' Anne admitted. 'I haven't a clue.' She turned to Russell. 'You've been unusually quiet, Colin. What

74

are you thinking about?'

'I was wondering,' said Colin, 'how Diana's parents came to christen her Euphemia.'

The words were lightly spoken, but there was no accompanying smile on his face. Now what's the matter, Anne wondered, recognizing the symptoms. I hope he isn't sickening for another broody spell.

# 4

## A Lamp Goes Bang

'When a man asks a girl to go for a walk,' said Anne, 'it seems reasonable for her to assume that he doesn't intend only to keep putting one damned foot after another. A little romantic conversation is the least she is entitled to expect. Yet during the last ten minutes the only word that has escaped you was when you tripped over a root. And there was nothing romantic about *that*.'

Colin grinned. 'Sorry, ducks. I was busy with me thoughts.'

'About me?' she asked hopefully.

'No. About J.C.'

'Oh.' And then, after a pause, 'What about him?'

'Only that his death has been a mighty convenient event for every one connected with the school.'

Anne considered this.

'Yes, I suppose that's true. For the Latimers certainly. Grandfather used to say there was nothing Mr Latimer wouldn't do to get Abbey Lodge back. Only there wasn't anything he *could* do, short of murder.'

'Not only the Latimers,' said Colin. 'There's Smelton too. Apparently he's had his eye on that flat for quite a while. And what about Diana? Three thousand quid is a tidy sum to a working girl.'

'It's a tidy sum to most people.'

'Yes. And then there's us. You're going to be absolutely rolling in the stuff, and I don't suppose you are likely to grudge me the odd quid or two when I'm short. Yet if J.C. hadn't been drowned we would probably have got married and been cut off without a shilling. Either that — or we should have had to wait until he pegged out naturally. And that might not have happened for years.'

'Or I might have been bludgeoned into marrying James,' Anne added.

'Yes, there's that too,' he agreed, not relishing the thought. 'And even the boys benefit by two thousand quid.'

'That only leaves Chris and the matrons. It seems a pity they should be left out, poor dears.'

'Chris isn't left out,' said Colin. 'Not if he's hoping to marry Diana.'

'Which he won't.' Anne spoke with conviction. 'Diana has an eye for the main chance. She won't throw herself away on a poor assistant master with no prospects.'

'Why not? You're going to.'

'I haven't got Diana's good sense,' she retorted, beginning to run, and then allowing herself to be caught, spanked, and kissed. When she had recovered her breath she said, 'It seems rather indecent, doesn't it, that so many of us should profit from the old man's accident.'

'If it *was* an accident.'

'Eh?' Anne was startled. 'But of course it was! Oh, I know the coroner hinted at suicide. But that was complete nonsense. If he'd known J.C. he wouldn't even have suggested it.'

'I wasn't thinking of suicide,' said Colin.

'Then what else . . . ' She stopped

suddenly, gripping his arm tightly. 'Colin! You're not suggesting he was *murdered!*'

'No, of course not. At least — well, yes, in a way I suppose I am,' he agreed reluctantly. 'That accident was just a sight to convenient to be true.'

'So you think we all got together and murdered him? Oh, come off it, darling. Whatever put that idea into your head?'

'It just grew on me, I think, starting with the wrist-watch. It wasn't like J.C. to forget it — you yourself said he was methodical. In all the years he's been taking an early-morning dip has he ever made that mistake before?'

'Not to my knowledge. But that only goes back to last March.'

'All right. But you have watched him bathing. What did he do with his watch?'

'Usually he put it on top of his clothes.'

Colin nodded eagerly.

'There! You see? And there's another thing. His clothes. It wasn't like J.C. to scatter them the way we found them. Or was it?'

'No,' Anne agreed, impressed against her will. 'He always folded them into a neat pile. But all the same, darling, you can't accuse people of murder on such trifling evidence as that.'

'I know I can't. All I'm saying is, that, with so many people eagerly awaiting his death, it's most suspicious that he should have died the way he did.'

'I wasn't eagerly awaiting his death,' she retorted with spirit. 'I hope you weren't either.'

'No, of course not. I wasn't thinking of us.'

'Then who *were* you thinking of?'

'No one in particular. But one could make out a case against most of them. Take Smelton, for instance. He had a motive, he was acting very oddly the evening before (remember how we saw him dashing off to Tanbury?), and he turned up late the next morning — the morning J.C. was drowned — looking perfectly ghastly, with water dripping from his hair and his suit looking as though he had slept in it. *And* his wife said she hadn't seen him that morning.' He glanced at her anxiously. 'Mind you, all this is between ourselves, Anne. If

Smelton got wind of what I've been saying he'd probably sue me for slander.'

The girl smiled to herself. She loved him when he became intense. It was absurd to believe that J.C. had been murdered, but Colin would be terribly hurt if she were to scoff at his fancies. They were real to him, no doubt. In a few days they would probably be forgotten — Colin was like that. But until they were she must humour him, if only to get them out of his system the sooner.

'I won't breathe a word,' she said soberly. 'Tell me more, darling. In spite of myself I'm impressed.'

Again he glanced at her, suspicious of this sudden change of mood. There was no trace of a smile on her pretty face.

'Well, old Latimer probably has the strongest motive,' he went on. 'J.C. must have been drowned shortly after seven o'clock, and it was a quarter to eight when I met Latimer outside the Fifth Form that morning. That would have given him time enough. Then there is Diana, with her three thousand quid. How do you fancy her?'

'Not at all.' If she were playing a game at least she would play it properly. Too ready an acceptance of all he said would spoil it; he needed opposition to bite on. And while there had been plenty of sense in what he had said about Smelton and Mr Latimer, there was no sense at all in suspecting Diana. 'I'm sure she had not the least idea that Grandfather was going to leave her that money. Besides, she was away at the cottage that weekend.'

'She was only four miles away,' said Colin doggedly, reluctant to release a suspect. 'She could do that easily on her bike. Her cottage is on the river, so she would know there was a mist that morning. Come to think of it, she might even have rowed down. Less conspicuous. I suppose it would take longer that way, but it could be done.'

'Longer than you think,' said Anne. 'It's not the same river.'

'Oh!' Colin was disconcerted, and decided temporarily to abandon Diana Farling. He could always return to her later. 'Well, there's James. He knew J.C. was in favour of your marrying him, and after the encouragement you apparently gave him last term he may have thought you were in favour of it too. You know how conceited he is. And with twenty-five thousand smackers in the bank you would be a pretty good prospect as a wife.'

'Thank you,' Anne said acidly.

'Don't get huffy, darling. You know I didn't mean it like that. Even if you were Cleopatra and the Queen of Sheba rolled into one — where looks are concerned, that is; I'm not referring to their morals or their habits — the money would still add a bit of extra glamour.'

'Of course. Don't worry, I'm not huffy,' she assured him truthfully. 'And I agree that James would be the ideal suspect — *provided* there had been a murder. He was closeted with Grandfather the evening before, and we didn't see him after that until lunch the next day. Anyone else?'

'Only Chris.'

'Chris?' Anne forgot the game in her genuine surprise. 'Why on earth should Chris want to murder J.C.?'

'I don't know. But it puzzles me that he

should have gone out so early that morning. It's most unlike Chris — he's the biggest lie-a-bed of the lot of us.'

'Pure coincidence,' said Anne firmly.

'H'm! I wonder. Is it also a coincidence that he chose to go past the Lodge and along the river?'

'Of course it is. And he certainly wouldn't have told us he went that way if he had anything to hide.'

'Well, I hope you're right. I like Chris as much as you do. But one has to face facts, Anne.'

'Yes, darling, of course,' she said soothingly. 'Still, I think you'd do better to confine your suspicions to Mr Smelton and the Latimers. They're far more suitable than Diana or Chris.' She looked at her watch. 'It's time we were making tracks for home. I don't want to miss my tea.'

They turned, and for a while there was silence between them. Then Colin said, 'You think I'm scatty, don't you? But what about the keys? You seem to have forgotten them.'

'Keys? What keys?'

'Your grandfather's. You thought it was J.C. who came back to the Lodge after you left it on Saturday morning. But it couldn't have been, could it? He was dead. So who — '

'Colin!' She stopped and looked at him, her face penitent. 'You're right, I *had* forgotten. And I never said a word about them at the inquest. Should I have done?'

'You should — but I think it's just as well you didn't,' he said grimly. 'And you're missing the point, darling. The keys weren't on J.C.'s dressing-table, they weren't in his trousers' pockets, and he certainly didn't take them into the river with him. Yet someone — or so you say — used those keys after J.C. was dead to enter the house and rifle his desk. And if that someone didn't murder J.C. — well, how did he get hold of the keys?'

Anne did not answer. There seemed suddenly to be less warmth in the October sun, and she shivered. Pulling her jacket around her, she walked on. The ground was hard underfoot; there had been no rain for some days. The hedgerows were thick and green, but already the trees were shedding their foliage, and their brown-tinted leaves carpeted the grass and the lanes. To Anne autumn was the most beautiful season of the year. Now she saw none of its beauty, for Colin's words had cast a blight upon her mind and her vision.

What if he were right? What if J.C. *had* been murdered? The suggestion did not now seem so absurd as when Colin had first made it. Against her will her mind played with the possibility that one of the people among whom she lived and worked was a murderer. It was a shattering and terrifying thought, the more so because she could not envisage any of them in that sinister rôle. She could not say 'it must be him,' and go warily in that person's presence. Every contact, every occasion, would be suspect. Only with Colin would she be able to relax, to talk and act naturally. And even then . . .

'What are you going to do?' she asked, as they turned into the lane leading to the school.

'What *can* I do?' He did not query her

reference, for his own thoughts had never left the subject. 'If I consulted the police they'd laugh at me. One couldn't blame them either. The coroner was satisfied, and I can't produce any fresh evidence. Not *real* evidence.'

'What about the keys? Isn't that evidence?'

'To you, yes. But not to the police, I imagine.' He kicked petulantly at a stone. 'No, it would have to be stronger than that for them to sit up and take notice. Yet I must do *something*.'

'Couldn't you find fresh evidence?'

'How? By asking every one what they were up to that morning? A fine mess *that* would land me in!'

Yes, thought Anne unhappily, they must do something. It was no longer a game, it was terrifyingly real. Even if they wanted to they could not ignore it now. Colin might be wrong — but if either of them were to have any peace of mind in the future they had to *know*.

'Why not mention it to Mr Latimer?' she asked. 'If you had his authority to question the staff, wouldn't that make it easier for you?'

'It might — although I don't see that he *has* any authority in that respect. And don't forget that he's under suspicion himself. And even if he's completely innocent he's still likely to refuse. Think of the harm it would do the school if I were proved right. You can't expect him to acquiesce in his own ruin.'

'I don't like him much,' Anne confessed. 'I think I'm a little afraid of him, too. But I don't believe he would refuse to co-operate if you could convince him that you may be right.'

'*If!*' Colin said with emphasis.

'Well, you have practically convinced me,' she said sadly. 'But I wish you hadn't.'

★ ★ ★

At tea-time Diana Farling had a surprise for them.

'Mrs Bain has changed her mind. She no longer wishes to be alone, and is prepared to accept one of us as a lodger.

The headmaster favours you, Chris.'

The Bains lived in a small cottage about ten minutes' walk from the school. At intervals since the previous April Mr Latimer had suggested to them that their spare bedroom could profitably be occupied by one of his staff. Mr Bain had had no objection to this, but his wife, an independent, out-spoken woman, had hitherto obstinately refused.

'Me? Why me?' asked Chris.

Diana shrugged. 'It has to be you or Colin, I suppose. And the daughter is at home weekends. She's quite pretty, I'm told. Maybe Joseph thinks you're more dependable than Colin.'

'But why does *anyone* have to go? Why can't we stay as we are?'

'The headmaster has spoken,' said Diana. 'Who are we to question why?'

'Oh, Chris, I'm so sorry. It's all my fault,' said Anne. 'I suppose Mr Latimer doesn't like to refuse the offer in case both sickrooms are needed later in the term. But it's a shame that you should be turned out of your room on my account.'

'It's all right,' Chris said. 'I don't mind.'

But it was evident from his expression that he minded very much. Anne guessed it was because he feared he might see less of Diana. 'What made Mrs Bain change her mind?' she asked the girl. 'She has always refused before.'

'Her old man is doing a spell of night-work. She doesn't like being alone in the cottage at night.' Diana smiled at Chris, an intimate smile that caused the young man to blush furiously. 'What time do you finish this evening, Chris? We could go down and see the old girl.'

'I'm free at six-fifteen. Would that do?' he asked eagerly, the end lost to him in the means.

'That'll do fine. If you're feeling thirsty we could call in for a drink at the Plough on the way back.'

At six-thirty, when Diana and Chris had eventually departed to visit Mrs Bain, Anne and Colin were left alone in the common room. But that evening they had no leisure for romance or detection. Their afternoon walk had occupied time snatched from work, and they were forced to busy themselves with corrections.

An exclamation from Colin caused Anne to look up from her books.

'What's the matter?' she asked.

'It's Tony Cuttle's essay. I told the form to write on 'The Most Exciting Day in My Life,' and Tony, of course, has written about his accident.'

'What does he say? Let me look.'

Colin tossed the exercise book across. Anne read it as he watched her.

*One day I got up to go to school*, the boy had written, *and came out of my house, and began to walk down the road, and as I came near a bend in the road, near the river I heard a shreek for 'Help!' When I heard this, I thought somebody must be drowning. I tried to cut through the brambles and marsh but I could not because it was so bogy, so I went back and ran down the road till I came to the brige. Then I went along the path beside the river, but when I got to where I thought the shreek came from, it was so misty when I got there, that I couldn't see to the other side of the river. Then I thought I better be getting along to school. So I ran back along the path to the brige and on the road and I cracked into the side of a car, and when I woke up I was in hospitle and . . .*

There was more, but Anne did not bother to read it. 'It doesn't tell us anything fresh, does it?' she commented.

'Not really. There's the cry for help he says he heard; that must have come from J.C.' He frowned. 'Tony doesn't mention Chris, so I suppose the two didn't meet. Chris didn't hear J.C., either. Yet I would have thought . . . Anne, do you think it would be okay to ask Chris a few pertinent questions? I can't see him murdering anyone, but he may have seen or heard something that's important.'

'You would have to do it very tactfully,' Anne said dubiously. Tact, she knew, was not Colin's strong suit.

'Yes, of course. Well, I'll think it over.'

Tony Cuttle's essay had caused the dread word 'murder' to loom large once more in the girl's mind, and she found difficulty in concentrating on Form One

Arithmetic. Few of the figures behaved as they should, and after a while she abandoned the task. She would get up early and tackle them in the morning.

Her eyes shut, she relaxed against the back of the settee and gave her thoughts full rein. And then suddenly she was sitting upright again, a startled look in her grey eyes.

'Colin!'

'Yes?'

'Tony couldn't have heard Grandfather calling for help. Don't you remember? He had lost his voice!'

Troubled, they stared silently at each other. It seemed such a little thing that neither quite knew why it should frighten them. Yet frighten them it did. The shadow overlying Redways seemed suddenly to have become bigger and somehow more threatening.

They were still staring at each other with troubled eyes when Diana and Chris erupted into the room. Chris's hands were black; there were black streaks on his cheeks; his duffel-coat was filthy. Even the normally immaculate Diana looked dirty and bedraggled.

'What on earth — ' began Colin.

'Mrs Bain tried to blow herself up,' said Diana, slumping wearily into a chair. 'She lit a lamp, and it went off bang. We've been picking up the pieces.'

Despite the attempt at nonchalance, Anne guessed that the girl was nearly all in. She turned anxiously to Chris.

'Is Mrs Bain badly hurt?'

'Pretty badly, yes. Burns and shock. The doctor seemed to think she would get over it, though. They've carted her off to hospital.'

'But how did it happen?' Colin demanded.

'Well, there is no gas or electricity in the cottage, you know. It's like Diana's, no mod. con. Mrs Bain went through the kitchen to get a lamp from the shed, after which she was going to take us upstairs to show us the room. Diana and I were in the hall, and we saw a glow in the kitchen — and then there was this almighty explosion, and we dashed in. The old lady was alight and screaming like billy-o, but we managed to smother the flames and get her out of the room. Then I went back to deal with the fire. The oil on the floor was blazing like merry hell. Luckily there wasn't much of it — the lamp must have been nearly empty — or I should never have been able to cope.'

'Poor Mrs Bain,' said Anne. 'Was her husband there?'

'He'd just left. The police were going to let him know.'

'But paraffin lamps don't blow up like that,' Colin said, bewildered.

'This one did, believe me.' Diana stood up. 'Well, I'm for a bath and bed. Be an angel, Anne, and bring me up some hot milk later. I don't want any dinner.'

'Of course. How about you, Chris?'

'Oh, I'm all right. But I'd better go and clean myself up.'

When they were alone again Colin said, 'Well, that settles one little problem. Chris won't be sleeping at Mrs Bain's now.'

'No,' Anne said absently. 'But what a ghastly thing to happen. I wonder if . . . ' She stopped, mouth agape, horrified incredulity reflected in her eyes. 'Colin!

You're not suggesting — '

He nodded. 'I certainly am! He didn't want to move, and now he doesn't have to,' he said grimly. 'Wonderful, isn't it, how nicely things turn out for some people? First J.C., and now Mrs Bain. I wonder who is next on the list.'

# 5

## Murder Under Discussion

'And do you mean to tell me that on such flimsy evidence you really believe J.C. was murdered?' asked Mr Latimer, his heavy eyebrows lifting and puckering the skin above them into deep ridges.

'Yes,' said Colin.

'Extraordinary! Most extraordinary!' Mr Latimer gazed at him as though he were a specimen under the microscope. 'I can only surmise that you have an unusually fertile imagination, Russell — fed, no doubt, on the wrong type of Sunday newspaper. You say Miss Connaught shares your opinion?'

'Yes,' Colin said again. Eloquence had temporarily deserted him. Sarcasm always took the wind out of his sails.

'Odd,' mused the headmaster. 'I had supposed her to be a young woman with both feet on the ground. And which of us, may I ask, do you fancy as the murderer? Or are you keeping an open mind on that point?'

Colin shook his head feebly. Why was it, he wondered, that Mr Latimer could always reduce him to this state of goggle-eyed dumbness? It had not gone too badly at the start, when the headmaster had allowed him, either from astonishment or from politeness (and the last was most uncharacteristic), to say his piece without interruption. But now —

'I don't think there is sufficient evidence to show,' he managed to answer.

'Well, at least we are in agreement there. I am much relieved — I had feared you might have your eye on me.' The eyebrows dropped. 'The obvious candidate would, I imagine, be Miss Connaught herself. Does she appreciate that?'

'Of course.'

'Good. It may cause her to hedge before you go too far.' The headmaster took a cigarette and offered one to Colin, who accepted it gratefully. A cigarette might help to restore some of the confidence which was so rapidly deserting him. 'Now let us try to dispose of this farcical fancy of yours. It should not be difficult. Take, for instance, your preoccupation with J.C.'s wrist-watch and scattered belongings. Do you suggest that someone attacked him on the river-bank, stripped the poor man of his clothing — not forgetting, of course, to put on his swimming-trunks in the interests of decency — and then threw him, all alive-o, into the river to drown? For he was drowned, you know; no rough stuff, no bumps on the head. The medical evidence made that quite clear.'

'No, I don't suppose it happened like that,' Colin said doubtfully. He had not given much thought as to *how* the murder had been committed, he only knew that it had taken place.

'Right. Well, then — perhaps you feel that the murderer did not use force at this stage? That he merely requested — no, ordered is the better word — his victim to remove his clothing and enter the water (again suitably attired, of course — one never knows who may discover the body, does one?) to await his end?'

Colin flushed angrily and stood up.

'I think that's enough, sir,' he said, his voice not entirely under control. 'I came to you because I thought it was the proper thing to do. I was prepared for incredulity and non-co-operation, but I'm damned if I'm going to stay here and let you make a fool of me. You are treating the whole thing as a huge joke, and — '

'Sit down, Russell.' The headmaster's voice was peremptory, and from force of habit Colin obeyed. 'I'm not trying to make a fool of you — you are doing that for yourself, if you will forgive my saying so. Nor am I treating this as a joke. It is no joke, believe me, when one of my staff accuses a colleague — even though he leaves that colleague unnamed — of so foul a crime as murder. If I spoke lightly it was to impress on you the absurdity of your hypothesis.'

Colin was not at all sure that he wanted the absurdity impressed on him. He knew he was right. By a skilful use of words the headmaster might confuse his convictions, but he could not dispel them. And a confused mind would merely handicap him in his search for the truth.

'Good man,' said Mr Latimer, apparently interpreting the other's silence as a willingness to listen. He sounded almost genial. 'Now, you seem to consider yourself something of a detective, but I say you are out of your depth in that rôle. For if we are agreed (as I think we are) that J.C. was not forced into the water it follows that he went in of his own free will and with no premonition of impending disaster. And in that case neither the wrist-watch nor the scattered belongings have any significance whatsoever. Can't you see that?'

He saw it only too clearly. And if old Latimer can make mincemeat out of me like this, he thought dismally, what would the police have done?

But Colin was stubborn. One thrust, however piercing, was not going to make him capitulate out of hand. 'Yes, I see that,' he conceded. 'But there may be an explanation that has not occurred to either of us. And you can't get away from the fact that J.C. had never before been so careless or so unmethodical.'

'How can you be sure of that? Miss Connaught accompanied him occasionally in the holidays, but nine times out of ten there was no witness. How do you know what he did then?' The headmaster threw his cigarette into the fire and lit another. This time he did not offer one to Colin. 'I suspect, Russell, that you do not *want* to be convinced. However, let us take your next point — this call for help that Cuttle is supposed to have heard. Personally, I would say that he imagined it.'

'No, sir, he didn't.' For once Colin felt himself on firm ground. 'I've questioned him closely, and he is positive he heard it.'

The headmaster's eyebrows shot up.

'So you have questioned him already, have you? Wasn't that rather presumptuous?'

'But I was correcting his essay,' Colin expostulated indignantly. 'There was no harm in making sure he had his facts right.'

'Form is more important than fact, Russell, when it comes to correcting a boy's essay.'

'I corrected that too, sir.'

'Well, we will let that pass for now. We will even suppose that Cuttle was *not* mistaken. What of it? Isn't it natural that a drowning man should call for help?'

'But the point is, sir, that he couldn't. He'd lost his voice.'

'So he had,' Mr Latimer agreed, in no way discomfited. 'Which brings us back to where we started — that Cuttle was mistaken. Or are you suggesting that it was the murderer who shouted for help?'

It's no good, Colin thought despairingly. The old man has an answer to everything — I'll never make him understand.

'You're dissecting these points individually, Mr Latimer,' he said indignantly. 'Of course they seem weak if you do that. But take them all together and they amount to something.'

Mr Latimer shook his head sorrowfully.

'Your mathematics appear to be as weak as your flair for detection, Russell,' he said. 'If each of these points amounts to nothing, then their sum is also nothing. And we haven't finished yet; there are still the keys to dispose of. Because they are missing you assume they have been stolen. Why?'

'Because they were neither in his pockets nor on the dressing-table,' said Colin. 'And someone other than Anne used them to enter the house after J.C. was dead. That's why.'

'But my dear fellow! There are a host of other places where J.C. might have left his keys. He might even have lost them. As for Miss Connaught's assumption (based solely on one misplaced chair, you say) that someone entered the house — well, frankly, I don't believe it. I'm sorry, but I don't. She must be mistaken.'

There was only Mrs Bain now, and to mention her would be to court ridicule. Despite what he had said to Anne the previous evening, calm reflection had made Colin aware that it would be very difficult indeed to establish any connection between the death of J.C. and the accident to Mrs Bain. There could be none.

'It's no go, sir,' he said, not attempting

to hide his annoyance and disappointment. 'I agree with much of what you say, but I still think I'm right, that J.C.'s death was no accident. But as I can't make you see it my way . . . ' He stood up. 'Good night, sir.'

The headmaster eyed him thoughtfully. He had met men of Russell's stamp before. They might appear submissive to authority, but there was a dogged streak in them that drove them, often against their better judgment, to persevere in a seemingly hopeless cause — underground, if necessary. He did not want that to happen here.

'What did you expect me to do?' he asked. 'Call in the police?'

'No, sir. I appreciate that there is not enough evidence for that. But I did hope that you would see my point of view, and perhaps give me your authority to question the staff and make a few inquiries.'

'The staff might say I had not the necessary authority to give,' Mr Latimer said drily. 'But as I am certainly withholding it, what do you propose to do now?'

Colin sensed his anxiety, and drew from it a little bitter consolation. Let the old blighter stew for a while, he thought. Why should I consider his peace of mind when he doesn't care a damn for mine?

'Do a bit of sleuthing on my own,' he said, and left the room before the other could question him further.

His consolation was only temporary. By the time he had sought and found Anne he was in a dismal mood. 'The old man knocked 'em down all along the line,' he told her. 'He applied common-sense and logic where I used my imagination, and common-sense and logic won in a canter. He fairly shrivelled me.'

Anne was uncertain whether to be sorry or relieved at this set-back. If Colin bowed to the common-sense point of view, would he come to accept it as the truth? Would he be completely converted, or would he accept it under protest? And where did *she* stand? Her mood at the start had been as sceptical as the headmaster's — it was the lost keys which had brought her round to Colin's way of thinking. And there she had the better of the headmaster. Mr Latimer might say she was mistaken in thinking that the chair had been moved, but he was wrong. And if he were wrong in that might he not be wrong elsewhere?

And yet with Mr Latimer against them what hope had they of achieving anything? Murder or no murder, they would be banging their heads against a brick wall; there would be nothing ahead of them but frustration and disappointment. Might it not be wiser to accept defeat now, considering that it was inevitable? There were less than seven weeks to the end of term; surely they could suffer their doubts and fears as long as that? Presumably the murderer had achieved his purpose, whatever that might have been; he was unlikely to strike again. By keeping silence they would not be condemning another innocent person to death.

'I'm sorry Mr Latimer was so beastly to you, darling,' she said, 'but perhaps it is all for the best. We shall soon have to start making plans for our wedding, and that will be a wholetime job. No time then for chasing a will-o'-the-wisp murderer who may not even exist. So let's forget it, eh?'

It was a reasonable if unethical decision. But Colin stared at her in dismay.

'Forget it? What — give in to that old so-and-so? No ruddy fear.'

The reproach in his voice puzzled her. 'But you said — ' she began.

'I said he beat me hands down on argument, that's all. I didn't say he was *right*. He's not, either — I'm sure of that. What's more, I'll prove it. I'll make the old buzzard apologize if it's the last thing I ever do.'

She smiled at him, suddenly glad. He had not chosen the easy way out. He might be up against a brick wall, but that didn't matter; it was his resolution, his refusal to accept the odds against him, that warmed her and filled her with pride in him. And — well, who knew? Colin was tough and a fighter. It might be the brick wall that gave way first.

'Good for you,' she said, hugging him after a quick glance to ensure that no small boy was watching. 'I can't see any real road to success, but I'm glad you didn't let that sarcastic old iceberg get you down. What do we do next? And I mean *we*.'

He kissed her. 'Chris, I suppose. He's the only one I can hope to tackle without being told to mind my own business.'

'Only if he's innocent — as I suppose he must be? I can't imagine Chris wilfully harming a flea, let alone a human being.'

Colin frowned. 'I would have said that too a fortnight ago. But now — well, we'll see. You don't suppose he would have confided in Diana, do you? Couldn't you try to pump her? Indulge in a spasm of girlish confidences?'

Anne smiled. 'Diana isn't given to girlish confidences; she's as close as a clam. If anyone is going to pump her it had better be you, darling; a presentable male would have more success with Diana than another woman. Even so I doubt whether you would discover anything she didn't want you to know.'

'I suspect something catty in that remark,' said Colin. 'But I might take you up on it. Diana is a remarkably good-looking female.'

Anne shuddered. 'Ugh! I hope you don't go around describing *me* as a good-looking female.'

'Well, you are, aren't you? But if you don't think you would get anywhere with Diana, how about Mrs Smelton? You're friendly with her, and I'd very much like to know what her husband was up to that morning. Incidentally, have you noticed that he's gone all gloomy again?'

'Probably had another row with Dorothy. All right — if the opportunity offers I'll see what I can do. But don't expect too much. She may not know, and she may not talk even if she *does* know.'

Colin took Chris Moull down to the local that evening for a drink before dinner. Unlike Smelton, Chris had not returned to the gloom that had enveloped him prior to the inquest. Anne ascribed this to Diana's kindlier manner towards him, but Colin wondered at times whether the verdict itself might not have something to do with it. If Chris had anything to hide that verdict must have made him feel more secure.

In the pub the talk was of Mrs Bain. Chris seemed taken aback at being regarded by the landlord and his customers as something of a hero, and vehemently denied the label. It had been a simple job to put out the fire, he said — and asked how the old lady was progressing.

'She'll do,' said the landlord. 'She ain't all that bad, I'm told. What beats me is how she come to make such a stupid mistake.'

'What mistake?' asked Colin.

'She'd been and filled the lamp with petrol in the shed where they keep the paraffin, but you'd think the old dear would know the difference after all these years.'

'What does he keep petrol for?'

'He's got one of them auto-cycles,' said the landlord.

It was not until they were on their way back to the school that Colin mentioned Tony Cuttle's essay. 'It explains how he came to run into the side of the car instead of the front of it,' he said. 'I wondered about that. Incidentally, how was it you didn't see him down by the river?'

'Goodness knows,' said the other, after a slight pause. 'We weren't there at the same time, I suppose.'

'Well, you ought to have seen him after the accident. They had to wait for the ambulance.'

This time the pause was longer. Then, 'I didn't come home along the Tanbury road,' said Chris.

'Eh? But what other way is there?'

'None, old boy. I turned round and came back the way I'd gone.'

'Quite a lengthy trek,' Colin said cheerfully, trying not to expose his growing suspicion. 'You didn't hear J.C. shouting for help, did you?'

'You've asked me that before.' Chris sounded somewhat testy. 'You or Anne, I can't remember which. What's all this in aid of? Why the interest in my comings and goings that morning?'

Colin decided to give a little. A show of confidence might be reciprocated.

'I'm intrigued by the number of unusual things that happened that morning,' he confessed. 'Tony Cuttle heard a man who had lost his voice shouting for

112

help, and then got knocked down by a car and was taken to hospital; J.C. broke the methodical habits of a lifetime by leaving his clothes all over the place and forgetting to take off his wrist-watch; you turned back and retraced your steps when it would have been so much quicker to come by the bridge; and the three of you — J.C., Tony, and yourself — must have been within a few yards of each other and didn't realize it because of the mist.' He lowered his voice confidentially. 'And here is something you don't know, old man. J.C.'s keys are missing. They should have been in his trousers' pockets, but they weren't. What's more, Anne is certain that someone was in the Lodge later that day; she didn't mention it at the inquest because she forgot about it. So you can see now why I'm slightly curious about what happened that morning.'

'I don't blame you,' said the other. 'Of course, Tony was knocked down by the car *because* J.C. called for help. That's cause and effect. There may have been cause and effect in J.C.'s death too; perhaps he was drowned simply *because* he wasn't his methodical self that morning. But the keys — that's queer, I agree. I suppose Anne couldn't have been mistaken in thinking someone got into the house?'

He did not, as Colin had hoped, volunteer any further information on his own behaviour that morning.

'She seems quite confident about it,' Colin said.

'What's all this leading up to? You're not suggesting there was any funny business, are you?' asked Chris, his voice low.

'That's what I want to find out. Did you meet anyone on your walk? That might be important, you know.'

'Not along by the river,' Chris said slowly. 'There was a chap on a bike near the bridge — the far bridge, not the Tanbury road one.'

'Anyone else?'

'Only Mrs Smelton.'

'Mrs Smelton? What the devil would she be doing so far from home at that hour? I'm told she never gets out of bed until after nine.'

'Well, there she was. She turned up the track leading to the Lodge. When I passed the house a few minutes later her bike was leaning against the hedge, but the lady herself had vanished.'

'Well! Well! Well!' said Colin. 'If you ask me, Chris, that's just about the oddest of all the odd things that happened that Saturday morning.'

When they entered the common room the staff were already sitting down to dinner, and he had no opportunity to tell Anne the news of Mrs Smelton. Several times during the meal he caught Chris eyeing him speculatively, and wondered. Was Chris merely curious — or was he uneasy? Whichever it is, thought Colin, I bet he could tell me a bit more if he wanted to. There's *something* he's keeping to himself.

James Latimer came in to speak to Smelton, who was on duty. They had asked James to sound his father on Diana's suggestion that a new swimming-pool should be built with the boys' legacy, it being generally agreed that this was the most sensible way of spending the money.

'He doesn't object,' said James, 'provided you convert the duckpond and don't start excavating elsewhere.'

Smelton frowned. 'The contractors say it would be cheaper to build on a fresh site,' he protested.

'Sorry. It's the duckpond or nothing. He won't have it anywhere else.'

The frown deepened. 'If you'll forgive my saying so, James, your father is being unnecessarily obstructive over this,' Smelton said irritably. 'We didn't frame the blasted will, and a new swimming-pool would improve the property, duckpond or no duckpond. He's taking it out of us simply because he can't get at J.C.'

'He certainly can't do that,' James agreed. 'That has been done already.'

Something in his voice caught their attention. 'What do you mean by that?' asked Diana.

'Simply that, according to Russell, J.C. was murdered. By one of us, too.'

He looked maliciously at Colin. The others looked at Colin also, too astonished to speak.

Miss Webber was the first to recover.

'What are you talking about?' she asked. 'I'm sure Colin doesn't think anything of the sort. Do you, Colin?'

Colin said nothing. Flabbergasted at this betrayal, red in the face with anger, he sat glowering at James.

'He does, you know,' said the latter, never taking his eyes off his victim. Colin Russell was broad and solid, and had a reputation for preferring action to words. Anne watched them both, fearful of what Colin might do.

'Is this true, Russell?' Smelton demanded.

'Yes,' Colin said bluntly. His wrath was too great to attempt to appease them. 'I don't know who killed him, but it was someone from Redways. I'm sure of that.'

'Well! Well! Well!' said Diana. 'What a snake in the grass!'

Smelton stood up, pushing his chair back so that it rasped along the floor. 'I demand an explanation of this foolery,' he said curtly. 'And I warn you, Russell, that slanderous statements such as that are highly dangerous.'

Colin took no notice of this outburst. He was watching James, he did not care about Smelton or the others. Anne looked at them each in turn, hoping to see on one or another of those staring faces something that might give her the information Colin wanted. James, delighted with the success of his bombshell, was still smiling. So was Diana: it was a situation, thought Anne, which would appeal to Diana's rather peculiar sense of humour. Miss Webber was goggling; Miss Dove, who was rather deaf, had placidly picked up her knife and fork and resumed her meal. Smelton was unmistakably angry, the more so because his anger was ignored. Only Chris Moull gave a seemingly guilty reaction, his restless eyes darting uneasily from one to another of the people round the table.

If I were a detective and I had to make an immediate arrest, thought Anne, it would have to be Chris. But I do so hope he didn't do it.

'It's partly my fault, I suppose,' James said. 'I put the idea into his head.'

That he should seek to take credit for a perspicacity that was wholly Colin's made Anne gasp. She did not suppose that he was endeavouring to mitigate Colin's offence in the eyes of his colleagues by shouldering some of the blame, since to Anne Colin's behaviour warranted praise, not blame. 'You did nothing of the sort,' she said furiously. 'It was entirely Colin's idea.'

All eyes turned to her.

'So you're in it as well,' Diana murmured. 'We might have guessed.'

James Latimer shook his head.

'I hate to contradict you, Anne, but you're wrong, you know. Only a few days after the accident I remarked in Russell's hearing that it was too good to be true. Somebody must have bumped him off, I said; J.C. was too unpopular to die unaided. A poor joke, perhaps — but it *was* a joke. And I don't see why I should hold myself responsible if some brainless ass takes me seriously.'

Anne glanced quickly at Colin, but his eyes avoided hers. So it's true, she thought; James *did* put the idea into his head. Furious with both of them, she fell silent.

Colin stood up. He had had enough.

'I don't joke about murder,' he said to

James, his voice cold with venom. 'And maybe you won't think it's so funny by the time I'm through. But right now I propose to have a few words with your father. It seems that he doesn't know when to hold his damned tongue any more than his son does.'

He marched out of the room amid a shocked silence. Whatever they might think or say among themselves, the staff were careful to utter no disrespectful word about the headmaster in James's hearing. Even Smelton allowed himself no more than an occasional mild criticism.

James flushed. To Anne's surprise he began to make excuses for Colin.

'He's right, you know. I did talk out of turn. I never can resist pulling his leg when the chance offers. But I think it might be better if you all forgot about this — otherwise complications may ensue.'

As if they could forget, thought Anne.

Smelton was of the same opinion. 'You know damned well that's impossible,' he said. 'Nobody is going to accuse me of murder and get away with it.'

'He didn't accuse you. Not specifically.

He probably thinks I did it.'

'But why murder?' asked Miss Webber, thrilled. 'And why one of us?'

'Goodness knows.' James frowned at their persistence. 'I suppose it was because so many of us benefited, directly or indirectly, from J.C.'s death. But forget it — he'll get over it. Lay off the topic for a few days and it will die a natural death.'

'Like J.C., eh?' commented Diana, still smiling.

*   *   *

Joseph Latimer knew he was unpopular with the staff. The knowledge did not perturb him. Popularity bred familiarity, and familiarity led to incomplete control and lack of discipline. But although in the past he had had to cope with dissatisfaction and dissent, even with indignation, he had never before been confronted by a member of his staff in the full flood of a righteous and uncontrolled wrath. In no uncertain terms Colin told Mr Latimer exactly what he thought of him and his offspring. He went on for so long, his

121

language was so violent and his bearing so threatening, that the headmaster became slightly apprehensive; and when Colin eventually paused through sheer lack of further material Mr Latimer forgot his dignity and abandoned the scathing reply he had intended making. It was an occasion, he hastily decided, when soft words should be given a chance to prove their efficacy.

'I appreciate your annoyance, Russell,' he said, with masterly understatement. 'But you must understand that I had to consult James. He is a director of the school as well as being my son. Naturally I had no idea he would be so foolish as to repeat what I told him. He had no right to do so, and I apologize on his behalf as well as on my own.'

This restrained, conciliatory, and unexpected reply tended to deflate his accuser. His anger having spent its first full flush, Colin began to wonder at his own temerity in speaking thus to his employer. Not wishing to show weakness now, he resorted to bluster to supplant his wrath.

'That's fair enough as far as it goes,' he

conceded. 'But what happens next? Thanks to James, my name is mud with the rest of the staff. There's going to be a pretty grim atmosphere in the common room when I'm around.'

Mr Latimer said he appreciated that, but could offer no solution. 'And yet — well, isn't this what you wanted?' he asked, bending his long body forward to look more searchingly at his listener. 'You asked me this afternoon for permission to question the staff. I couldn't give it then and I cannot give it now — and I still think you are behaving foolishly. But now that the gloves are off and they know what you have in mind there is nothing to prevent you from asking as many questions as you wish. Whether they will answer them is, of course, another matter.'

Somewhat doubtfully Colin acknowledged the truth of this. So did Anne when he consulted her later. 'If they are not too angry with you you might get the truth from those who have nothing to hide,' she said. 'If there are any such persons in the school, that is — which I very much doubt.'

Her voice was cool. 'What's up now?' he asked. 'Is it me?'

'Of course it's you. I'm furious with you, Colin. Why didn't you tell me at the beginning that it was James who started you off on this inquiry? You made me look an absolute fool at dinner.'

He flushed. 'I'm sorry,' he said. 'But what difference does it make? The truth's there. He didn't see it and I did.'

But it *did* make a difference, although she was not certain where the difference lay. As a second-hand theory it became less valuable, it detracted somehow from Colin's honesty of purpose. Into her mind flashed the dread thought that he might have adopted it in self-defence, to lead the war into the enemy's camp before it was taken to his. But the conclusions to which that thought might lead were frightening, and she forced herself to ignore it. She could not begin to doubt him now.

A cocktail party at the Smeltons' the next evening gave her the desired opportunity to speak to Dorothy. Anne was the only member of the staff to be invited, and she suspected that, had Philip Smelton had any say in the choice of guests, she certainly would not have been on the list. The lack of enthusiasm with which he greeted her on arrival confirmed this suspicion.

Most of the guests were strangers to Anne, and she did not greatly enjoy the party. Smelton at first seemed to enjoy it even less. He drank heavily and talked little, standing moodily alone and glowering at those who tried to engage him in conversation. He is probably reckoning up what all this costs, thought Anne, and has taken fright at the figures.

But as the gin took effect Smelton's tongue loosened and his mood changed, and presently Anne noticed that he was engaged in a heavy flirtation with an under-dressed and over-decorated blonde. Anne was surprised — she had never envisaged him in that guise. He did not make a dashing Don Juan, she thought; he was no Apollo for looks. His suit was ill-fitting and he needed a haircut, and wisps of ginger hair stood out like a fringe above his collar.

The guests began to drift away, and Smelton and the blonde disappeared together. 'He's taking her home in the car,' Dorothy told Anne; she had completely ignored her husband's flirtation. 'Stay for another drink, and I'll drive you back when he returns. He won't be long.' She went into the hall with the last of the guests. When she returned she said, 'Now, tell me all about this boyfriend of yours. Philip is absolutely furious with him. He says he's been accusing all and sundry of murdering J.C.'

Anne tried to make light of it; she did not want Dorothy to connect J.C.'s death with the questions she intended to put to her. There was nothing to it really, she said; the murder theory had been mooted simply because so many persons seemed to benefit, but it still remained just a theory. So far as she knew it was unlikely to proceed further than that.

'No smoke without fire,' said Dorothy. 'I suppose your young man has put *us* on his list, eh? Or Philip, rather. Personally, I'm not in the least interested in what becomes of the Lodge. I refuse to live in a

126

poky flat on the school doorstep, with a lot of hearty young men creating merry hell above. I told Philip so, too.'

'It's not poky,' Anne told her. 'Have you been inside the house?'

'No. But I had a look at it from the outside the other day. That was enough for me.'

It was an ideal opening. 'That was the morning J.C. was drowned, wasn't it? The Saturday before last,' said Anne. 'One of the masters told me he'd seen you there about seven o'clock.'

'I dare say. I don't remember.'

Anne got the impression that Dorothy did not want to remember. 'Pretty early for *you* to be abroad,' she said with a laugh. 'And Chris said you were on a bicycle. I didn't know you rode one.'

'I don't if I can help it. I loathe the things. But it's the only way I can get around when Philip has the car.'

He had had the car that Saturday morning, Anne reflected. *And* the evening before. 'You must have to cycle quite a bit, then,' she said. 'He uses it every morning to come to school, doesn't he?'

127

'He does, blast him!' The expletive sounded good-humoured, not vindictive. 'I have to do my gadding about of an evening.'

'What happens if he wants it in the evening also?'

'He seldom does, thank goodness. I don't think he's stirred out after dinner for months.'

'We saw him about ten days ago,' Anne said. 'Colin and I. Colin was seeing me home. It was getting on for ten o'clock, and we wondered where he could be going in such a hurry at that hour.'

'He wasn't going anywhere.' Mrs Smelton's voice had an edge to it. 'He was here. I told you, he hasn't been out of an evening for months.'

'But we saw him, Dorothy.' Anne realized that her persistence was out of place, but she did not greatly care. This was important, Colin had said. 'We were standing by the side of the road as he went past.'

'At ten o'clock? Don't be silly, my dear. At that time of night you couldn't possibly recognize anyone in a closed car.'

'She's right, too,' Colin said the next day. 'We didn't actually see him. We assumed it was Smelton because we recognized the car; but it might have been his wife.'

'She didn't say so.'

'There wasn't any reason why she should. How about the next morning? Get any gen on that?'

'No. She wasn't anxious to talk about her dear Philip after that.'

'If her dear Philip killed J.C. it seems he did it to no purpose,' said Colin. 'I mean, if she refuses to move to the flat. Maybe that explains his present gloom.'

'Maybe. Did you speak to the others?'

'Only Diana and Chris. The two matrons are obviously out of it, and I hadn't the nerve to tackle James or Smelton. But as Diana seemed to treat the whole thing as a joke I reckoned I was on fairly safe ground with her.'

'What did she say?'

'What you might expect, knowing Diana. She said she had not been overfond of J.C., but that her idea of a free weekend was to get up late and take life easy. It did not include rising in the small hours of the morning in order to drown a more or less harmless old gentleman. When I asked if she could prove she was in bed at the time she pretended to be shocked.'

'I don't blame her. It was a stupid question. What about Chris?'

'I apologized to him. I thought I ought to. He was the only person I'd tried to pump, you see, before James let the cat out of the bag. And the odd thing is that he seemed more worried than annoyed; wanted to know if I really believed J.C. had been murdered. When I said I did he went as white as a sheet.' Colin himself looked worried. 'I don't like it, Anne. Chris is a damned good chap, and I'd hate like hell to get him into trouble. I'd rather drop the whole thing.'

'He isn't a damned good chap if he killed J.C.,' said the girl. 'But I don't believe he did. Are you going to drop it, then?'

'It looks like dropping me,' Colin said gloomily. 'Barring a miracle, I'm scuppered.'

# 6

## A Glass of Milk

The miracle, as Colin saw it, arrived after lunch the next afternoon, although no one would have recognized in David Lane a messenger from the gods. He was a scruffy little boy who seemed in imminent danger of losing his shorts. His stockings sagged round his ankles, the tail of his shirt flapped loosely behind him, his knees and legs were grimy. At Colin's bellowed 'Come in' he opened the common room door a few inches and pushed his head through the narrow slit thus formed.

'Can I speak to Mr Smelton, please, sir?'

'What is it?' growled Smelton, from the depths of an armchair.

Thus encouraged, David Lane sidled round the door, closed it carefully, and tiptoed across the room with a grubby fist held out before him.

'I was told to give you this, sir,' he said, opening the fist.

Smelton reached out a languid hand, plucked the object from the boy's sticky palm, and examined it.

'Where did you get this?' he asked sharply.

'I found it by the river, sir. On Sunday, when we were out for a walk with Mr James.'

'Mr James wasn't on duty last Sunday.'

'No, sir. It was the Sunday before.'

The word 'river' had caused Colin to sit up and take notice. For him it had only one significance. But Smelton sat with his back to him, and he could not see what it was that Lane had found.

'Why didn't you hand it in before?' Smelton asked.

'I didn't know I had to, sir. Not until Barrett told me.'

Prudence struggled with curiosity in Colin's breast as the door closed behind the boy. At last he said, his voice casual and friendly, 'What was it Lane found by the river?'

Smelton did not answer. He placed the object in a waistcoat pocket, picked up his newspaper, and continued reading. Colin, red in the face, got up and walked out of the room. Smelton could have and enjoy his snub, but he was mistaken if he thought he could keep the matter a secret.

Barrett was one of the school prefects, a tall, serious boy. Colin found him in the Fifth Form room. 'It was an identity-disc, sir,' he said. 'It had Mr Connaught's name on it. That's why I thought Lane ought to give it to Mr Smelton.'

'Quite right, Barrett. Exactly where did he find it?'

'Just off the towpath, I think, sir.'

David Lane, when run to earth in the gym, said he had picked it up on the grass between the towpath and the river; about half-way between the two bridges, he thought. But Colin was not interested in the exact spot; it was enough that he now had something more tangible with which to support his theory of murder. J.C. himself would certainly not have dropped the disc on the far bank, for he would have no cause to be there. Moreover, it seemed to establish an idea that had been forming in Colin's mind — that the murderer had come from the far bank and not from the same side of the river as J.C.

Filled with a renewed zest for detection, he hurried down to the towpath as soon as he was free. Somewhere along there the murderer must have waited, have changed into and then out of his swimming-costume. He would not do that on the path, but in the concealment of the bushes. Even at seven o'clock in the morning there was always the possibility that someone might be using the path.

His search did not take long. Almost opposite the spot where J.C.'s clothing had been found he came on a small clearing screened from the path, where the bushes and long grass had been trampled and had not fully recovered. But although this, to Colin's mind, proved the correctness of his theory, he found nothing in the clearing which could be used as concrete evidence of murder.

Dusk was falling as he reached the

bridge on his way back to the school, and he nearly collided with a cyclist as he hurried on to the road.

Shades of Tony Cuttle! he thought, apologizing as the man dismounted. Then he recognized him. 'You're Mr Bain, aren't you?' he asked. 'How's your wife?'

'Not too good, thank you, sir,' said the man. 'It'll be some weeks afore she's out of hospital.'

Colin expressed his sympathy.

'What beats me,' said Mr Bain, who seemed in no hurry to continue his journey, 'is how petrol got into that there lamp. A real mystery, that is.'

'But wasn't there a tin of petrol in the shed? That's what I was told, anyway. I thought your wife must have used it in mistake for paraffin.'

Mr Bain shook his head emphatically.

'She don't fill the lamps,' he said. 'She puts them out in the shed of a morning, and I does them afore I goes to work. I just done them now. And, seeing as I filled all the lamps out of the same can — well, you tell me how that one lamp come to blow up and the others didn't.'

'I didn't realize it was like that,' Colin said thoughtfully. 'Is the shed kept locked?'

Mr Bain said that there was no lock fitted, and added, in a voice that showed his mind to be running on much the same lines as his questioner's, that his wife was usually out of an afternoon.

'But you are there, aren't you?' said Colin.

'Asleep upstairs,' said the man. 'With the doors shut and the curtains drawn. I wouldn't hear nothink.'

At dinner that evening Colin took little part in the conversation, his mind busy on the new problems that confronted him. Smelton too was silent. Colin wondered whether guilt had prompted the senior master to conceal the identity-disc from him, or whether he was just being bloody-minded. If Smelton were guilty would he dare to destroy the disc? That would be a dangerous game to play. Both Lane and Barrett, and doubtless several other boys, had seen and would be able to describe it.

His thoughts turned to James. Lane

had said he had found the disc during the Sunday afternoon walk on the day after J.C. had been drowned. Why had James chosen that walk on that day? Was it morbid curiosity — or was it another instance of a criminal being drawn to the scene of his crime? Had it no significance, or had it every significance?

Colin wished he knew.

After the meal he went upstairs to ponder the problem in the quiet of his own room. Even Anne was excluded from his thoughts and his company. He had told her of the identity-disc and of his search by the river that afternoon, of Mr Bain and his dark suspicions; but, although Anne appreciated that all these might be important, she was no wiser than he as to their exact significance.

As Colin saw it the main obstacle to enlisting the support of the police was Joseph Latimer's interpretation of the known facts. It was the common-sense interpretation, and would therefore be more likely to appeal to the police than his own. Doubtless Latimer could provide an equally innocent explanation for J.C.'s identity-disc having been found on the far bank; and if he could not explain away the explosion in the Bains' cottage he would certainly be scornful of the suggestion that it was linked in any way with the death of J.C.

What he had to do, Colin decided, was to discredit Latimer's interpretation by making all the facts fit neatly into a theory of his own. But what *was* his theory? Obviously the murderer must have come from the far bank, from which it followed that J.C. could not have been forced into the water. Not forced physically, that is. Yet there must have been some urgency involved, or why the forgotten watch, the scattered clothing?

What, then, was this urgency? It was that above all else which he had to decide.

There was also that mysterious call for help. J.C. had lost his voice, therefore he could not have shouted loud enough for Tony Cuttle, nearly two hundred yards away on the road, to have heard him. Yet it was surely too much of a coincidence to suggest, as the headmaster had suggested, that Tony had imagined if? If one believed

138

in telepathy one might conceivably put it down to that. But not to imagination.

Well, I'm damned if I'm going to accept telepathy, thought Colin. Yet what else was there, apart from Latimer's sarcastic suggestion that perhaps it had been the murderer, and not J.C., who had called for help? And that . . .

He had been lying on his back on the bed, hands behind his head, staring thoughtfully at the ceiling. Now with a sudden spring he sat up and swung his feet to the floor, a gleam in his eye. By Jiminy, that was it! That was how it had happened! Latimer's silly crack had hit the nail bang on the head. It *was* the murderer who had called for help!

For a few moments he stayed where he was, excitement mounting in him as he realized how much was now explained, how so many previously inconsistent facts now fitted harmoniously together. Then, exultant, he made for the door. Anne must be told. And as he scurried down the stairs in his stockinged feet there flashed into his mind the happy picture of an adoring Anne engulfed in admiration of her fiancé's genius.

But the picture faded instantly as he burst into the common room. James Latimer stood with his back to the door, his outstretched arms barring Anne's exit. The girl's face was flushed, and Colin knew that she was near to tears. His love for her, his dislike and jealousy of James, the frustration and excitement of the past few days, welled up inside him and spilled over. Acting on impulse, he caught hold of James's outstretched right arm, swung him sharply round, and hit him with all his force full on the point of the chin.

James went down and stayed down. Anne, consternation struggling with relief, turned first to Colin and then to prostrate man. Colin knelt beside her guiltily. Anger had vanished with the blow, and the likely consequences of his impetuosity began to crowd upon him.

'He's out cold,' he said. 'Must have hit him harder than I thought. But there's no damage done, I fancy; he'll come round in a moment. Thank the Lord he didn't crack his skull against anything.'

'You shouldn't have hit him, darling,'

said Anne, still struggling with her tears. 'It was a dreadful thing to do.'

Colin knew she was right, but refused to admit it. 'It may teach him to leave you alone in future,' he said.

'But he wasn't doing anything,' she protested. 'He asked me to have dinner with him tomorrow, and I refused. Then he said he wouldn't let me out of the room until I changed my mind. I was furious, of course, and terribly glad to see you; but I don't believe he would have used actual force to stop me leaving. I imagine it was his idea of a joke.'

'It isn't mine,' said Colin.

James sat up and rubbed his chin, looking vacantly at the two figures kneeling beside him. Then, as memory returned, he rose unsteadily to his feet and slumped into an armchair.

The others stood up. 'Are you all right, James?' Anne asked anxiously.

Colin, feeling extremely uncomfortable, muttered a shamefaced apology. 'Afraid I lost my temper,' he said.

James glowered at them. He was in no mood for forgiveness. 'Apart from giving me no chance to defend myself, who the devil gave you the right to interfere?'

'Anne and I are engaged,' Colin said briefly.

'Oh!' James was momentarily non-plussed. 'Well, that doesn't entitle you to assault any other man who happens to speak to her, damn you. You had better learn to control your temper, my lad, if you hope to remain a schoolmaster. That is one of the essentials.' Gingerly he caressed his chin with his fingertips. 'You can say goodbye to Redways. You've asked for trouble and now you're going to get it. Once my father has an earful of your behaviour this evening you'll be out, and out sharp. I'll see to that.'

'I wouldn't stay in this ruddy dump if you trebled my salary,' Colin retorted. He had been prepared to eat humble pie in order that the incident might be hushed up, but as James was clearly in no mood to be magnanimous he saw no further need for humility. 'And from where I'm standing it looks as though *you've* been in trouble, not me.' He rubbed the knuckles of his clenched fist significantly. 'As for

Mr Latimer — well, he may be your father, but I doubt if he would approve of your molesting a lady.'

'That's a damned lie!' the other protested hotly. 'I wasn't molesting her. Ask Anne.'

'Forcible restraint, then. You can call it what you like, but it amounts to the same thing. And if I catch you at it again you'll get the same treatment.'

'Try it when I'm looking and see what happens.' James turned to the girl. 'I'm sorry about this, Anne. When your hot-headed fiancé returns to his senses (if any) you might inform him that I neither molested nor restrained you. Good night.'

Anne did not answer. When James had stalked from the room she looked at Colin in consternation.

'I'm dreadfully sorry, darling. It's torn everything.'

Colin was more annoyed than sorry, and said so. 'It doesn't matter two hoots,' he assured her. 'James and I were due for a bustup sooner or later. Just as well to get it over.'

'But you'll lose your job.'

'What of it? There are plenty more jobs, most of them a damned sight better than this one. The only attraction at Redways is you; and, to be on the safe side, I think I had better take the attraction with me.'

Anne hugged him, relieved that he should accept his probable dismissal so cheerfully. 'What made you dash into the room like that?' she asked. 'Did you know James was in here?'

'Good Lord!' Memory returned to him. 'No, it wasn't anything to do with James. I have seen the light, darling. I mean, I know how J.C. was killed.'

'Really? How?'

'It was something old Latimer said that pressed the button, although it didn't click at the time. He was trying to be funny, as usual. He said that if Tony wasn't mistaken in thinking he heard someone shouting for help, and if J.C. had lost his voice, was I suggesting that it was the murderer who called out? Well, I wasn't. But I am now. For that's who it was, you see. It couldn't have been anyone else.'

Anne shook her head in bewilderment.

'I don't understand,' she said. 'Surely that's the last thing a murderer would do?'

'Not this one. Look — this is how I think it happened. The murderer waited on the opposite bank until J.C. was due, then slipped into the water, swam out to the middle of the stream, and started to splash around and call for help. Tony Cuttle heard him — and so did J.C. And that is why J.C. didn't wait to take off his wrist-watch or fold up his clothes — he just chucked his things off and went to the rescue. And when he reached the supposedly drowning figure . . . ' Colin shrugged his shoulders. 'J.C. wasn't a big man. It wouldn't call for much strength to push him under and keep him there.'

Anne shuddered.

'How horrible! Anyone who could do that would have to be an absolute monster. I can't believe it of any of the staff, Colin. I just can't.'

'Murder is always horrible. I don't see that drowning is any more so than poison, come to that.'

'Perhaps not. But all the same . . . ' A

thought occurred to her. 'What about the identity-disc and the keys?'

'I think the murderer swam over to this side of the river after he had finished with J.C., and took the keys from his pocket. But the disc is more difficult. There must be an explanation as to how it got to the far bank; I just haven't thought of it yet, that's all. But it'll come to me in time.'

'Do you think J.C. knew who it was when he went to the rescue?'

'No. Too misty. That mist was in the murderer's favour from start to finish. If someone else came on the scene before J.C. reached him he could pretend that he himself was drowning; feign cramp, or something like that. And if the someone else turned up during the struggle, or before he had had time to leave the water and hide, the mist would have obscured what was really happening. The murderer could have explained — if he was ever asked to explain — that J.C. was in difficulties and he had gone to the rescue. Unsuccessfully, of course. He'd be quite a hero, in fact.'

'I still don't believe anyone at Redways

could have behaved like that,' the girl persisted. 'It's too horrible to contemplate.'

'You don't want to believe it, you mean.'

She knew that to be true. Ever since Colin had persuaded her that J.C.'s death was no accident she had deliberately shut her mind to all that the word 'murder' implied. If there was a murderer among them, she had told herself, he was a murderer by accident and not by design; a murderer who, having killed, would be filled with instant remorse. But how different it looked now! If Colin were right there must have been cool, calculated planning and execution — followed, no doubt, by satisfaction in success. It implied the work of a monster; and that monster, according to Colin, was one of themselves. *Any* one, from Mr Latimer down to Miss Dove.

No, not Mr. Latimer. He at least was ruled out. He couldn't swim.

'Are you sure?' asked Colin when she mentioned this.

'Well, he didn't bathe at all last term.

The rest of the staff did — even Webby. But not him. And it's well known that he hates cold water.'

'That doesn't mean he can't swim,' Colin said obstinately. 'I'd want stronger evidence than that before ruling him out. And talking of Latimer — I suppose I'd better see him now and get it over.'

'Not tonight, darling,' said Anne. 'Leave it until tomorrow morning. It will give him time to cool down after James has had his say.'

The door opened slowly, and Diana's head appeared. There was an air of suppressed excitement about her as she came into the room.

'What happened?' she asked. 'A bust-up? I heard an almighty row going on in here, and then James came out looking absolutely black with rage. Since then I've been hanging around waiting for my curiosity to overcome my finer nature. Do tell.'

'James was pestering Anne,' said Colin, before Anne could stop him.

'Did you hit him?'

Anne spoke quickly. 'I don't think we

ought to discuss it, Diana. I'm sorry — but you do understand, don't you?'

'Okay, we won't discuss it.' Diana laughed. 'So Colin hit him, eh? Good for you, Colin. But I wonder what our Joseph will have to say about it.'

'Goodbye, I imagine,' answered Colin. 'Only I intend to say it first.'

The headmaster had obviously reviewed the matter well before Colin spoke to him the next morning. 'I am not greatly concerned with the rights or wrongs of this unfortunate incident,' he said, his voice cool and unfriendly. 'I have now heard both James's version and your own, and it seems probable to me that neither of you is without blame. But I cannot tolerate such sharp discord between members of the staff; obviously one of you must go. I hope you will absolve me from undue favouritism when I say that that can hardly be James.'

'I appreciate that, sir. That is why I offered you my resignation.'

'Thank you. I can in all honesty give you an excellent testimonial. This antagonism between you and James will not affect it, and you have carried out your duties here satisfactorily.' Mr Latimer sighed. 'I hope you will both manage to control and, if possible, conceal your dislike of each other for the rest of the term. We cannot have a recurrence of last night.'

'It won't happen again, sir,' Colin assured him, voicing a confidence he did not feel. James, he knew, would be out for revenge. That knock-down in front of Anne was an affront to his dignity that James would neither forgive nor forget.

The headmaster stood up.

'James tells me that you and Miss Connaught are engaged to be married,' he said. 'It seems rather hasty — you have not known each other long. But I hope you will be happy. Miss Connaught is a charming girl — and, of course, a wealthy one,' he added drily.

Colin flushed, and muttered his thanks for the good wishes. He did not like the final crack, but he had a firm grip on his temper that morning.

'Shall we be losing Miss Connaught

also?' asked Latimer.

Colin said he did not know. He would have to talk it over with Anne.

'I should like to know as soon as possible. We are nearly half-way through the term, and it is not always easy these days to find new staff.' He cleared his throat noisily. 'Oh — one more point, Russell. About J.C.'s death. I don't know whether you have thought any more about this, but under the circumstances you will, of course, drop any further exploration of your absurd hypothesis.'

Now for the fireworks, thought Colin. But with the loss of his job much of his former dread of his employer had vanished. The old boy can't do me much harm now, he told himself. Even a testimonial isn't all that important with . . .

He flushed guiltily. Was he already counting on Anne's new wealth to keep him in idleness? But his voice was firm as he answered.

'No, sir, I can't do that. There's nothing vindictive about it, you understand. It's purely a matter of conscience.'

The heavy eyebrows wobbled ominously.

'Are you sure of that, Russell? It seems to me — '

Colin interrupted him before he could get fully into his stride.

'There's new evidence, sir. I think you'll agree that makes a difference.'

He had considered very carefully what he should say, and now he rattled it off concisely and clearly. It was, he thought smugly, a masterpiece of deductive reasoning. Even the headmaster must be impressed by its logic.

But Mr Latimer, although his look grew more baleful and his frown deepened, did not appear at all impressed.

'Very clever,' he said, with heavy sarcasm. 'But what you fail to appreciate, Russell, is that in nine cases out of ten it would be possible to twist the details surrounding an accidental death such as this to give it the superficial appearance of murder. Provided, of course, that you had the necessary imagination — and time to spare. You, unfortunately, appear to have plenty of both.'

'I haven't done any twisting,' said Colin, unabashed.

'You have not accounted for all the facts, either. You suggest that this identity-disc — I must accept your word that it exists, although this is the first I have heard of it — you suggest that it somehow hooked itself on to the murderer during his struggle with J.C., and then dropped on to the bank as he was climbing out of the water. But tell me exactly what is there in a bathing costume to which it could have attached itself'

Trust the old man to put his finger on the weak link, thought Colin. But he refused to be discouraged. He was no longer drifting aimlessly, waiting for a light to guide him. Now he knew — or thought he knew — where he was going.

'Search me,' he said cheerfully. 'It depends on the costume, I suppose.'

His ready acceptance of criticism disconcerted the headmaster. Mr Latimer, alarmed at the other's self-assurance, descended from his pinnacle and abandoned sarcasm for persuasion. He did it awkwardly and with obvious reluctance and to no avail.

Colin, happily aware that he was being wooed, refused to budge. He had no wish to bring harm or discredit to Redways, he said sententiously, but personal considerations could not be allowed to interfere with justice. All he would promise was to take no drastic step, such as consulting the police, without first informing his employer.

At this declaration of independence, and with the hateful word 'police' ringing loud in his ear, Mr Latimer played his trump card.

'In that case, Russell, you allow me no alternative but to terminate your engagement forthwith,' he said haughtily, back on the familiar pinnacle. 'I should be glad if you would leave tomorrow. You will receive half a term's salary in lieu of notice — although I doubt whether your behaviour entitles you to such consideration.'

And that, as Colin ruefully admitted later to Anne, left him high and dry. However certain he might be that murder had been committed, there was little he could hope to accomplish in the few hours left to him. 'And I can't hang around the district indefinitely,' he said. 'I can't afford to.'

'I'm not staying here without you,' she said nervously, near to tears. 'I'd go crazy, wondering which of them had killed J. C. and knowing I could never hope to find out. I'd be terrified someone might try to murder me. If you go I go.'

'That would fox the old man good and proper,' Colin said, with a relish of which he felt a little ashamed. 'How on earth would he manage for the rest of the term?'

That was the thought uppermost in the minds of the rest of the staff when they heard the news, which neither Colin nor Anne saw any reason to hide. Despite the anger which had previously been aroused by Colin's talk of murder, there were few who had taken him seriously. This new announcement hit them harder, for the consequences were only too plain to all. There would be larger classes to cope with, duty-days would come round more often, free periods and long weekends would become only a memory.

'I've met some outsize bounders in my

time, Russell, but you beat the lot,' said Smelton, discarding his attitude of silent scorn in favour of an all-out attack. It was the short interval before lunch, when most of the staff were gathered in the common room. 'Life was reasonably smooth here until you erupted with this tomfoolery about murder, blast you!'

Colin eyed him speculatively. That identity-disc — why had not Smelton handed it over to Latimer? According to the latter, Smelton had not even mentioned it. Or had Latimer been lying? Colin disliked them both, and it irritated him almost beyond endurance to know that if either of them had murdered J.C. he was going to get away with it. After tomorrow all talk of murder would vanish from Redways; the murderer could again breathe freely, and even the innocent would feel relief at the easing of tension. And he had less than twenty-four hours in which to accomplish what seemed to him at that moment like a small miracle.

And then, only a few moments later, it was no longer a miracle but a very real possibility. It was as quick as that.

'Well, I'm off tomorrow. You can go back to your smooth life — if it ever was smooth in this dump, which I take leave to doubt.' He spoke slowly, spinning out the idle, stupid words so that he might gain time for thought, time in which to make a decision. 'You can all live happily for ever and ever, amen.'

'Can we hell! We'll have your damned work to do as well as our own,' growled Smelton.

'And Anne's,' Diana put in blandly. The extra work would not fall on her, but she saw no reason why Anne should escape the brick-bats being thrown at Colin. Colin had been sacked, but Anne was leaving of her own choice. That made her desertion the more heinous. 'I can just see you teaching the babes to read, Mr Smelton.'

The senior master glowered at her, and turned away in disgust.

'Yes, I'm afraid you are all going to be rather busy for the rest of the term,' Colin agreed cheerfully. 'No time for early-morning murders and other sporting pastimes. But then you can't have it both ways, can you? It's either me or work.'

James Latimer eyed him sourly, suspicious of his good humour.

'It won't seem quite so funny to you when you're out of a job,' he said. 'You won't find headmasters falling over themselves to engage a man who has been sent packing halfway through the term.'

'Nice of you to worry,' said Colin. 'The memory of it will help to comfort me when I'm drawing the dole.'

Like James, Anne was surprised at his mood. He had been angry and despondent at having to abandon his self-appointed task, he had railed at Joseph Latimer for his refusal to co-operate. But there was no sign of despondency now, and he had not hitherto exhibited a talent for acting. What was behind his sudden change of front?

Diana wondered too. 'You seem in remarkably good spirits, Colin,' she said. 'What's up? Of course, we know you are engaged to Anne and that you will have J.C.'s money to keep you in idleness. Is that it? Or have you by any chance decided which of us murdered the old man?'

'As a matter of fact, Diana, I have,' Colin said lightly.

They were all, Anne included, startled into silence. No one questioned him. They just stared — incredulous, frightened, angry. Colin watched them, noting their reactions, savouring his moment of triumph.

'Don't expect the police to make an arrest right away,' he went on, with a cheerful assurance that irritated more than one of his listeners. 'There's a bit of routine spade-work to do first — by them, thank goodness, not by me. I'll just hand them my report in the morning, and then it's up to them. I'm out of it.' He sighed extravagantly. 'It's a pity I can't see my way to include a few words of gratitude to the staff for their co-operation,' he concluded, shaking his head in reproof. 'It would have looked well on paper.'

Smelton was the first to recover.

'I don't believe a word of it,' he said loudly, defiantly. 'It's merely another of your blasted attempts to cause trouble. Well, it won't work this time.'

'Won't it? I shouldn't bank on that if I were *you*, Smelton,' Colin said with emphasis.

The other flushed. Chris Moull, who had so far taken no part in the conversation, asked quietly, 'Who are you accusing, Colin?'

Colin hesitated. Then he said slowly, his voice serious again, 'I can't tell you that, Chris. I'm sorry — but it wouldn't be right for me to do so.'

'Have you written this report of yours?' asked James.

'Not yet. I'll do it this evening.'

'And does my father know what you're up to?'

'No. But he will.' Colin faced them, his expression grim yet somehow boyishly appealing. 'Oh, I know you all think I'm the last word in cads — but why? What's wrong with you? I've only done what I imagine any one of you would have done had he or she felt the way I feel. You think J.C.'s death was an accident, you're mad at me because I can't let well alone. But I *know* it was murder, I tell you. I don't think, I *know*.' He paused for effect. 'All right, then. Do you expect me to sit tight and let the murderer get away with it? I'm sorry for the rest of you; it won't be much fun having the police around, poking their noses into your private affairs. But I can't help that. I'm not going to stand aside and allow a murderer to escape just because his arrest may cause some people a little inconvenience. And if you weren't such a pack of moral cowards you'd back me up instead of looking down your noses at me,' he ended emphatically, his voice rising above the clangour of the lunch bell.

'Famous last words, I shouldn't wonder,' Diana murmured to no one in particular, as she led the way out of the room. None of them had much to say at lunch, for the proximity of the boys forbade conversation on the topic uppermost in their minds. Colin was relieved that neither Mr nor Mrs Latimer was present. If the headmaster knew what was afoot he would probably order him to leave Redways that very hour, and that would

161

wreck everything he had planned. James would spill the beans as soon as his father returned, of course; but by that time Colin hoped to be out of Mr Latimer's reach. It was his free afternoon; he intended to clear off after lunch and to stay away from the school until it was too late in the day for the headmaster to take action.

Anne found him unusually evasive when she tackled him outside the common room after lunch.

'What are you playing at now?' she demanded. 'You're not *really* going to the police tomorrow, are you?'

'I certainly am.'

'But why? Only this morning you were complaining that you hadn't enough evidence to do that. What has happened to make you change your mind?'

Colin shook his head, smiling at her.

'Sorry, ducks, but I'm not telling. Not even you.' He bent to give her a hasty kiss, but she turned her head impatiently away. 'Sore, eh? Well, I don't blame you. I suppose it does seem a trifle mean, my holding out on you like this. But I can't help that, I'm afraid. This is something I must keep to myself.'

Anne lost her temper. She had had a trying twenty-four hours, and her nerves were on edge.

'For Heaven's sake, stop being so mysterious and smug; it may impress the others, but it's wasted on me. You are behaving like an overgrown schoolboy, Colin; you're so puffed up with conceit that you've no time now for anyone but your own stupid self. All right, go ahead without me. I don't care. Only don't come running to me for advice when you discover that you're not as clever as you thought you were.'

Taken aback by this violent outburst, Colin caught her arm as she made to leave him. 'That's damned unfair!' he said indignantly. 'You know perfectly well that — '

He fell silent as Diana emerged from the common room. Anne took advantage of the moment to break away and run up the stairs.

Diana gazed after her thoughtfully. Then she turned to Colin.

'So Anne's annoyed with you too, is she? You *are* making yourself unpopular today, aren't you? Well, it's none of my business, but if I were you I'd go after her and apologize for whatever it is you've done or said.'

Colin, to whom the same thought had occurred, promptly changed his mind.

'I imagine you're trying to help, Diana, but I wish to blazes you wouldn't interfere,' he said stiffly. 'As you say, it's none of your business.'

'Damn all women, eh?' Diana laughed. 'What I admire in you, Colin, is your subtle tact. I expect that is what endears you to Anne. How are you spending your free afternoon? Compiling someone's death warrant?'

'If you mean my statement for the police I shall do that this evening. This afternoon I'm going out.' It occurred to him that Anne might be listening at the top of the stairs, and he raised his voice. 'I've got a date with a girlfriend in Wisselbury, so I'll probably be late back.'

'I'll tell Anne,' Diana said. 'She'll be delighted.'

Anne *was* listening. She knew that Colin's friend at Wisselbury was the science mistress at the college there and nearly twice his age, so no pangs of jealousy assailed her. But she became increasingly miserable as the afternoon wore on and Colin did not return, and began to reproach herself for having been childish and petty enough to pick a quarrel with him. Maybe he *had* been annoying and smug, but men were like that. Particularly Colin. She should have made allowances. And had he only followed her up the stairs instead of rushing off in a tantrum she would, in her own time, have been perfectly content to allow him his stupid little secret — it could not really be important; there had been no time or opportunity for further developments — in return for his company. This was their last day together at the school, and when they left on the morrow it would be to go in opposite directions. It was stupid of them both to have wasted precious hours by behaving so childishly.

She was in the First Form room,

correcting work while the boys were at tea, when James Latimer joined her. He was wearing a raincoat, and Anne idly wondered where he had been. Only Colin had free periods on a Thursday afternoon.

'You must think me an awful bounder,' James said, without preamble.

Anne was surprised. It was most unlike James to belittle himself. And this apologetic, almost penitent air was even more unlike him.

'Don't be silly, James,' she said, uncertain how to treat him in this unfamiliar mood. 'You know I don't think anything of the sort. Let's forget it, shall we?'

He looked at her searchingly.

'I want to, of course. But I'd like to thank you first, Anne, for being so sporting over this. It's damned decent of you.'

Anne blushed, wondering in what way she had been sporting but reluctant to dispute the fact.

'All I want is for the three of us to be friends,' she said sweetly, involuntarily

166

warming towards him. 'I don't harbour any ill feelings on account of last night, and I hope you don't either. Colin was wrong to hit you, and I told him so; but there was nothing personal in it, James — I mean, it wasn't just because it was *you*. He would have treated any other man the same way under those circumstances.'

James looked puzzled; almost, she thought, disappointed. Then he laughed.

'A trifle impetuous, Colin, don't you think?' He was the old James again, bantering, cynical. 'It should take him far — the farther the better, from my point of view. I only regret your foolish determination to accompany him. And now I must away to my chores. Forgive the rather sickly sentiment that escaped me a moment ago. Definitely a lapse — I can't think what came over me.'

He strolled airily from the classroom. Anne gazed after him blankly, her mouth agape. What an extraordinary performance, she thought. And why the sudden drop in temperature? She had said nothing to offend him — unless it were that the very name of Colin offended him. If that were so it was well that Colin was leaving before the skirmish developed into a major war.

She went upstairs to finish her packing. When that was done, and when dinner came and went and still there was no sign of Colin, self-reproach changed to annoyance. It was unfair of him to stay away so long because of a few angry but justifiable words, to leave her unprotected against possible insults from the staff; he knew how they resented her decision to leave with him the next day. And if he could so neglect her now, how would he behave when they were married?

Filled with self-pity, she sat in the common room with Diana, reading little of the novel in her lap, but brooding over the reproaches she would heap on him when he did eventually return.

At nine-thirty Diana shut her own book with a snap and stood up. 'I'm off to bed,' she declared. 'Coming?'

'Not just yet.'

'You might as well. I don't suppose Colin will be back for hours. He is probably delaying his return on purpose to make you wait up for him.'

'I have no intention of waiting up for him,' lied Anne, her manner distant. 'I merely want to finish my book.'

'Well, unless you turn over the pages considerably faster than you have done up to now you won't finish it this side of Christmas,' Diana said, and left her.

By ten o'clock Anne had had enough. It was eerie sitting there alone, believing as she did that a murderer was at large in the school; if there was to be another victim she made a sitting target. Let Colin come home and find her gone to bed. It might teach him to think more of her and less of himself in the future.

Outside the common room she met one of the maids with a glass of milk in her hand. 'Is that for Mr Russell, Doris?' she asked.

'Yes, miss. I was just taking it up to his room.'

'I'll take it. I'm going up now.'

She put the milk on Colin's dressing-table. A large framed photograph of herself confronted her, and she tiptoed from the room with a slightly guilty feeling. As she passed the matron's open door she saw Diana and Miss Webber talking together. She bade them good-night and went to her room, prepared to toss and turn in her bed until she heard Colin's footsteps on the stairs.

She fell asleep almost as soon as her head touched the pillow.

★   ★   ★

It was nearly eleven-thirty that night when Mr Latimer was disturbed by a knock on the study door. 'Sorry to disturb you at this hour, sir,' said Colin, 'but something very serious has occurred. Would you mind coming up to my room?'

This extraordinary request caused the eyebrows to lift abruptly. The look on Mr Latimer's face indicated a belief that his visitor had either taken leave of his senses or indulged too freely in alcohol.

'I am becoming tired of your eccentric behaviour, Russell,' he said sternly. 'This is going too far. What is more, I understand that you have expressed the intention, despite your promise to do nothing without first consulting me, of making a report to the police.'

'Yes. I did mean to inform you, sir; but you weren't in to lunch, and this afternoon I had to go out. And now this has happened.'

'What has?'

'If you'll come upstairs I'll show you.'

Slowly and deliberately, a look of acute annoyance on his lean face, the headmaster rose and stalked out of the room, leaving Colin to follow. Outside the young man's bedroom he stopped.

'Well? What now?'

Colin pushed open the door and pointed. 'There you are, sir,' he said. 'Over there by the bed.'

Mr Latimer's gaze followed the pointing finger to where the school cat lay outstretched on the floor.

'If you are allergic to cats I will remove it for you,' he said, as one humouring a lunatic. 'But I fail to see — '

'That cat's dead, sir.'

'Oh! I'm sorry — I believe my wife was attached to it. But was it really necessary

171

to bring me up here to look at it?'

'It was poisoned,' said Colin. 'Somehow or other it got into my room and drank from that glass of milk on my dressing-table. That's what killed it. And but for the cat I'd have drunk the milk myself.'

Mr Latimer sucked in his breath noisily.

'What are you inferring, Russell?' he asked quietly.

'Isn't it obvious, sir? Someone doped the milk in a deliberate attempt to poison me. If the cat hadn't sampled it first I'd be a dead man by now.'

# 7

## The Swollen Door

Colin sat on the edge of his bed and watched the police at work. Mr Latimer must have telephoned them at a very early hour that morning, for it was not yet eight-thirty and already the room seemed to overflow with policemen. So far they had asked him only the minimum of questions. He wondered when the real business of the day would begin.

The old man had taken it remarkably well, he thought, as he fumbled with his tie (the mirror was hidden from him by policemen). No fuss, extremely dignified. 'I will inform the police myself,' Latimer had said, sniffing at the milk. 'But tomorrow morning, not tonight. I can see no point in disturbing the school at this late hour, and the — ah — culprit will, I presume, still be among us. You agree?' Colin had agreed, and Latimer had walked sedately from the room, pausing at the door to say, in a completely detached tone, 'Under the circumstances it might be better if you and Miss Connaught did not leave tomorrow, Russell. I have no doubt the police will require your presence here. But your notice for the end of term will, of course, still stand.'

He's an unfriendly, remote old devil, Colin thought, as he heaved himself off the bed. He may even be a murderer. But at least he has dignity, a poised presence that we lesser mortals cannot reach.

He was too late to see the small boy who had watched, fascinated, from the corridor. But Robert Cramp's eager eyes had missed nothing — until a sudden move towards the door by one of the policemen had sent him scurrying down-stairs before the heavy hand of the law could descend upon him.

'Pass it down!' Cramp whispered hoarsely to his neighbours at the break-fast table. 'Mr Russell's been murdered! His room is absolutely full of policemen, and I heard them talking about poison.

174

They were taking fingerprints, too, and photographs.' His voice cracked in excitement as he added with a shudder, 'Mr Russell's legs were hanging over the edge of the bed. I saw them — it was horrible.'

As the information passed rapidly from boy to boy and from table to table all eyes turned in swift succession to the empty chair normally occupied by Colin. The noisy chatter sank to a hissing whisper, and Smelton, aware of the change, looked up from his porridge and glared suspiciously round the room. But no mischief seemed to be afoot, and, after barking at one or two boys to sit more squarely on their chairs, he continued with his breakfast. Neither he nor the rest of the staff had as yet been told of the attempted poisoning.

The subdued hum grew louder as excitement and conjecture replaced the awe induced by the first shock of Cramp's startling news.

'I bet Miss Connaught will be sorry,' said Oakes. 'She's sweet on him. I saw them kissing once.'

'Soppy things,' commented a youthful

misogynist; and added, as though following his train of thought to its inevitable conclusion, 'P'raps he committed suicide.'

'Not if the police were taking finger-prints. They only do that when you've been murdered.'

'Hurray! No more Maths!' exclaimed Dicken, suddenly awake to the personal angle. 'How smashing!'

'Don't be silly,' said Fellowes. 'We'll just have a new Maths master, that's all. I'd much rather have Mr Russell. He was jolly decent. And he was absolutely wizard at games.'

'I bet he hasn't *really* been murdered,' said Rodgers. 'I bet you a million pounds Cramp was having us on.'

There were no takers.

'He saw Mr Russell's legs hanging over the bed,' Dicken reminded them; 'so he jolly well must have been. And there wouldn't be policemen in his room if nothing had happened.'

'P'raps they weren't Mr Russell's legs,' Oakes said. 'P'raps he lured someone else into his room and then poisoned him.'

'Who?'

'Not the Stinker, worse luck,' said Fellowes, glancing resentfully at Smelton. It seemed to him in extremely bad taste that, with first J.C. and then Russell coming to an untimely end, the senior master still managed to survive. 'But the Mule hasn't come in to breakfast yet.'

Only among this small group was scepticism expressed. Elsewhere Cramp's news was accepted as gospel; and while speculation on the murderer's identity and on the possible consequences to themselves of his crime comprised the general reaction, there were those who looked fearfully about them and lost interest in their food. Astonishment was therefore tempered with relief when Colin walked into the room, unscathed and unfettered, and sat down to eat his breakfast.

The meal over, there was a rush of boys to his side.

'Sir! Sir! Cramp said there were policemen in your room. He said you'd been murdered.'

'Did you believe him?' asked Colin.

'I didn't,' said Rodgers. 'I *knew* he was having us on. He ought to be jolly well bashed.'

Robert Cramp, small but agile, was in the forefront of the press. 'But there *were* policemen, sir,' he protested earnestly. 'I saw them. I saw your legs too.'

'That settles it then. I *must* have been murdered if you saw my legs.'

'No, but please, sir, what happened? Why were the policemen in your room?'

Colin pushed his chair back against the beseiging bodies and stood up. 'Out of here, all of you,' he ordered. 'You ought to be in your classrooms. Go on, clear off. I'm not answering any more questions.'

To Anne this was the first intimation that anything untoward had occurred. Grasping Colin's arm, she hurried him away from the excited boys to the seclusion of the common room, and demanded to be told the news.

The previous day's quarrel was forgotten by both. As Colin told her of the poisoned milk Anne clung to him in terror.

'Oh, Colin!' she exclaimed, bursting

into tears. 'If it hadn't been for the cat you might be dead!'

Awkwardly he tried to console her.

'It doesn't necessarily follow, darling. Even if I had remembered to drink the damned stuff — and I often don't — I might not have liked the taste. Anyway, I'm alive. So why worry?'

But she refused to be so easily comforted. Remembrance of their quarrel returned, and it occurred to her that but for her stupid bad temper he might not have been exposed to danger. He would have come home earlier, Doris might . . .

She stopped crying and, holding him at arm's length, looked up at him in sudden horror.

'Colin! I put the milk in your room myself!'

He laughed. 'You did, eh? I suppose you didn't add a dash of cyanide to improve the flavour?'

Instantly he regretted this remark, resulting as it did in tearful reproaches and a further paroxysm of grief. He was relieved when the entry of Smelton and Diana caused Anne to dry her eyes and attempt to repair the damage to her complexion.

'I hear someone tried to do you a bit of no good,' said Diana. 'You're getting quite unpopular around these parts, aren't you? Just as well for you that you're leaving today.'

'I'm not. I'm staying till the end of term.'

Diana did not seem surprised. 'You'll have to watch your diet, my lad, if you hope to survive that long. Any idea who pepped up your nightcap?'

'None at all.'

'Whoever it was, he had the right idea,' growled Smelton.

\* \* \*

'An admirably detailed statement, Mr Russell,' said the Inspector. 'I congratulate you.'

Colin leaned back in the armchair and tried not to look as pleased with himself as he felt. He had lavished much loving care on his report, detailing the various points, distinguishing fact from fancy, trying to make the police view the case through his own eyes; it was gratifying to be told that his work had been well done. Nothing had been omitted, he thought. Even the fire at the cottage and his subsequent talk with Mr Bain had been included. As he had told the Inspector, there was no reason to suppose a connection between the fire and J.C.'s death. But it had happened, and it was unusual; and he therefore considered it worthy of mention.

Inspector Pitt, after his few words of praise, fell silent, occasionally rattling the end of a pencil between his teeth as he gazed thoughtfully at Colin. He was tall and thin and solemn-looking, with greying hair and an unhealthy, sallow complexion. Only his eyes gave him distinction; there was in them a youthful alertness that belied his age.

The stare became embarrassing, and Colin looked down at his wrist-watch. Five-past ten. He had already missed one lesson, and seemed well on the way to missing another. He wondered why that should concern him, seeing that he was under notice to leave and had not, he thought, been considerately treated by head or staff. But it *did* concern him, and he shifted restlessly in his chair, hoping by movement to bring the Inspector out of his trance.

The action succeeded.

'I want to be quite certain on one point, Mr Russell,' said Pitt. 'Am I to understand that the rather startling announcement that you made to the staff before lunch yesterday was not founded on fact? You don't know who murdered Mr Connaught, you don't even know that he *was* murdered? Yes, yes — I know you *think* he was,' he said hastily, as Colin opened his mouth to protest. 'We'll go into that later. The point is, you deliberately deceived them, eh? Threw them a bait, as it were.'

'That's right. I was hoping to put the wind up them.'

'Risky, wasn't it? It never occurred to you that if there *did* happen to be a murderer in your audience he might be tempted to dispose of you before you unmasked him?'

182

'No, I can't say it did. I just hoped to panic someone into giving himself away. It was a sort of final gamble before I left.'

'Before you left?' As Colin flushed the Inspector nodded shrewdly. 'Sacked, eh? The headmaster didn't share your views on Mr Connaught's death, I presume.'

'No, he didn't.' Colin was annoyed with himself at having given away this piece of information. 'He thought I was churning up scandal to no purpose.'

'I don't entirely blame him.' Pitt smiled slightly. 'A bit thin in parts, isn't it?'

'I didn't think so. I think so even less now.'

The Inspector nodded. 'Yes, I can understand that,' he said. 'Now, about this glass of milk. You didn't suspect it might be poisoned? You weren't trying it out on the cat first?'

'Of course not.'

'And you think the poison was added by someone who wanted to prevent your telling the police what you knew about Mr Connaught's death?'

'Obviously. What other reason could there be?'

'You're the best judge of that, sir,' Pitt said drily. 'Any idea who the someone was?'

'No.'

'Do you always drink a glass of milk at night?'

'I have it. I don't always drink it.'

'Do you take it up with you?'

'No. Doris, the maid, puts it in my room. It's always there when I go up to bed.'

'And everyone knows it's there, I suppose?'

'I suppose so. The staff treat it as a joke (or did — they're not given to joking with me now); fatuous remarks about the weaning of babies formed the substance of their humour. Incidentally, I suppose I should tell you that last night it was Miss Connaught, not the maid, who put the milk in my room. She happened to meet Doris on her way up. But don't start connecting her with the poison, Inspector. Miss Connaught and I are engaged.'

The Inspector made no comment, but the pencil rattled faster. 'You made this announcement of yours just before lunch,

Mr Russell; and immediately after lunch you cleared off for the rest of the day. You didn't give yourself much opportunity to observe reactions, did you? Wouldn't you have done better to stay here?'

'I don't think so. I expected the reactions to be immediate, you see; but, apart from causing quite a lot of surprise and annoyance all round, my bombshell didn't seem to have much effect.'

'That must have been rather discouraging for you.'

'It was, rather. Then I thought, well, the chap may be a good actor, but he can't *know* I'm bluffing. Ten to one he'll decide to do a fade-out before the day is over.' Colin grinned. 'I didn't anticipate he'd try to fade me out instead.'

'Where did you go?'

'To Wisselbury. A friend of mine is on the staff of the college there; I hoped she might be able to wangle a job for Miss Connaught and myself. It's co-educational — one of these progressive schools.'

'Any luck?'

'I don't know yet.' Emboldened by the

other's apparently non-professional interest in his fortunes, Colin said, 'If you need any outside help, Inspector, I hope you'll call on me. After all, I more or less started this business, if you see what I mean.'

'You nearly provided the finale as well,' was Pitt's comment. 'All right, sir, we'll bear you in mind.'

For some minutes after Colin's departure the Inspector stood, silent and thoughtful, staring at the fire. The constable waited placidly for orders. Sergeant Maddox, a bull of a man with a weather-beaten face and ears that protruded like fins, walked across to the window. There had been heavy rain throughout the night and early morning, but a break in the clouds promised fairer weather. Raindrops dripped from the trees, which in their November garb no longer screened the school from the road.

At the Inspector's cough Maddox turned from this rather depressing outlook. 'A rum go, eh?' he said, his booming voice tinged faintly with the local accent. 'What do you make of it, sir?'

'Nothing yet. Except that it is, as you say, a rum go. I imagine Russell was telling us the truth as he sees it. But is it the *real* truth? Was Connaught murdered? If he was, then the motive for last night's affair was probably as Russell said. But if Connaught's death was an accident . . . ' Pitt shrugged. 'Well, bang goes your motive.'

'I'd say he's right,' said Maddox. 'He threatens to spill the beans, and someone promptly tries to poison him. Too big a coincidence if the two aren't connected.'

'I dare say. But coincidences happen. And the poisoner didn't have much time to get hold of the poison, did he? A few hours only — and where would he go for it? Russell says he was the only member of the staff who was free yesterday afternoon; and I can't see him being given *that* errand. 'If you're passing a chemist's, old man, pop in and buy me some cyanide, will you?' A bit unlikely, isn't it?'

'The chap might have had it by him,' the Sergeant persisted.

'You think so? Do schoolteachers usually keep cyanide handy?'

'Not as schoolteachers, they don't. Not unless they teach chemistry, which I'm told isn't usual in prep schools. But it's used in photography.' The Sergeant nodded meaningly at the library walls, plentifully decorated with framed photographs — some of formal school groups, but others containing more artistic merit. 'Those aren't oil paintings, are they?'

'Not in the literal sense. But metaphorically — well, yes, some of them are. I particularly like . . . ' Pitt turned reluctantly from the photograph that had caught his eye. 'All right, Maddox, that's certainly a line to follow. We will take up the matter of photography with the headmaster. And now, back to the grindstone.'

Diana Farling was not at all perturbed at being called to the presence of the police. She reduced them to their lowest common denominator; they were only men, and men had seldom been a problem to Diana. She gave her evidence calmly. On the previous evening, she said, Christopher Moull had gone up to his room soon after dinner. Mr Smelton had left the common room later, but she and Miss Connaught had sat there reading until half-past nine. 'I went upstairs then; I had finished my book, and Miss Connaught was not in a mood for conversation. She was a little upset, I think; she and Mr Russell — they're engaged, you know — had quarrelled after lunch. I think she hoped to see him when he returned.'

The girl paused — for him to ask a question, Pitt thought. When he did not she went on to explain that she had gone into Miss Webber's room to return the book she had been reading. 'We got down to a bit of gossip,' she said, with a slight, rather apologetic smile, 'and I stayed there until eleven o'clock. It was not until I heard Mr Russell come upstairs that I looked at my watch and realized how late it was.'

'You didn't see him?'

'No. But I knew it was Colin. He's a heavy man, and he always takes the stairs two at a time. I recognized the thuds.'

'Anyone else come up those stairs while you were with Miss Webber?' asked Pitt.

'Only Miss Connaught. That was about ten o'clock — I suppose she had got tired of waiting. I heard her go into Mr Russell's room — the door sticks, you have to give it a bang before it will open — and then she went along to her own room. She said goodnight to us as she passed.'

'And you are certain no one else went into Russell's room during the hour and a half you were talking to Miss Webber?'

'Quite certain,' the girl said firmly.

The Inspector indulged in another bout of staring. It was completely impersonal; the recipient was a focus for his thoughts, not his eyes. Diana wondered uneasily if her nose was shining.

'When Mr Russell announced yesterday that he was making a statement to the police did that surprise you?' Pitt asked, still staring.

She smiled. 'It certainly did. Of course, we all knew he had this odd fixation about J.C.'s death, but none of us took it seriously, I imagine. I didn't, anyway.'

'Do you take it seriously now?'

'Because someone tried to poison him,

you mean?' Diana considered this. 'No, I don't think so. Frankly, I can't even believe in the poison.'

'Why not?' asked Pitt, surprised. 'I can assure you that that at least was real enough.'

'Was it? Well, if you say so . . . but it's all so impossible, Inspector, so out of place. That sort of thing just doesn't happen in schools.'

'Obviously you don't know your Ronald Searle,' said Pitt, the flicker of a smile on his gaunt face. 'Is Mr Russell popular here?'

Diana laughed. 'In other words, who do I think tried to poison him, eh? Well, to be candid, I wouldn't say we were a particularly matey bunch. We have our little squabbles. But they don't usually wind up with a dose of poison.'

Pitt wondered if this was an attempt to evade the issue, but he let it pass. As the door closed behind the girl Sergeant Maddox smacked his lips appreciatively. 'Nice bit of homework, Inspector. What you might call a strapping wench.'

'You might,' Pitt agreed. 'Though I

doubt whether she herself would take kindly to the description.'

Miss Webber was able to confirm much of what Diana had said. She had made her customary round of the dormitories at nine o'clock, finishing in the sickroom — of which Duke, a suspected case of measles, was the only occupant. She had found him restless and tearful, and frightened at being alone in the dark. To calm him she had given him a night-light, and had left his and her doors ajar so that she might hear him if he called.

'He didn't call — or if he did I didn't hear him,' Miss Webber admitted. 'He was sound asleep when I went into the sickroom at eleven.'

'Perhaps your conversation with Miss Farling was particularly engrossing,' Pitt suggested.

'It was, rather. Love and passion are always heady topics for us spinsters,' she said. 'When they take place under one's very nose, so to speak, we like to make the most of them.'

The Inspector admitted that his knowledge of such matters was limited, being confined to the police courts and the Sunday newspapers. Looking at Miss Webber's plain face and dumpy figure, he doubted whether much love or passion had come her way either.

'I'm learning a lot about schoolteachers,' he said. 'Their lives appear to be much less monotonous than I had imagined. Whose romance were you discussing? Or perhaps I shouldn't ask?'

'Oh, it's no secret,' she assured him. 'Every one knows about it.'

'Except me,' he pointed out.

Miss Webber happily expanded on the triangle that was James and Colin and Anne, and on the animosity that had flickered between the two men throughout the term and had culminated in a blow. This was interesting news to Pitt, and he asked for more. But Miss Webber had no more to give. 'Mr James told his father,' she concluded. 'That was why the poor boy — Mr Russell, I mean — got the sack.'

It wasn't the reason the poor boy had given *him*, Pitt thought grimly.

Miss Dove, the under-matron, had

remained in her room throughout the previous evening and had heard nothing; her deafness was reason enough for that. Doris — a pert little teenager with an engaging confidence in herself — declared that she had poured the milk for Russell from a sealed quart bottle and that the glass had not left her hand until she had given it to Miss Connaught. 'I usually puts it in his room during staff supper,' she said, her sharp eyes darting with interest from one to the other of the two policemen. 'But last night I was all on me own. Didn't remember it until I'd done the washin' up.'

'All of which seems to point to Miss Connaught,' said Pitt. 'She put the milk in Russell's room, and there are two witnesses to prove that no one entered the room after that until Russell returned. We'd better have her in.'

'Russell's door sticks all right,' said Maddox. 'I tried it.'

Although Anne had recovered from her earlier hysteria she was still nervous and upset and in no condition to think clearly. Pitt, realizing that here was a very different witness from the composed Miss Farling and the garrulous Miss Webber, allowed her to tell her story in her own way and at her own pace. Some of her nervousness disappeared as she did so, and she seemed comparatively calm when he began to ask questions.

'Did you share Mr Russell's views on your grandfather's death?' he asked her.

Anne hesitated before replying.

'Not at first,' she said. 'Not until he reminded me about the keys. I *knew* someone had been in the house, you see. But even then I couldn't believe it was anyone from here. It's not that I like them all — I don't, really. But it's so impossible to imagine someone you know and work with doing such a horrible thing.'

He nodded. 'I know, miss. But what about last night? No one from outside the school could be responsible for that.'

'No,' she said, distressed. 'It must be one of them.' She was not considering the police angle; her thoughts were all of Colin and the danger that threatened him. 'He believes the poison was meant to stop him from telling you about my grandfather. Now that he's told you, he says, the murderer won't be interested in him any more. Well, I can see that, of course, and I hope he's right. But supposing he's wrong? Suppose Grandfather *wasn't* murdered? That means somebody wants to get rid of Colin for quite a different reason — though I can't think why, he's never harmed anyone. They may try again, and . . . '

Anne dissolved into tears. Sergeant Maddox fumbled in his pocket for a handkerchief, looked at its soiled greyness, and hastily put it back. He was as relieved as Pitt when the girl eventually dried her eyes and looked at them contritely.

'I'm sorry,' she said, swallowing hard. 'It was silly of me to cry.'

'That's all right, miss,' Pitt said. 'And there's no need to frighten yourself about what may happen to Mr Russell. He's safe enough. People don't go around committing murder with the police on the premises.'

'Thank you,' said Anne, blinking her long lashes at them so that the sergeant instinctively squared his broad shoulders and looked for someone to hit. 'I do feel happier now you are here. But I wish he wasn't so confident.' She told them how Colin had teased her after breakfast that morning. 'He can't *know* there won't be another attempt.'

'Perhaps he has more confidence in us than you have,' Pitt suggested.

'Oh, no, it isn't that.' Anne was unconscious of the sting in her words. 'It's because he's so sure that J.C. was murdered.'

Pitt decided he had humoured her long enough. She might be a damsel in distress, but he was no knight errant, and there was sterner business afoot than mopping up a girl's tears. When he had got from her all she could tell him of the day her grandfather died he said — rather hesitantly, fearful that the tears might flow again — 'Suppose Mr Russell is wrong, Miss Connaught. Suppose last night's attempt to poison him has no connection with your grandfather's death — can you name anyone who might want your fiancé out of the way?'

His fears proved to be groundless. 'No,' said Anne, dry-eyed. 'Every one likes him. That is, they did until he told them he thought J.C. had been murdered. Some of them were annoyed about that.'

'Including Mr James Latimer, I suppose?'

'Yes.'

'There's no point in beating about the bush, Miss Connaught,' Pitt said briskly. 'We know all about the row between Mr Russell and James Latimer on Wednesday evening. Didn't it occur to you that Mr Latimer might try to retaliate in some way?'

'Yes, of course. But not that way. He wouldn't try to *kill* him.'

'He might if he hoped to marry you. Paying Mr Russell back in his own coin — giving him a clout on the jaw — wouldn't simplify that problem, would it? But poison might.'

Anne reddened. 'It wouldn't — and he knew it wouldn't. Anyway, Colin was leaving today. James didn't have to use poison to get rid of him.'

'If James Latimer hoped to marry you,

miss, your fiancé would be an obstacle even if he were in Timbuktoo,' said Pitt. 'However, that's by the way. Luckily, most quarrels don't end in poison. Er — you had some sort of a disagreement with Mr Russell yourself yesterday, I'm told.'

'Yes, I did. I was peeved at his holding out on me.' She smiled faintly at the recollection. Then her eyes widened. 'How on earth did you know that, Inspector? Did Colin tell you?'

Pitt shook his head, ignoring the first question. 'How long were you in Mr Russell's room when you took his milk in last night?' he asked.

'Only a few seconds. I just put the glass on the dressing-table and came straight out.'

'Was the cat in the room then?'

'I didn't see it. But it might have been under the bed or behind the furniture.'

'Did you go directly to your room after that?'

'Yes. I meant to stay awake until Colin got back, but I must have dropped off to sleep almost immediately. I didn't hear a thing until Doris brought my tea the next morning.'

'Nobody seems to have heard anything,' Pitt grumbled, when Anne had gone. 'I wonder when the cat was last seen alive. If we can pin that down it might help.'

The Sergeant nodded. 'You don't think the girl did it, do you?' he asked anxiously.

'I'm keeping an open mind,' said Pitt — adding, as an afterthought, 'No, not really.'

Maddox sighed his relief.

Smelton was in one of his more irritable moods. He was curt to the point of rudeness, volunteered nothing, and gave it as his opinion that the whole wretched business was just another instance of 'that young fool Russell's impudent meddling.'

'You think he tried to poison himself?' asked Pitt.

'No, of course not. But it would never have happened if he had minded his own business from the beginning.'

By dint of patient questioning the

Inspector learned that Smelton had stayed to dinner at the school the previous evening because his wife was away for the night, and that afterwards he had gone up to Christopher Moull's room to borrow a book. As the young man was not there he had returned to the common room, had read for half an hour, and after a further fruitless visit to Moull's room had gone home. It was then, he said, just after nine o'clock.

'Did anyone see you leave?'

'I didn't go round saying goodnight, if that's what you mean.'

It wasn't, but Pitt let it pass. 'Were you surprised at not finding Mr Moull in his room?' he asked.

'No. Why should I be?'

'Any idea where he'd got to?'

'Dammit, man, no! He had said he was going up to write letters, but if he chose to do otherwise it was no business of mine. No business of yours either, if you ask me.'

'I didn't,' Pitt said curtly, tired of the other's ill humour.

Smelton was startled. He was not

accustomed to being answered back. 'That all?' he demanded, recovering.

'Not quite. I'm told you don't subscribe to Russell's belief that Mr Connaught was murdered?'

'No.'

'Why not?'

It was too much for Smelton in his present mood.

'It may be your duty to inquire into the events of last night,' he said violently, causing Pitt to wonder anew how such a melancholy and moth-eaten exterior could house so irascible a being. 'But my opinions are my own concern, not yours. I refuse to discuss them.'

'We'll stick to facts, then,' said Pitt. 'Where were you at seven o'clock on the morning of October the twenty-second — the day Mr Connaught was drowned?'

'I don't remember. In bed, I imagine.'

Pitt wondered if he were mistaken in thinking he saw a flicker of apprehension in the man's eyes. 'I'm told you were late for school that morning,' he said, feeling his way.

'Was I? Probably overslept, then. But

let me warn you not to accept as gospel everything that fellow Russell tells you. He's out to make mischief.'

His tone was surly, but it lacked its former bite. Remembering what Colin had told him, Pitt took a leap in the dark.

'If I were to suggest that you were *not* in bed,' he said, 'but that you had left home soon after nine o'clock the previous evening and did not return either that night or the next morning — would that surprise you?'

This time there was no mistaking Smelton's anxiety. His pale eyes clouded, the fingers of both hands twitched nervously. And when, after a long pause, he answered the question he avoided the detective's eyes and his voice was flat and measured.

'It would not only surprise me, Inspector; it would arouse in me grave concern for your sanity,' he said. 'And now, if you will excuse me . . . '

Pitt excused him.

'Maybe Russell isn't so far out,' he said to Maddox. 'Maybe there *was* something fishy about Connaught's death. Smelton wasn't anxious to discuss it, anyway. Definitely evasive. But not unduly concerned about last night, I thought. Irritable and obstructive, yes; but then I guess he's that by nature. One might infer, I suppose, that he was involved in one and not the other — which would seem to sink Russell's idea that the first crime led to the second.'

'Probably had a night out with the boys and didn't want it broadcast,' Maddox suggested. 'That sort of thing wouldn't do a chap in his position any good. But what about Moull, sir? Where was he last night when Smelton went up to his room?'

'In the bathroom or the lavatory, most likely. Not that it matters. Miss Connaught didn't take the milk up until ten o'clock, and after that, if those two women can be relied on, *nobody* went into Russell's room.'

'That's just it,' the Sergeant said eagerly. 'I was thinking he might have sneaked in *before* ten. Perhaps even before Miss Farling came upstairs at nine-thirty. That's why she didn't hear the door open.'

'But the milk wasn't there then.'

'No. But he'd expect it to be. The maid said she usually took it up during dinner. And he wouldn't want to leave it too late, not knowing what time Russell might be back. When he finds the milk isn't there he's in a spot, of course. He knows Doris may arrive at any moment — and so may Russell. So what does he do?'

'All right, I'll buy it,' said Pitt, beginning to be interested. 'What *does* he do?'

'He stays put,' Maddox said with conviction. 'It's safer. Every time he pops in and out he's in danger of being spotted. If the maid turns up before Russell (he'd recognize Russell's tread on the stairs; Miss Farling said he always runs up two at a time) he can hide under the bed until she's gone. But if Russell arrives first — well, he can say he just popped in to borrow a book or something. Nothing suspicious in that. Not that it would matter if there were, since the poison hasn't been used.'

'It's an idea,' Pitt agreed. 'What causes that door to stick, by the way?'

'The wood seems to have swollen. Russell says it's been like that all the term. He's still waiting for someone to fix it.'

'Does it also make a noise when you open it from the inside?'

'It groans a bit,' the Sergeant admitted. 'But not too loud if you take it gently.'

'I'd like to hear it,' said Pitt.

The upper corridor was deserted. With Maddox inside Russell's room and the door firmly closed, the Inspector tapped on Miss Webber's door. He was surprised when she opened it. He had not expected to find anyone upstairs at that hour.

'More questions?' she asked brightly.

'Not this time, ma'am. We want to try an experiment. May I come in?'

'Please do.'

The room seemed to overflow with the garments of small boys. They were on the bed, on the chairs, even on the floor. 'A bit of a mess, I'm afraid,' Miss Webber apologized, as she cleared a chair. 'I've always had the small sickoom for my mending, but since Miss Connaught moved in I've had to make do with this.

What's the experiment, Inspector?'

'We just sit down and wait. But talk if you like.'

Miss Webber found herself unable to talk to order, and there was silence in the room. Then came the sound of boots creaking along the corridor, and Sergeant Maddox appeared in the open doorway.

Pitt shook his head and turned to the matron. 'Did *you* hear anything, Miss Webber?'

'I heard the Sergeant, if that's what you mean.'

'Did you hear a door open?'

'No. I didn't hear him come upstairs, either. Where *did* you spring from, Sergeant?'

'It's me fairy feet, ma'am,' said Maddox, grinning. 'They've got wings on them, like that Atlantic chap.'

'Atalanta,' said Pitt. 'And it's a she, not a he. *And* she didn't have wings on her feet. You're confusing her with Mercury.'

The Sergeant's grin grew broader. 'That's what comes of working in a school. It gets you, doesn't it? I'll be spouting that sort of stuff myself if I'm not careful.'

A gong sounded in the hall.

They left Miss Webber to ruminate on the strange ways of policemen. Pitt slipped quickly into the sickroom to speak to Duke, leaving Maddox on guard against the matron's possible wrath. As they descended the stairs they looked down on a noisy sea of boys' faces, and out of the sea Colin Russell came bounding up to meet them.

'Mrs Latimer has arranged for you to have lunch in the library,' he told them. 'If you want to avoid the mob I'll take you round by the side door.'

They followed him out on to the terrace. Boys were still drifting in from the grounds. The sun had come out, and, although small pools of water twinkled among the uneven flagstones, the air was warm and dry.

'Hi!' shouted Colin, so loudly and suddenly that Sergeant Maddox, lost in a delicious dream of promotion, was startled back to reality.

At the far end of the terrace two small boys were furiously engaged in a mock battle. At Colin's shout they lowered their weapons, after a final cut and thrust, and walked sheepishly towards the three men. One boy held an old cricket stump, the other what appeared to be an iron bar.

'Yes, sir?' Iron Bar asked innocently.

'You know perfectly well that you are not allowed to fence with sticks,' Colin said sternly. 'It's dangerous. If you'd caught Stewart with that iron bar, Locking, you might have killed him.'

'It's not iron, sir — it's wood. That's just black paint on it.'

'Oh! Well, you were still disobeying the rules. Now give them to me and get indoors. You'll be late for lunch.'

As the boys departed Colin threw the two sticks into a shrubbery and then led the detectives round to the front door and into the library, where a table was already laid for lunch. He was curious as to what they had achieved, but Pitt refused to discuss it.

As the young man reluctantly turned to leave them Pitt said, 'Exactly where was the cat when you first noticed it, Mr Russell?'

'Half under the bed. No, more than that. I could just see its hindquarters.'

'Could it have been in that position when you went into the room?'

'I suppose so. But I didn't shut the door until I'd hung up my coat, so it could have come in after me. I should say that's more likely. I put the milk on the floor, out of the way, while I wrote a letter to the scholastic agents; and it was after I'd done that that I looked under the bed for my slippers and saw the cat. It was dead then.'

'I suppose it was you who put the glass back on the dressing-table?'

'Yes.'

And effectively messed up any likely prints, you clot, thought the Inspector irritably as the door closed behind Colin. *And* on the door-handle. The poison bottle would be about the only important thing you couldn't get your big mitts on — and that, of course, is missing.

He ate his meal in silence, allowing Sergeant Maddox to drift happily back into his dream of promotion. That brainwave of his about young Moull had been a masterpiece. The only cloud on the sergeant's visional horizon was the Inspector himself. He had never worked with Pitt before. How much credit, he wondered anxiously, would Pitt allow him when he came to make his report? Would he be generous, or would he hog all the glory for himself?

He came out of his reverie to hear Pitt say, 'That kid in the sickroom told me he *did* call out last night. But Miss Webber didn't hear him — and she didn't hear you this morning either. So we can't place much reliance on *her*. That throws it all on Miss Farling. Well, that's fair enough — if it were not for one little snag.'

'What's that?'

'Russell says Moull is sweet on the girl, but that she doesn't reciprocate his affection. But he may be wrong there; the young lady strikes me as having her emotions well under control. Not the demonstrative, clinging type. And if she *is* keen on Moull — well, you see where that leads us?'

Sergeant Maddox said he wasn't sure that he did.

'It means that if she had the least reason to suppose that Moull was the poisoner her evidence is as valueless as Miss Webber's,' Pitt said sorrowfully.

# 8

## Man With a Bicycle

Few of the staff had been able to hold the interest of their respective forms that morning. But if mental control was difficult physical control was even more so. During the breaks between lessons boys thronged the corridors and the hall, pestering every one for information, darting to the library door each time it opened in the hope of catching sight of one or other of the detectives. Mr Latimer and the duty-master shooed them away with threats of punishment if they returned, but neither shooing nor threats were of lasting avail. The tide momentarily receded and then flowed back again. It was not until nearly the whole staff was on permanent duty downstairs that curiosity was baulked and order restored.

During lessons it appeared that the

school had suddenly become afflicted with incontinence. The procession from classrooms to lavatory (and always via the hall) seemed never ending until the more hardened and experienced members of the staff adopted a complete and callous disregard of even the most importunate pleas. The weaker members, however, such as Anne and Chris, could not resist the dervish-like antics and agonized expressions with which they were confronted on refusing to allow a boy to leave the room. The procession was checked, but there were always a few boys missing from their classrooms.

Lunch at the staff table was therefore in the nature of an impromptu council of war.

'I am afraid there can be neither rest nor relaxation for any of us while the police are here,' said Mr Latimer. He looked worried and harassed, but Colin could not help suspecting that this statement must have given him some satisfaction. Mr Latimer liked to get his money's worth. 'I cannot allow this morning's disgraceful exhibition to be repeated. The boys must be kept away from the hall and, as much as possible, out of the corridors. And I want you all to discourage any discussion on this wretched business. I believe some most extraordinary rumours are circulating in the school.'

'They can't be more extraordinary than the truth,' said James. 'Or perhaps I should say, what we are allowed to know of the truth.'

Colin was silent. Silence, he decided, should shroud him in council and discussion — at least in the presence of the headmaster. He had been conspicuous in bringing them to the present crisis. Now that it was upon them he preferred to remain inconspicuous.

'You can't avoid rumours,' Smelton said peevishly. He had reached an age when the solace of rest and a cigarette between classes had become almost an essential in the daily routine. The prospect of unrelieved duty appalled him. 'They'll get worse, too, unless the boys are given a reason for the police being here. Incidentally, their letters home on

Sunday should make interesting reading.'

James gave a low whistle. 'Yes, that's a point. We'll have to censor them. Parents will be swarming here on Monday like bees if we don't.'

Mr Latimer frowned, but made no comment; and for some time there was little talk at the staff table. The boys, however, made up for the silence of their elders. Never before had they had such a topic for discussion. The rumours which had already reached the ears of the headmaster were as milk and water compared to the fiery brews now being concocted.

For once Mr Latimer took no account of the noise. He was deep in thought. But with the sweet he reached a decision.

'We cannot censor the boys' letters,' he said weightily, but speaking in a low tone so that those furthest from him had to crane their necks to listen. 'Apart from being wrong in principle and purpose, it would merely heighten the tension and delay the scandal. It would be equally wrong . . . ' He paused, considered again, and then plunged. 'No, there is no alternative. I shall send the boys home.'

'The parents won't think much of that either,' said James. 'It's only half-term now.'

'I can't help that. It may be possible for them to return when this business has been settled, but I will not accept the responsibility for keeping them here under existing conditions.' Mr Latimer looked angrily to where a group of shrill voices rose suddenly above the general din, reached a crescendo, and then subsided as one of the culprits caught the headmaster's look. 'You had better send the notices out this afternoon, Miss Farling.'

'Will you tell them the reason?' asked Smelton.

'I shall give them a reason. Duke has measles. The doctor confirmed it this morning.'

'That won't pacify the parents,' said James. 'A few moments alone with their precious offspring and they'll know there is a hell of a lot more to it than measles. You'll have to do better than that, Dad.'

Smelton agreed. Only an official

announcement, he said, could counteract the lurid stories likely to be invented by the boys. The headmaster listened, uncertainty writ plain on his usually poker face. Anne thought she knew why he hesitated. He was wondering whether there was still some slight chance that the affair might be hushed up, that the truth need never come out. If he told the truth now he would be burning his bridges behind him.

Diana's cool voice broke into the discussion for the first time. 'What is there to tell?' She asked simply. 'Nothing has actually happened, has it?'

It was too much for Colin.

'Thanks very much,' he said, with a poor attempt at sarcasm. 'Somebody tries to poison me and you call that nothing!'

'But the attempt didn't succeed,' the girl answered, smiling at him. 'That's the point. There's no corpse, no one is missing. As far as the boys are concerned, therefore, nothing *has* happened.'

Mr Latimer did not heed Colin's renewed protest. He clutched eagerly at the proffered straw.

'Miss Farling is right,' he said. 'Apart from the presence of the police, there is no visible evidence to support any tales the boys may choose to tell their parents. We can deny them all with a clear conscience.'

'Apart from the presence of the police!' mimicked James. 'And how do you propose to explain that insignificant item?'

His father did not answer. Anne wondered whether, if the police were not in evidence when the parents called, he would deny that they had ever been there. She had always regarded him, with some awe, as a tin god lording it, in his metallic, unfeeling way, over a little world of paper subjects — a tin god who if he did wrong could do it with impunity. Now she knew that he was as vulnerable as they were. If he were made of tin he was either buckling or melting. And if he were a god, then there were other and more superior gods to whom he was answerable. He was no longer the master of his own fate and of his own world. His world had been invaded.

Colin, having once broken his resolution to keep silent, broke it again.

'You'll have to let the Inspector know that you want to send the boys home, sir,' he said.

Mr Latimer glared at him. Since he must, he would accept this interfering young jackanapes; it did not follow that he would forgive him. 'I imagine it is no concern of the police how I run my own school,' he said icily.

'But you'll have to get their permission,' Colin persisted. 'The Inspector may want to question some of them.'

That, thought the headmaster, was a very good reason why the boys should go. Still glaring, he rose to say grace.

As they stood watching the now silent boys file from the dining-hall Diana said, 'What happens to us? Are we to be sent home too?'

James laughed. 'You're a bigger optimist than the old man,' he said. 'We stay put. The Inspector won't let any of us out of his sight until he discovers who prepared Russell's nightcap for him. It seems a pity,' he went on, with a backward glance at Colin, 'that we should suffer all this inconvenience for nothing. Now, if only Russell had drunk the ruddy stuff . . . '

Anne, for one, had not realized that they were virtually prisoners. Upstairs in her room after lunch she wondered about it. Surely the police could not keep them at Redways indefinitely? The atmosphere in the common room had been unhappy enough before. With the boys gone and nothing to occupy their time it would become unbearable.

The boys were resting on their beds, and for a little while the staff were at liberty. On the drive in front of the house Diana and Chris were walking together. Still busy with her thoughts, Anne watched them idly. They were of equal height, and Chris never took his eyes from his companion's face. He seemed to be pleading with her; but to no avail, for the girl shook her head repeatedly. Once she turned to leave him, but the young man caught her arm and held it, still pleading. Poor Chris, thought Anne; he's terribly in love, and Diana so obviously cares nothing for him. Obviously to every one but Chris, that is. Now and again she seems to soften a little — through boredom, perhaps, or because she can't help feeling sorry for him; but that only makes it worse — it makes him see hope where there is none. If she doesn't want him she should tell him so, cut out all this blowing hot and then cold. Chris would get over it in time, thought Anne. Men always do.

Sergeant Maddox appeared from under the jutting eaves and walked across the terrace to the couple on the drive. After a moment's conversation he and Chris went back to the house. Diana hesitated, started to follow them, and then, apparently changing her mind, went off in the direction of the kitchen.

Poor Chris, thought Anne again. If Colin is right in suspecting he had something to do with J.C.'s death he is going to hate the next half-hour or so. She wondered how she could feel sorry for a man who might have murdered her grandfather, and decided it was because, no matter how black the evidence might appear against him, she could not visualize Chris Moull as the cold-blooded monster that the killer of J.C. must have been. He might kill — but not like that.

As she turned away from the window she wondered if Inspector Pitt would be more successful than Colin at prising the truth out of Chris.

★　★　★

Inspector Pitt was wondering much the same thing. Apart from exonerating Miss Farling and Miss Webber from the attempt to poison Russell, the evidence he had so far collected did not amount to much. But there were still the Latimers, father and son — and Christopher Moull. And Moull, Pitt had decided, looked like being his best bet.

But Chris, despite a certain wariness at odds with his cherubic countenance, did not at first seem perturbed by the Inspector's questions. He knew nothing of the poison, he said. He had gone upstairs to his room almost immediately after dinner, had read for some time, and had then retired to bed and to sleep.

'Miss Connaught left the milk in Russell's room at ten o'clock. I dare say you already know that,' said Pitt. 'Now, your room is next to Russell's. If anyone entered his room either before or after ten you should have heard him. Did you?'

'No. I can't honestly say that I heard Miss Connaught either — though I suppose I must have done.'

'Did you leave your room at all before going to bed?'

'No.'

There had been a slight pause before that second 'no'. Pitt hesitated. Should he lay his cards on the table now, or should he seek to entangle the young man further?

He decided on the former alternative.

'Would it surprise you to learn, sir, that twice during the course of the evening someone visited your room, and that on both occasions you were absent from it?'

Moull flushed. 'I may have gone to the bathroom,' he said.

'I don't think so, sir. The bathroom was empty at the time.'

He spoke with conviction. The other did not argue.

'You still say you did not leave your room?' Pitt persisted.

'I'm not saying anything. Who was this mysterious visitor, anyway? It looks as if one of us needs his head examined.'

'It looks as if one of you isn't speaking the truth,' the Inspector corrected him, ignoring the question. 'That is a serious matter in a case of attempted murder.'

'Murder?' The other looked aghast. Then his face cleared, and he smiled. 'Good Lord! You don't think I was responsible for doping Colin's milk, do you? Why, he and I are the best of friends. You ask him.'

His serene assurance unsettled the Inspector.

'Even friends can be dangerous if they know too much,' Pitt said harshly. 'You know Russell believes that old Mr Connaught was murdered?'

The wariness came back to the young man's eyes as he nodded.

'Do you agree with him?' Pitt asked. 'Do *you* think it was murder?'

'I don't know enough about it to form an opinion,' said Chris.

'H'm! Mr Russell does not appear to confide in his *friends*,' Pitt could not resist saying. 'You went for a walk by the river that morning, didn't you?'

'Yes.'

'Do you often go walking before breakfast?'

'Not often. It just happened that I woke early and couldn't get to sleep again.'

The young man was vague about time, but that, if he were innocent, was understandable. It was a fortnight now since John Connaught had died. He had seen Mrs Smelton on her bicycle, said Chris, and he remembered passing a stranger as he crossed the far bridge. He had gone a little way along the river-bank, and had then retraced his steps to the school.

'Why?' Pitt asked bluntly. 'Why didn't you go on? What happened to make you turn back?'

'Nothing happened. But I was in no hurry, and it was pretty misty along the river.'

'Did you meet anyone on the return journey?'

'No.' And then more firmly, after a pause. 'No. No one.'

Pitt asked him about his visit with Diana Farling to Mrs Bain's cottage. The petrol-filled lamp was something that intrigued the Inspector out of all proportion to its apparent importance. If, as seemed certain, the Bains had not been guilty of carelessness, how had it happened? Had Mr Bain tired of his wife and chosen that rather clumsy method of disposing of her? Or was it, as the man had hinted to Russell, the work of an outsider? Whatever the reason, it seemed to lie beyond the sphere of the Inspector's present investigations. Yet it was an incident so senseless and incomplete in itself that surely it had to be part of a larger and more comprehensive crime? And that scattered country district could not be so steeped in crime that it could boast another more serious than those he was now investigating.

Yet, if there were a connection, where did it lie? There had been time and opportunity enough for any member of the staff to set the scene, for Miss Farling had announced at tea that Moull was to be boarded out at the Bains', and it was not until two and a half hours later that the lamp had exploded. But what was the motive? Russell had said . . .

'You were not very pleased at the prospect of sleeping at the cottage, were you?' Pitt asked.

'No, I wasn't. It would have meant going out night and morning in all weathers. Besides, I — ' Chris stopped with a jerk, biting off the last word. His eyes narrowed, and when he spoke again his voice carried a pugnacity normally foreign to it. 'I don't think I like that last question, Inspector. Are you suggesting that I deliberately tried to blow up the cottage — to say nothing of Mrs Bain — simply to avoid having to sleep there? If you are, then let me tell you . . . '

'You need not bother, sir,' Pitt said placidly. 'I can guess. Well, we will have your statement typed, and I'll let you know when it is ready for signing.'

'Statement?' The young man stared at

him. 'I've made no statement.'

'We would like your signature, Mr Moull, to a summary of what you have said in this interview. That is a customary request, although you are not bound to comply with it. And if you wish to modify or alter any part of your statement . . . '

He paused. The stare was a troubled one. So troubled that for a moment the Inspector had wild hopes of a confession — or of at least an approach to the truth. Then Moull shook his head slowly and walked out of the room.

'I'm not sure I didn't bungle that,' Pitt said thoughtfully. 'Though I can't think how.'

Sergeant Maddox clucked sympathetically. 'He didn't take kindly to signing that statement,' he said. 'And for why? Because it's as full of lies as a colander is of holes.'

'He may be lying, but unless we know where and why he's lying we aren't much forrader. The only concrete evidence against him is Smelton's statement that he was out of his room at eight-thirty and nine o'clock last night. And Smelton may be lying. Smelton himself may be the poisoner. You suggest Moull may have slipped into Russell's room before ten and waited there. Well, so could Smelton. No one saw him leave the school, and no one can say when he arrived home. Not if his wife was away for the night, as he says.'

'They may have a maid.'

'I doubt whether schoolteachers can afford maids. However, suppose Smelton *was* speaking the truth — where was Moull?'

'In Russell's room, as I said.'

Pitt nodded impatiently. The Sergeant, he thought, was exercising that particular horse too often and neglecting the rest of the stable.

'Supposition only. He might have been in someone else's room.'

'Wouldn't he say so in that case?'

'I can think of reasons why he might not,' said Pitt. 'But there is one factor here that points to Moull, and not Smelton, as the liar. I didn't tell Moull *when* his visitor called. Therefore, since he must realize that the vital time was after ten o'clock, he would, if he had been in his room then, assume that his visitor called *before* ten. But he didn't assume that — presumably because he couldn't. He was out of his room both before and after ten. Get me?'

'I'm not sure that I do. A bit involved, isn't it?'

'All right, skip it,' said Pitt. 'It's probably irrelevant.'

Now that he had met and talked with the staff he needed inside information about them from the headmaster. It would have helped him in his interviews had he been able to get it earlier, but Joseph Latimer was not an easy man to corner. Nor, when the Inspector eventually succeeded in cornering him, was he particularly informative. With the exception of Smelton and the two matrons all the staff were comparative newcomers, he said, and he knew little about them. Diana Farling had come the previous January; she had good references from a school in Ireland, where her mother lived. Mr Latimer thought that her father was dead and that her mother had remarried, but he could not be certain of that.

'I understand she has a cottage out at Chaim,' said Pitt. 'Has she an income apart from her salary? Even small cottages cost a tidy sum these days.'

Mr Latimer did not know. Miss Farling was an efficient secretary, and he was not concerned with her private life. Nor was he any more informative about the rest of the staff. Anne Connaught and Christopher Moull had joined Redways at the beginning of the summer term. Moull's home was in Kent; he was a shy young man and a poor disciplinarian, though willing. Pitt gathered that it was only his willingness that restrained Mr Latimer from sacking him. As for Russell — here the headmaster grimaced — 'I know nothing of his past, apart from one reasonable reference, and I hope that I shall not in any way be connected with his future. This is his first term here, Inspector, and his last. Since I feel that I am perhaps biased against him I would prefer to keep my opinion of him to myself.'

'And Mr Smelton?' asked Pitt.

Here the headmaster's knowledge went a little deeper, but only in respect of Smelton the schoolmaster. Of Smelton the man he could say little, apart from some rather scathing comments on the man's inability to manage either his wife or his financial affairs. Pitt wondered how such an impersonal and cold-blooded creature as Joseph Latimer could run, apparently successfully, such a personal institution as a private boarding-school.

'Did any of these people have cause to dislike Russell?' he asked.

The headmaster struggled between personal animosity and a regard for the truth. 'Not so far as I know,' he said cautiously. 'Not until he started accusing all and sundry of murder. I imagine they liked him then no more than I did.'

And that, thought Pitt, was a minus quantity. 'Where were you yourself last night, sir? Until, say, eleven o'clock?' he asked. He realized that he had to tread warily here. But, headmaster or no headmaster, the question had to be put.

Mr Latimer told him. He obviously considered the question an impertinence, but he told him. He had spent the evening, he said, as he spent most evenings during term-time, working in his study. His wife and son had also been in the room until ten-thirty. After that he had been alone until Russell disturbed him.

Pitt decided to leave it at that, and not to brandish a further red rag by delving into the circumstances surrounding the death of John Connaught. He knew from Russell what cause Latimer had had to dislike the old man. He knew too how Latimer and others had benefited from Connaught's death. And, although he was beginning to suspect that Russell had been right in designating it as murder, he needed to know more about it before voicing his belief, either to the headmaster or to his own superiors. His job was to discover who had tried to poison Russell. Connaught's death was at present no concern of his unless it helped him to do that.

But he did ask about the identity-disc. To his surprise Mr Latimer promptly produced it from his desk. It was of plastic, and stamped with the late owner's name and address.

'Mr Smelton gave it to me, Inspector. He admitted that he could see no reason for preserving it — it has no value — but thought that, in view of Russell's extraordinary accusations and apparent loss of sanity, it might be wiser to do so. And I agreed with him.'

There was one more stretch of thin ice to negotiate. Pitt introduced it by admiring the photographs on the library walls, and was surprised to see a faint enthusiasm in the other's face.

'I took them myself,' Latimer said, his voice less frigid. 'I am — or was — a keen photographer. But nowadays I seem to have little time for it.'

'You do your own developing and enlarging, I suppose?'

'Of course. No true photographer would dream of doing otherwise.'

There was a slight pause. It's no good, thought Pitt; you can't skate round the damned thing, you've got to go at it baldheaded. 'I hope you won't misunderstand this, Mr Latimer, but isn't potassium cyanide used in photographic processes? Isn't it a fixative?'

'I don't think I misunderstand you, Inspector,' the headmaster said grimly, standing stiffly erect. 'I can assure you that there is no potassium cyanide in my darkroom and that I did *not* attempt to poison Russell last night. Isn't that what you wanted to know?'

'Not exactly, sir.' Pitt was relieved at the lack of fireworks. He had anticipated a more vigorous reaction. 'I was not suggesting that you yourself were impli-cated. But cyanide was used — and obtained at short notice, apparently. If there had been a supply in the build-ing — '

'Well, there was not. In any case, I keep the darkroom locked.'

Pitt rose to go. But if he had finished with the headmaster the headmaster had not finished with him. 'Perhaps you should know, Inspector, that I intend to send the boys home on Monday,' he said curtly.

'I've no objection, sir. The staff will have to remain, of course.'

'Yes. And I should be obliged if you and your colleagues would be as unobtrusive as possible when parents are here. I do not wish to advertise this unfortunate affair.'

We might be the broker's men, Pitt thought angrily. 'You won't be able to hush it up,' he said shortly. 'Not after the newspapers have got wind of it.'

Mr Latimer winced.

'I see no reason why they should,' he said. 'I shall give orders that no reporters are to be admitted. And I presume it is not customary for the police to indulge in gossip.'

It was too much for the Inspector.

'It's about time you faced the facts, Mr Latimer. This isn't a tuppenny ha'penny theft or common assault; when we make an arrest it will be on a charge of attempted murder. It's news, Mr Latimer. It will make the big dailies, and it'll be splashed all over your local paper, I shouldn't wonder. And there's nothing you or anyone else can do to stop it.' He laughed grimly. 'As for barring the place to reporters — well, try it and see what happens. They'll get the news somehow. If they don't get it from you or your staff they'll get it from the boys. Over fifty boys here, aren't there? So that if you close down the school on Monday there will be that many fresh sources of information for the reporters to get at. Not very reliable sources, perhaps; but talkative, I imagine. Have you thought of that?'

Mr Latimer had not. Not in connection with newspapers.

'Do you expect to make an arrest shortly?' he asked, considerably chastened.

But Pitt was not prepared to commit himself on that.

James Latimer showed surprise and annoyance at finding the police already informed of his quarrel with Colin, but he did not attempt to deny it or to minimize its significance. Instead he practically went out of his way (in a spirit of bravado, the Inspector thought) to emphasize his dislike of his rival, and concluded by saying that, although he had not put poison in the milk, he was fully in sympathy with whoever had done so. The sharp rebuke which this remark elicited from the Inspector did not help to keep the interview on an easy footing.

On the previous evening, said James, he had been with his parents in his father's study until shortly after ten-thirty. He had then gone upstairs, via the main staircase, with his mother and, after saying goodnight to her outside her room, had retired next door to his own. 'And I can produce no witnesses, Inspector, to testify that from then on I was in bed,' he mocked. 'That makes me a marked man, I shouldn't wonder.'

Pitt took no notice of this crack. He had already decided that James had a rather warped sense of humour. 'I'm told you were away the night before Mr Connaught was drowned,' he said. 'Is that correct?'

James slapped his thigh noisily.

'Good Lord, Inspector, don't tell me you've joined Russell on *that* old hobby-horse! With the two of you in the saddle it must be buckling at the knees. You'll kill it if you're not careful and what will Russell do then, poor thing?'

'Were you away that night, Mr Latimer?'

The other stared at him thoughtfully, the smile fading. 'Yes,' he said, with unusual brevity.

'Where?'

'That, Inspector, I am not prepared to say. Not, at any rate, until you start rattling the handcuffs in earnest.'

'Handcuffs don't rattle, Mr Latimer — they snap. And perhaps I should have said, where did you go after leaving Mr Connaught?'

The black eyebrows lifted. 'Good Lord! So you know that too, do you? What it is to have friends! But I'm afraid the answer is still the same.'

'What was your business with Mr Connaught that evening?'

James shook his head. 'Sorry, Inspector. You'll have to rattle harder than that before you can persuade me to discuss my private affairs with strangers.' He frowned. 'What's biting you, man? You know damned well that J.C. was alive the next morning — so what the devil does it matter what happened the evening before?'

* * *

Pitt was glad to get away from the school. He did not like small boys in large quantities, he did not like the Latimers, he did not like witnesses who apparently went out of their way to confuse and annoy. He felt frustrated and peevish. The only item of the day he could recall with genuine pleasure was the look on the headmaster's face when he had told him that a constable would remain on duty at the school overnight.

He was surprised at the size of Philip Smelton's house and the elegance with which it was furnished. No wonder the man is hard up, he thought, and no wonder he wanted that flat. A place like this must cost a packet to run. Certainly more than a schoolteacher is likely to earn.

Dorothy Smelton surprised him too. He had dismissed her husband as an insignificant, pompous little man notable only for his irascibility. That Smelton could have inspired the affection of such a charming and vital woman seemed incomprehensible.

Smelton had telephoned the news to Dorothy that morning, explaining that it might delay his return — a return which, for once, Dorothy was eagerly anticipating. She was not abnormal in her love of gossip, but little happened in Wainsford to stimulate conversation. It had never occurred to her that she might be interviewed by the police; all her information, she had thought, would have to be gleaned from her husband. Now, with a Detective-Inspector actually in her house, she saw herself as the centre of interest for many a party to come. Mobilizing all her considerable charm and powers of persuasion, she went to work on her visitor.

But Pitt was accustomed to dealing with the curiosity of females. Firmly he cut short her questions and supplanted them with his own — which Dorothy, so rapidly had the tables been turned, found herself meekly answering. No, they had no maid. No, she could not say at what time her husband had returned the previous evening; she had spent the night with her parents in London. No, she did not think Philip harboured any enmity towards Colin Russell — realizing, with a quickening pulse, the threat behind the question. Philip, she said, usually spoke disparagingly of young masters. He did not consider they had sufficient respect for the experience of their elders.

When Pitt mentioned John Connaught's death her answers came less readily. That, he thought, might be due to the strain on her memory imposed by the lapse of time. But it puzzled him that, whereas practically every one connected with Redways grew cautious when Connaught's name was mentioned, none, with the possible exception of Christopher Moull, displayed any sign of guilt when questioned about the previous evening. One would suppose, thought Pitt, that they had all had a hand in disposing of the old man (whose death had already been dismissed by the coroner as accidental), and that no one had put poison in Russell's milk — neither of which suppositions could possibly be true.

'I'm told you were out early on your bicycle that morning,' he said.

'I dare say,' she agreed. 'I know I went over there one morning, but I can't remember which.'

'Meet anyone you know?'

'No, I don't think so. Only the old man in the garden. That was Mr Connaught, I suppose; I'd never come across him before.' She laughed, remembering. 'He was in his dressing-gown. He wasn't very big, but he looked so threatening that I turned tail and bolted.'

'Did he say anything?'

'No. That was odd, wasn't it? He just stood there shaking his fist at me. Of course, he had every reason to be angry, seeing a perfect stranger wandering round the house and peering in at the windows.'

So it had been to Mrs Smelton, and not to his granddaughter, that the old man had been expressing his displeasure. Knowledge of that might please Miss Connaught, thought Pitt — and was promptly surprised that the thought should have occurred to him. 'What was the purpose of your visit?' he asked.

'Oh, just to have a look round. My husband had been telling me we might be offered the bottom floor as a flat when J.C. died. This house is so far from the school, and much too big for us.'

'Rather an early hour to go calling, wasn't it?'

'I wasn't calling. I went early on purpose to avoid meeting anyone. I could hardly ask to be shown over the flat with a view to occupying it on the old man's death. That would have been most indelicate. And it never occurred to me that people might be up and about before seven. *I* never get up before eight-thirty. Not even then unless I have to.'

'I thought Mr Connaught's morning swim was common knowledge.'

'Oh, yes, I knew about *that*. But I didn't know it took place at such an unearthly hour.'

'And why the bicycle, Mrs Smelton?

Why didn't you use the car?'

'My husband had it,' she said, unthinking.

'So your husband had the car, did he?' commented Pitt. 'And before seven o'clock in the morning. Where would he be going at that hour?'

Recognizing her slip, she realized she could do nothing to rectify it. Philip might already have been asked that same question and have given an answer. She must not try to invent one now.

'I don't know,' she said, feeling helpless and inadequate.

Pitt decided to force his hand. 'I have reason to believe that your husband was away from home that Friday night,' he said. 'Can you confirm that?'

'He may have been,' Dorothy admitted — and then, deciding that it was safer to tell the truth, 'Yes, I think he was. We had had a row that evening, and he went off in a huff.'

'At about nine-thirty?'

'About then, yes.'

'Do you know where he went?'

'No. I didn't see him again until the

246

next evening, and neither of us referred to it then.'

'Might he have stayed with friends?'

'I don't know,' she said again. 'He hasn't any real friends in this district. But if it's important why don't you ask him?'

'I have asked him, Mrs Smelton,' said Pitt. 'He told me he had spent the night here. He said he was late to school the next morning because he overslept.'

That shook her. She had not realized that Philip might find it necessary to lie. But she made no attempt to retract her statement or to excuse her husbands's. If Philip were in danger he must see to his own salvation. They had grown too far apart for her to do so.

To Inspector Pitt, whose experience had shown him more of the friction of married life than its bliss, Mrs Smelton's explanation of her husband's action seemed a very natural one. Even Smelton's lie did not arouse in him undue suspicion; Smelton was a man full of his own importance, he might consider it beneath his dignity to admit to a marital squabble. But Pitt was taking no chances.

Since Russell had seen Smelton's car heading for Tanbury that night, he despatched Maddox there to make inquiries. Then, feeling rather self-conscious at the assiduity with which he was chasing apparent red herrings, he went in search of Bain.

He found him clearing away the remains of his evening meal, and looking extremely miserable about it. 'I don't mind a bit of cooking, so long as it's easy like,' said the man. 'But washing and wiping! That's worse than housework, that is.'

Pitt commiserated, and inquired after Mrs Bain.

'She's coming along, but it'll be a week or two yet afore she's out,' said the other. He handed the Inspector a cloth. 'You dry them things while I wash, and we'll get along quicker. I gotta go to the 'ospital.'

The Inspector obeyed. 'What's your job?' he asked, gingerly rubbing a plate that still contained traces of egg and mustard. Mr Bain, he thought, was not a good washer-upper.

'Lampard's, out along the Kirten road.

I'm on nights — eight-thirty to six-thirty. They're long hours, but the pay's good.'

Pitt looked at his watch. 'You'll have to hurry, won't you, if you want to get to the hospital and back before eight-thirty?'

'I've got me auto-cycle,' said Bain. 'It don't take long on that.'

Pitt asked him about his wife's accident, but got little enlightenment and much suspicion. The suspicion, however, was not directed against any person in particular, and Pitt decided — somewhat regretfully, for he was still intrigued by it — that this red herring was not for him. Then an idea occurred to him and he said, 'The Kirten road, eh? Do you go by the towpath?'

The man nodded. 'That's the quickest way,' he said. 'But I don't use the motor along that bit. She's easy to pedal.'

'If you knock off at six-thirty, then, you must often have seen old Mr Connaught taking his early-morning dip.'

Mr Bain agreed. He had seen the old gentleman many a time. 'I remember the morning he was drowned, too. Same day as that kid from Redways got run over.

They was carting him off to 'ospital as I come to the bridge.'

'Did you meet anyone on or near the towpath that morning?'

'Well, there was the young gent from the school. I don't know his name. Round-faced, quiet-spoken chap.'

Pitt nodded. 'Short hair, like a Yank's? Was he wearing a duffel-coat?'

'He was. But I wouldn't know about his 'air. Always seen him in a beret.'

'Where did you meet him?'

'Far end of the towpath.'

'Was he coming this way?'

'He wasn't coming *or* going,' said Bain. 'He was standing leaning against his saddle and looking at the water.'

'Saddle? What saddle?'

'The saddle of his bike, of course.' The man laughed. 'You didn't think he was on a horse, did you?'

# 9

## Peregrinations of a Bottle

The school was strangely silent for a Saturday afternoon, thought Anne. Normally the boys would be playing football, and, although the building itself would be empty, there would be the sound of their excited voices, the shouted instructions of the masters, and the shrilling of whistles, drifting in from the fields. But today there was no football, for Mrs Latimer and the two matrons were busy packing and there were no football clothes available. The boys were down in the woods at the far end of the grounds, playing 'He' and leap-frog and other boyish games. Some whose homes were near were leaving that evening, and some on Sunday; but the majority would be there until Monday. After that it will be all silence, Anne thought. Probably in a few days we shall be longing to hear the noisy shouting we now complain of. A school empty of boys must be a horribly depressing place.

She wandered into a dormitory and offered her help to Miss Webber. But, as Miss Webber pointed out, by the time you had explained to someone else where everything was to be found it was usually quicker to do the job yourself.

Anne sat on a bed and watched the other's practised packing.

'What do you think of all this, Webby?' she asked. Not because she really wanted to know. She was depressed, and needed someone to talk to.

'I don't let myself think of it, dear,' said Miss Webber, rummaging under a pile of clothing. 'I'd probably go crazy if I did. But I locked my door last night. *And* I looked under the bed.' She stood up. 'No, it isn't there.'

'What isn't there?'

'Derwent's other boxing-glove,' said Miss Webber, holding up the one. 'I've never yet known that boy have everything ready for packing.'

'Why does he take them home?' asked

Anne. 'I thought they usually left them here.'

'He has boxing lessons in the holidays. Well, his trunk must wait. But I reminded him about his gloves before lunch. I suppose one was in its right place and the other wasn't, and he simply couldn't be bothered to look for it. That's just typical of Derwent.'

'I'll see if I can find it,' said Anne, standing up. 'It must be somewhere in the gym.'

'Don't bother, dear,' said Miss Webber. 'Let him look for it himself later.'

'I don't mind. I've nothing else to do.'

The boys' boxing-gloves were hung on pegs at the far end of the gymnasium. Anne examined them all; they were clearly marked, but none had Derwent's name on it. Looking round the bare walls, it seemed impossible that the missing glove could be anywhere in the gymnasium; apart from some coiled rope, the vaulting horse, and a few mats, there was nothing on the floor. The mats were heavy, but there was no need to lift them. They lay quite flat; there could be no lumpy boxing-glove hidden underneath.

Just to make sure, she laboriously tilted one end of the horse. She saw the glove at once. With some difficulty she fished it out, wondering how it had got there. Yes, it was Derwent's. Well, perhaps he had hidden it on purpose, she thought. Perhaps he doesn't like boxing. Imagining the boy's scared disappointment when he learned that his ruse had not succeeded, she felt rather mean.

Idly wondering what it would feel like to be punched on the nose with such a solid piece of leather, she tried to slip her hand into the glove as she went upstairs. Her fingers encountered something cold and hard, and she pulled it out. It was a small glass bottle, empty with a rubber stopper.

Funny place to hide a bottle, thought Anne.

It was not until she reached the open dormitory door that she connected it with the poison. Clutching the bottle tightly in one hand, she proffered the glove to Miss Webber with the other.

'Thanks, dear,' said Miss Webber.

'That's a great help. But I'll see that Derwent — ' She paused, eyeing with concern the girl's pale face. 'Are you feeling all right, Anne?'

'Just a headache,' said Anne. 'I think I'll go outdoors for a bit, though. The fresh air might blow it away.'

'I hope you're not sickening for measles,' said the other. 'If you don't feel better after tea I'll take your temperature.'

Anne escaped to her room and examined the bottle. It was hexagonal in shape, with a plain white label devoid of printed matter. Underneath embossed on the base, was what appeared to be the letter M. She pulled out the cork and sniffed warily. Was she mistaken, or was there really a faint odour of bitter almonds? Or was that the wrong smell for cyanide?

She pushed the cork back firmly, slipped the bottle into her jacket pocket, and, since neither the Inspector nor the Sergeant was about, went out into the grounds to look for Colin. There was no one in sight, but in the distance she could hear the boys' voices. They seemed to come mainly from the direction of the valley, and she ran down through the trees towards the wooden bridge.

Colin was there. He stood on the bridge, his hands resting lightly on the broken rail, gazing pensively down into the water foaming past underneath. Along the banks of the stream the boys were scattered, chasing each other and playing hide-and-seek among the trees.

Colin saw her coming and walked off the bridge to meet her. He caught her in his arms as she slid involuntarily down the slope and, forgetful of the boys, bent to kiss her.

Anne turned her head sharply and struggled out of his embrace.

'Colin, do be careful, *please!* The boys are watching us.' She put her arm through his and led him away. 'Come along, I've got something to show you.'

'Mustn't go far,' said Colin. 'I don't want those damned kids falling into the river in their Sunday suits.'

'If they fell in in their birthday suits they'd be no better off,' said Anne. 'They'd drown either way.' She fished the bottle from her pocket and held it out to him. 'There!'

He took it from her. 'Where did you find this?' he asked sharply.

'In the gym. It was inside one of Derwent's boxing-gloves, under the vaulting-horse. It's the bottle the police are looking for, isn't it? The one the poison was in?'

'Probably. You can tell by the shape that it's a medicine bottle.'

'I wouldn't call potassium cyanide a medicine,' Anne retorted, rather nettled that he had not commended her on her discovery. 'Come on, give it back. I'll keep it until the Inspector returns.'

'I suppose it never occurred to you that there might be fingerprints,' said Colin, still holding the bottle and ignoring her outstreched hand. 'Now it will be plastered all over with yours and mine.'

'They will be able to trace where it came from, anyway.' She was annoyed with herself at having forgotten so elementary a precaution. 'And I don't suppose the poisoner would be so careless as to leave his fingerprints on it.'

'You'd be surprised at the damned silly

257

mistakes criminals sometimes make. Even the cleverest of them.' He juggled the bottle up and down thoughtfully. Then, acting apparently on impulse, he slipped it into his pocket.

'I think I'll keep this for a while,' he said.

'Colin!' Anne was horrified. 'The police must have it. The Inspector said that if he could find the bottle he would be half-way home. Don't you *want* him to find out who tried to poison you?'

'I'd rather find out for myself — if I can. Anyway, I'm not going to keep it — I only want to borrow it. The Inspector can have it later.'

'Colin, you mustn't. It's wrong and it's dangerous. And you promised me you wouldn't meddle any more; you know you did. *Please*, darling, let me have it.'

'Why? You can't give it to the Inspector yet — he's not here. And I don't call it meddling to want to nail the blighter who tried to poison me. That's just getting my own back. I promise not to run any risks; but I might be more successful than the police simply because they *are* the police

— if you get me.'

'No, I don't. And the Inspector would be furious if he knew.'

'Then we'll see that he doesn't know. Don't you breathe a word about this to anyone, or we'll both be for it.'

He gave her a brief smile and then turned to walk back to the bridge.

'But what are you going to *do*?' asked Anne, following him; and, when he did not answer, 'If you don't tell me I shall go straight to the Inspector as soon as he gets back. I mean it, Colin. I won't have you — '

'I'll explain later,' he said. 'Not now. It's time these kids were indoors.'

She waited until he had rounded up the boys and herded them towards the school, and then walked beside him in silence as he harried and chivied the laggards up the valley slope. But once they were on level ground and the boys were well ahead she again pressed him to explain.

He seemed embarrassed.

'I will if you insist, of course. But honestly, darling, it would be better if you didn't know. You would react more naturally, you see. Of course, if you don't trust me . . . '

It was mean of him to put it like that, she protested. It was the wisdom of his intentions, not the intentions themselves, that she distrusted. 'I don't want last Thursday night all over again, Colin. You were lucky then, but next time — '

He gripped her arm. 'There won't be a next time, ducks, I promise you that. Nobody's going to — hallo, what's up with Brother James? He looks rattled.'

James Latimer bore down on them with long, purposeful strides.

'I have been wanting a word with you two since last night,' he said, his tone suiting his expression. 'Someone has been telling tales out of school. I found the police extremely well informed on our little fracas of Wednesday night.'

'I didn't even consider it worth mentioning,' said Colin. 'What's the matter — wind up?'

'Somebody mentioned it,' said James, looking pointedly at Anne and ignoring the taunt. 'The Inspector had it all cut and dried, and only we three were in the room when it happened.'

'It wasn't me,' Anne said, slightly red of face. 'I certainly discussed it with him, but it was the Inspector who referred to it first, not me.'

'Probably Diana,' said Colin. 'She knew about it.'

'Diana?' James looked thoughtful. 'How did *she* come into it?'

Colin told him.

As they continued on their way back to the school James said, 'I can't make that fellow Pitt out. One moment I think he's sound, the next he seems completely crackers.'

'He's all right.' Colin was prepared to defend anyone attacked by James. 'Not spectacular, perhaps, but he knows his job.'

'Does he? He asked me some pretty pointless questions this morning, I thought. When did Dad last go up to London, for instance, and where did he stay? What in Hades can he want to know that for?'

'Obviously gunning for the male

Latimers,' Colin said cheerfully, 'and can't decide which is the worst. Neither can I.'

'I thought at one time that he'd picked on me as the villain of the piece,' said James. He looked doubtfully at Anne. 'Had that idea occurred to either of you?'

'Of course not,' Anne said at once, the blush returning as she recalled her talk with the Inspector. 'Don't be silly, James.'

'It occurred to me,' said Colin. 'I dismissed it because I considered you hadn't the necessary guts.'

'Thanks. And, not to be outdone in old world courtesy, may I say that, although I did not actually add the fatal dose, all my sympathies are with the fellow who did. I only deplore his lack of success.'

Anne looked reproachfully at her fiancé as James Latimer stalked off.

'Why do you always have to rub him up the wrong way?' she asked. 'It's so silly. There's no reason at all why the two of you shouldn't be friends.'

Colin scowled. 'There is, and you know it. Come on, let's get some tea before Chris scoffs the lot. What puzzles me,' he said, frowning, 'is why Diana blabbed to the police. Do you think she considered it to be her duty? Or was she just out to make trouble for James?'

'It may not have been Diana,' said Anne. 'It could have been Webby. *She* knew — she wormed it out of Diana on Thursday night. That's what the two of them were discussing when I went up to bed. Yes, I bet it was Webby. She's a dear, but she does love to talk.'

★   ★   ★

In later years Sergeant Maddox was to remember that particular Saturday as one of his luckier days. Out of the blue he had to produce witnesses who would confirm or deny Bain's statement that Chris Moull had had a bicycle with him on the morning of October the twenty-second. Neither Pitt nor Maddox could say why the bicycle was important; but since Moull himself had made no mention of it, had stated categorically that he had been on foot, and had been seen by Russell to return without it, important it must be.

But the question still remained — why?

Where, pondered Maddox, should he look first for information? Postmen? Milkmen? Roadmen? Newsboys? They were all likely to be abroad early in the day.

He decided to try the milkmen first. That was Lucky Strike Number One.

There were two dairies serving the district that lay to the north of Abbey Lodge; Lucky Strike Number Two was when he chose Haddyn Farm instead of wasting time at the Chaim Road Dairy. And Lucky Strike Number Three came up when Bill Mander, the first roundsman called into the office by the dairy manager, recognized Christopher Moull's description.

'Yes, I seen him,' said Mander, a little man with a face pointed as a ferret's. 'Nearly ran me down, he did. Not that I'm blaming the chap, mind you,' he added in all fairness, suddenly remembering to whom he was speaking. 'It was me own fault. No, come to think of it — it was the old woman's fault. She'd got me that wild I didn't look where I was going.

But that's the geyser, Sergeant. Duffel-coat, blue beret — couldn't be anyone else, could it?'

'You're sure it was the same morning?' asked Maddox.

'Sure? 'Course I'm sure. Here!' He rummaged among a pile of ledgers and papers on the untidy office table, and produced a printed slip which was headed 'Haddyn Farm Dairy. Account for week ending Friday, October 21st.' 'See that? That's what caused the rumpus.'

'What rumpus?'

'With Mrs Grant, same as I'm telling you. Some of 'em leaves the money with the empties, and some of 'em — them what's up early enough — pays me when I call on the Saturday. Well, Mrs Grant's one of the early ones.'

'How early?'

'I don't know when she gets up, mate, but it's about half-past six when I reaches her place. That's out along the Chaim road, t'other side of the bridge.'

'Okay,' said Maddox. 'Let's have the rest of it.'

'Well, we've had trouble with the old

girl before, see; so the boss says not to take any chances. Most mornings she has a pint, others it's two; and I enters it in me book before I leave the house, just to make sure. That week she'd had ten pints; but soon as I bangs on the knocker she whips open the door, swearing like ruddy hell and saying as how she'd only had eight.'

'Very tricky,' murmured the Sergeant.

'I'll say! Made me hopping mad, it did. I told her straight she wasn't getting away with it this time. 'Either you pay me for the ten,' I says, 'or you don't get no more milk until you do.' Then she starts calling me names and saying as how she'd report me to the boss; so I just pops the milk back in me basket and lams.'

'And that was when you nearly collided with the cyclist, eh?'

'That's right.' Lost in his recital of Mrs Grant's duplicity, the man had temporarily forgotten the question that had prompted it. Now he regarded the Sergeant with bright, inquisitive eyes. 'What's Duffel-coat done, mate?'

'I don't know that he's done anything.

He's wanted for questioning, that's all. Ever seen him before or since Mr Mander?'

'I didn't rightly see him *that* time,' the man admitted. 'I wasn't looking where I was going, see? I had me head down — swearing like a trooper, I was — and suddenly this here chap's almost on top of me. I just sees the bike and a pair of brown trousers and his white coat, and then he's gone.'

'You didn't see his face, then?'

'No. Only his back view, like. That was when I noticed he was wearing a beret.'

'How big a chap would he be?'

'Well, now.' The man considered this point. 'Well, I don't rightly know. Not easy to tell, him being on a bike. A bit bigger'n me, perhaps.'

That would fit Moull, thought Maddox, satisfied. 'Which direction was he going?' he asked.

'Towards the bridge. Must have come from out Chaim way,' said Mander.

Why should Moull be cycling along the Chaim road at six-thirty in the morning? wondered Maddox. More important still, why should he try to hide the fact that he had done so? Recalling all that Russell had told them about the various members of the staff at Redways, the Sergeant decided to prowl farther afield. Since Moull had been coming from Chaim, since Diana Farling had a cottage there, and since Russell had declared that there was at least 'something' between those two young people, the Farling cottage might offer a clue to the mystery.

He had some difficulty in finding it, since he did not know the address and few people in Chaim appeared to have heard of the girl. It lay down a muddy track about a mile outside the village; a small grey stone building with a sharply pointed roof. There were, he judged, peering through the gaily curtained windows, two rooms on the ground floor, with one or possibly two attic bedrooms above. At the back a stone washhouse had been converted into kitchen and scullery, and an outside earth-closet and well indicated that the cottage had not yet been blessed with the comforts of modern plumbing.

Primitive but attractive, he thought, as he wandered through the unkempt garden to where a stream bordered the small orchard. An old fisherman's punt, badly needing a coat of paint, was moored to the bank, where a patch of grass had been trimmed to form a rough lawn. Does her sunbathing here, no doubt, thought Maddox, and entertains her boyfriend. Well, if it's privacy she's after she's got it here.

He walked back along the track to where the police car waited on the road. At the junction stood a large Georgian house, its ordered garden surrounded by a tall, close-clipped box hedge. A man was working at the front, and Maddox pushed open the drive gates and padded across the smooth lawn to talk to him.

'Police, eh?' said the man, startled. 'Yes, I've seen her. Tall, red hair, good-looker. What's the trouble?'

'No trouble,' said Maddox. 'And I'm not interested in the girl. I'm just trying to contact one of her boyfriends. He may be able to give us valuable information.'

'I wouldn't know about her friends,' the

man said doubtfully. 'I don't see her much, anyways. I'm told she just comes for weekends, and I'm not here then.'

'The chap I'm interested in,' said Maddox, 'was out this way on a bicycle about a fortnight ago. *Exactly* a fortnight ago.'

'What time of day?' asked the other.

'I'm not sure. Either some time after dark on the Friday evening or very early on the Saturday morning, around six o'clock.'

'Then I wouldn't have seen him,' said the man. 'I don't start work till eight and I finish at five. Sorry.'

Disappointed, Maddox thanked him and turned away. But before he had reached the gates the man called after him.

'Hey! Wait a minute.'

Maddox waited.

'A fortnight ago, eh?' The man came close to him, a flicker of excitement on his rather bovine countenance. 'That'd make it the twenty-first of October, wouldn't it?' And when Maddox nodded hopefully he went on. 'There *was* a chap went up the lane that night on a bike. About twenty-past ten, it'd be. The family were away that weekend, and the guv'nor asked me to come in nights and do the boilers. I was just leaving when I saw him go past.'

'What did he look like?'

The other shook his head. 'I couldn't say. It was dark, you see, and there was the hedge between us. Looked like he was wearing some sort of light-coloured mackintosh.'

'Could it have been a duffel-coat?'

'Could have been, I suppose. I'd say it looked more like a mackintosh, though.'

'Was he wearing any sort of headgear?'

'I don't know,' the man said. 'All I saw was this here mackintosh moving along behind the hedge. I can't tell you no more than that.'

It was six o'clock by the time Maddox had completed his various missions and was able to return to the school. The clouds that had been gathering all day brought heavy rain late in the afternoon, and the Sergeant grunted with relief as he stood in the front porch and shook the water from his raincoat and trilby. Inside, at the far end of the hall, James Latimer and Miss Farling appeared to be engaged in argument, but the Sergeant was too intent on reporting the result of his day's labour to waste time in eavesdropping.

As he stepped into the hall the two looked round and saw him. James, an angry expression on his face, disappeared towards the study. Diana, smiling sweetly, bade the Sergeant good evening.

'Evening, miss,' said Maddox. 'Is the Inspector here?'

'In the library, I think. Mr Latimer left him about ten minutes ago. If I may say so, Sergeant, you look very pleased with yourself. Like a cat full of cream. Or should I say a policeman full of clues? Are you? Full of clues, I mean?'

Maddox laughed. 'We don't give away trade secrets, miss. But I'm certainly not full of cream.'

★   ★   ★

Pitt had had a trying and unprofitable day. It was some consolation to him to learn that at least one of the team had met with success.

'Moull must have spent the night at Miss Farling's cottage, I suppose,' he said. 'He was without his bicycle when Russell saw him return the next morning, but he could have dumped it somewhere and collected it later. I wonder what reason he gave the girl for leaving so early.'

'We could ask her,' Maddox suggested.

Pitt nodded. 'We could — but I don't think we will. Not yet, anyway. Are there any other houses down that lane of hers?'

'No. It's completely isolated.'

'It's a pity the identification isn't clearer,' said the Inspector. 'A cyclist who may or may not have been Moull was seen going down the lane to Miss Farling's cottage on the Friday night: at six-thirty the next morning another cyclist — who probably *was* Moull, from the description of his clothing — was seen coming from the direction of the cottage towards the river: and at about seven-twenty (Bain isn't very certain of the time, I'm afraid) a cyclist who definitely *was* Moull was seen, dismounted, on the towpath.' He frowned. If Moull killed him why should he hang around? Why didn't he clear off at once?'

'Maybe he heard Bain coming, jumped off his bike intending to hide, but wasn't quick enough.'

'Perhaps. Well, the first step is to establish whether Moull slept in his own bed that Friday night. The maid might know. She takes Miss Connaught an early morning cup of tea, so maybe they all have one. And if Moull wasn't in his room she would at least know if his bed had been slept in.'

'It's over a fortnight ago,' the Sergeant reminded him.

'Let's hope she has a good memory,' said Pitt. After a pause he went on, 'Now we know why Moull refused to take prep for James Latimer that Friday evening. Remember Russell told us about that? They all expected him to volunteer, and he didn't.'

'Do you think he had already planned to murder the old boy?'

'Go easy,' warned Pitt. 'Just because he took a bicycle-ride that morning it doesn't make him a murderer.'

'Why be so secretive about it, then?'

'Miss Farling might be responsible for that. She would probably object strongly if he let every one know that he had spent the night at her cottage. And who could blame her?'

'You don't think he did it?' asked Maddox, incredulous.

'I didn't say that. I admit the bulk of the evidence is against him, but I'm not rushing my fences. And don't forget that Moull was one of the few who did *not* appear to benefit by Connaught's death.'

'We don't have to establish a motive, thank the Lord!' the Sergeant said piously.

'No. But it helps. Well, you rustle up the maid, Maddox, and we'll see what we can get out of her.'

As the Sergeant left the room he had the impression that something was wrong. But there was no one in sight, and everything appeared to be as usual. 'Must be imagining things,' he told himself. 'Old enough to know better, too.'

But as he walked down the corridor

towards the kitchen the uneasy feeling that he had missed something still persisted.

Moments later there was a light tap on the library door, which opened slightly to admit the tousled head of Colin Russell. 'May we have a word with you, Inspector?' he asked.

'We?'

'Miss Connaught and myself. It's rather urgent, or we wouldn't have bothered you. incidentally, your constable seems to have disappeared.'

'Even policemen have to disappear at times,' Pitt said. 'We're all human. Now, what's the trouble?'

Colin, uneasy but defiant, told his story. Anne, distressed and tearful, stood beside him bravely, silent except when he appealed to her for confirmation. And as Inspector Pitt listened his cheerfulness vanished, his brow grew heavy with anger. By the time Colin had finished he was almost glaring at his two unhappy visitors.

'I wonder if you appreciate the seriousness of your position, Mr Russell,' he said, as Colin's lame apologies stumbled into silence. 'Both of you could be charged with wilfully concealing vital evidence and with obstructing the police in the execution of their duty. You should have handed that bottle to the police immediately you found it, Miss Connaught.'

'I know,' said Anne, still tearful. 'But you weren't here. Neither was the Sergeant.'

'No matter. You had no right even to show it to Mr Russell, let alone give it into his keeping. And you, sir — just what was your purpose in taking possession of the bottle?'

Colin, his face red, took his hands out of his pockets and then, not knowing what to do with them, stuck them back again. He began to feel as he imagined a boy must feel when confronted by an irate schoolmaster. I'll be a jolly sight more lenient with the little devils after this, he vowed fervently.

'I know it was stupid of me,' he said. 'But you weren't here, and I thought that if I could find the owner of the bottle before you returned it would be one up to me. After all, I'm the chap they tried to poison.'

'And I'm the chap who's supposed to catch the poisoner — not you, Mr Russell,' Pitt retorted. 'Tell me, how did you propose to become 'one up' on me, as you put it?'

'I was going to wait until all the staff were present — at dinner, say — and then produce the bottle from my pocket. I thought the owner might give himself away if suddenly confronted with it like that. I meant to give it back to you afterwards, of course.'

'Neatly labelled with the owner's name, eh? That was generous of you. Instead of which you leave it carelessly in your raincoat pocket, handy for the first person who happens to fancy it.'

'There's no need to be sarcastic,' Colin said hotly. 'How was I to know the damned thing might get pinched?'

'I should have thought it was highly probable. You are firmly convinced that someone murdered Mr Connaught, you know someone tried to poison you.

278

Stealing a bottle from a raincoat pocket is small beer after that. Particularly if the thief knew that his life might depend on its recovery.'

'Well, I'm sorry. But the bottle's gone, and pitching into me won't do any good.'

'It will if it teaches you not to meddle in police affairs. When did you last see this bottle?'

'Just before tea, when I hung my raincoat in the hall. About four o'clock. At six o'clock, or just after, it had gone.'

'Two hours,' mused the Inspector. 'During which time anyone in the school could have lifted it with the greatest of ease. Miss Connaught — who besides Mr Russell knew that you had found the bottle?'

'No one,' said Anne. 'I took it down to Colin at once — after I'd looked for you, of course. I wish you'd been here,' she added sorrowfully; 'then this wouldn't have happened.'

'So do I, miss. How about you, sir? Could anyone have seen it while it was in your possession?'

'Quite impossible, Inspector.'

Pitt went out into the empty hall, the others following. Against the opposite wall hung a miscellaneous collection of coats, raincoats, and other outdoor garments. At the Inspector's bidding Colin pointed out his own.

'Is it in the same position now as when you hung it up before tea?' asked Pitt.

'Yes, I think so.'

Pitt looked at the name-tabs on the coats on either side of Colin's. 'Mr Smelton's and Mr Latimer's,' he announced. 'Not that that has any significance. If no one knew you had the bottle it must have been discovered accidentally. Has anyone in the school got a raincoat similar to yours, Mr Russell?'

'No, not quite the same. James Latimer has a fawn one, but his is lighter in colour and not so heavy.'

The Inspector nodded absently, his mind momentarily elsewhere. But he listened attentively as Anne described the bottle to him in detail, and then dismissed the two culprits with no assurance that they would not later be called to account for their misdemeanour.

They were half-way across the hall when Pitt remembered something.

'Just a minute, Mr Russell,' he said; and, as Colin turned and came back, 'When you saw Mr Moull returning from his walk on the morning Mr Connaught was drowned — what colour were his trousers?'

'Eh?' Colin was startled. Then, realizing that detectives did occasionally ask questions which to the layman seemed pointless, and anxious to redeem himself in the Inspector's eyes, he stood silent, wrapped in thought.

'I don't think I can remember,' he said slowly, screwing up his eyes in a concentrated effort to visualize the scene. 'But I *do* know that he was wearing grey flannel trousers at breakfast. Someone — Miss Dove, I think it was — spilled tea on them, and he had to go up and change.'

Pitt was still fuming when Maddox returned to the library with Doris. The girl was delighted at this further tribute to her importance, but disappointed when told what was wanted of her. Early morning tea, she thought, could not rate very high when it came to murder; unless, of course, there was poison in it, the same as there had been in Mr Russell's milk.

'They all have it,' she said. 'All except Mr Russell — he don't drink tea. And Mrs Latimer has one of them electric things. You know — it tells the time and wakes you up and boils the kettle.'

'Do you remember the morning old Mr Connaught was drowned?' asked Pitt.

'I remember him bein' drowned,' said the girl. 'But if you was to ask me which day it was I couldn't tell you.'

'Well, can you remember any morning during the past three weeks when you went into one of the bedrooms and found it empty? What time do you take the tea up, by the way?'

'Just before seven.' There was a pause while Doris considered the first question. 'Yes, I can. I think it was about a fortnight ago that Mr Moull wasn't in his room.'

'He hadn't just gone to the bathroom, perhaps?'

'Well, his clothes wasn't on the chair, and he don't usually get up early. I mostly has to wake him. I left his tea on the table, just in case, but it was still there when I collected the cups.'

'Had his bed been slept in?'

'Oh, yes. Anyways, the bedclothes were pulled over the end, like he always does. I didn't see no pyjamas; they must have been under his pillow.'

'And you can't be certain which day that was?' asked Pitt.

To his surprise the girl nodded vehemently.

'Yes,' she said excitedly, her bright eyes sparkling. 'Yes, I can. I remember now — it was the weekend Miss Farlin' was away. The Saturday. He's sweet on her, Mr Moull is, and I thinks to meself when I see he's gone, I wouldn't be surprised, I thinks, if he hasn't cycled over to that cottage of hers to wish his lady love good mornin'. He's that barmy about her, it's just the sort of daft thing he'd do.'

'Had he done it before?'

'No, I can't say he had,' Doris admitted. 'But then I'd never known him get up that early before, neither.'

It takes us a little further, I suppose,

thought Pitt. It's not conclusive: Moull could have slept here and gone out early. But it's something. Then, switching to another train of thought, 'Were the others all in their rooms that morning?' he asked. 'Mr James, for instance?'

The girl looked at him in surprise.

'Funny you should ask that. Yes, the others were there. But Mr James — you see, he'd told me he'd be away that night, so I didn't take him any tea in the mornin'. That's how he come to give me such a shock later.'

'How did he give you a shock?'

'Well, you see, while they're at breakfast I goes upstairs to collect the cups. The empties, as you might say. I'm always in a bit of a hurry like — I just pops into the rooms, puts the cups on me tray, and pops out again. And that mornin', not thinkin'' — here Doris giggled at the memory — 'I went into Mr James's room, same as I always does — and there he was, fast asleep.'

# 10

## The Ginger Horse

The congregation of St John's, Wain-bridge, had just started on the *Venite* when Dicken, cap in hand and red in the face, his unevenly buttoned raincoat giving him a lopsided appearance, entered the church and slid into a pew as far removed as possible from the scowling Smelton. He had run most of the way to catch up with the others, having been delayed by a missing cap. He felt hot and uncomfortable, and his throat was dry, but none of these discomforts mattered when he thought of the momentous news he was about to impart to his school-fellows.

The Redways boys occupied a wing of the church well away from the rest of the congregation. The reason for this was not clear. It may have been the headmaster's wish to protect his charges against possible contamination by other worshippers, or a desire by the rector of St John's to shield his adult congregation from the boys. Certainly it enabled the master on duty, seated in the back pew, to keep a watchful eye on his flock.

But boys in bulk are very Daniels in their bravery, however abject and submissive they may appear singly when in the presence of outraged authority. And the Redways boys had long since realized that, whereas in secular surroundings a misdemeanour might call forth a roar of disapproval or a stinging buffet on the head, in church no such reaction on the part of authority need be feared. Retribution might follow in due course; but boys live mostly in the present, and the opportunity to misbehave unchecked right under the watchful but helpless eye of authority was too tempting to be withstood.

The favourite Sunday morning pastime of a select group, of which Dicken was a founder member, was to maintain a private conversation in tune with the airs and chants played by the organist, substituting their own words for those printed in the prayer-book.

'The sea is His and He made it; and His hands prepared the dry land,' sang the choir and congregation. But Oakes leaned towards the perspiring Dicken and chanted tunefully, 'Why were you late for church? The Stinker is in an awful bait.'

Dicken missed a verse to compose his answer.

'I don't care. I've got some absolutely wizard news. The Mule has done a bunk,' he sang, slightly off key in his excitement.

'How do you know?'

'I heard Mr Latimer telling the Inspector.'

Unmindful of his surroundings, Oakes had emitted a low but piercing whistle of surprise. Now, suddenly aware that he had become the cynosure of all eyes, he hid his crimson face behind his prayer-book in confusion. During the psalms, however, he recovered his composure sufficiently to pass the news on to his other neighbour. Before the first lesson all, with the exception of those in Smelton's immediate vicinity, were aware that Christopher Moull had fled.

The service over, there was a concerted rush outside the church to obtain further information from Dicken. But Smelton, seething with anger and indignation at the manner in which his authority had been flouted, broke up the crowd and called Dicken to his side. Keeping him there on the walk back to the school, he delivered a stern lecture on the virtue of punctuality and the sin of levity in church, mingled with threats of the punishment in store for the boy on their return to Redways.

The rest of the school were indignant at this bottling up of the fount of information. But Dicken could not have enlightened them further. That Chris Moull had gone was the sum of his knowledge.

\* \* \*

Inspector Pitt replaced the receiver and turned to face his subordinate.

'That's about all we can do for the present,' he said. 'I don't think he'll get far. I wish we'd known of this earlier, but apparently it's quite usual for the staff here to lie abed of a Sunday morning and miss their breakfast. Damned laziness, I call it.'

Sergeant Maddox made no comment. He had been all in favour of putting Moull under lock and key the previous evening, but he saw nothing to be gained by reminding the Inspector of this.

'He must have left in a hurry,' said Pitt. 'Not a thing missing from his room — didn't even take a toothbrush with him. But what scared him? That's what beats me.'

'No doubt now he's the guilty party,' said Maddox, delighted at this vindication of his hypothesis. 'It must have been Moull who found the bottle in Russell's coat pocket. That would have told him the game was up.'

'H'm!' Pitt's lack of enthusiasm surprised the Sergeant. 'Let's have that constable in again and see if we can learn any more from him.'

But Constable Prettyman, who had been on duty at Redways the previous night, had little further to report. Meticulously he went through his statement again. He had seen Moull leave the common room at eleven o'clock and go upstairs, but had not seen him come down again. At eleven-fifteen Miss Farling had gone along the corridor to the kitchen, returning later with a cup of tea. 'She'd made a pot for herself; said she was sitting up late writing half-term reports. Very nice and friendly she was, telling me about the boys and the funny things they said.'

'All pals together, eh?' the Inspector commented. 'Lucky your tea wasn't poisoned. What happened after that?'

'Well, Miss Farling went back to the common room, and about midnight Mr Latimer — the young one — came out of the study and said as how he was going to lock up and would I care to accompany him and see he did it proper. Which I did, sir. Regular tour of the premises, it was. He tried every door and window, even in the common oom where Miss Farling was working. Then he said goodnight and went upstairs.'

'What time did Miss Farling go to bed?'

'Just after one, sir. She was the last person I saw until the maids turned up in the morning.'

'And since none of the doors or windows was found unfastened this morning it follows that Moull must have left before midnight,' said Pitt, dismissing the constable. 'That gives him about twelve hours' start.'

'Unless he had an accomplice to lock up after him,' the Sergeant suggested. 'Miss Farling, for instance.'

'Yes, that's possible. Well, let's have another look at his room.'

'I wonder he didn't take his bike,' Maddox said, as they went into the hall. 'With the start he had he could have gone a long way on that by now, and it's safer than public transport. He must have known there'd be a check on buses and trains as soon as he was missed.'

'I wonder about a lot of things,' Pitt said irritably. 'I wish to hell we could get a line on that ruddy poison. I've got my own ideas about it, but I want to *know*.

Damn that interfering young fool Russell!'

It was at this unpropitious moment that Colin chose to accost them. His reception was not cordial.

'Well, sir, and what have you lost now?' asked Pitt, glowering at him.

'Cut out the ribbing,' said Colin, aware that ribbing was far from the Inspector's present mood, but anxious to appear casual. 'Have you heard anything of Chris yet?'

The glower merged into a thoughtful scrutiny. Dammit, he's scared, was Pitt's surprised decision. But — scared of what? Not of the possible consequences of losing the bottle, or he would have shown it yesterday. Yesterday he had been apologetic, embarrassed by his own stupidity, even defiant in admission of his guilt. But not scared. What had happened since, Pitt wondered, to frighten a man who, by the look of him, was not easily frightened?

'No,' he said. 'Have you?'

'Of course not.'

'Were you surprised to hear he had gone?'

'Very.' Colin was emphatic. 'I don't believe he's guilty, and I don't believe he would run away if he were. I know Chris.'

'But not very well, apparently. Was that all you wanted? To know if we'd picked him up?'

'No. But I thought it might help if you could fix the time he left, and I happen to know that he was still in his room at three o'clock this morning.'

'Eh?' The exclamation came in unison from the two detectives. 'How can you be sure of that?' asked Pitt.

'Because I heard him. I woke up suddenly — the walls are fairly thin, and I suppose it must have been some noise he made that disturbed me. I heard him moving about the room, and drawers being pulled out; I wondered what the devil he was up to at that time of night. Of course, I realize now that he must have been packing.'

Whatever he was doing he certainly wasn't packing, thought Pitt. 'Did you call out to him to make less noise?' he asked.

'No. You know how it is when you wake

up in the middle of the night; no matter what's wrong you're too damned lazy to do anything about it. I just looked at my watch, turned over, and went to sleep again.'

'And that's all you know, eh?'

'Yes, that's all.'

Pitt wondered why such an apparently innocent question should have brought fear back into the young man's eyes. Was Russell trying to mislead the police, to cover up for his friend? Was he, and not Miss Farling, the accomplice Moull must have had if he had left the building after midnight? Was that his fear — that by his words or actions he had irrevocably associated himself with Moull — and with what Moull had done? Or had he interpreted the question in a more general sense than had been intended? Was he, in fact —

Robert Cramp came round the corner at full speed and brought himself to a stop by using Colin as a buffer. 'I'm sorry, sir,' he panted. 'I was looking for Mr James.'

'Well, look for him a little less

energetically next time, will you?' Colin said pleasantly, glad of the interruption. 'Or we'll get the Inspector to arrest you for speeding. What did you want Mr James for?'

'I found this, sir.' The boy held out a folded sheet of quarto duplicating-paper. 'And it's got his name on it, so I thought it must be his.'

Colin took the piece of paper, opened it and glanced at the typescript, hesitated, and then said, 'Where did you find this, Robert?'

'Under the master's desk in the Fourth Form, sir. Mr James dropped a lot of letters and things there when he was taking us for Latin yesterday. I suppose he didn't see this when he picked the others up.'

'All right. I'll give it to Mr James when I see him. You'd better run along.' And as the boy started off, 'No, not run. Walk, Robert.'

As Cramp disappeared Colin glanced again at the paper in his hand and then handed it to the Inspector. 'I suppose I'm interfering again,' he said, 'but I think you ought to see this.'

Surprised, Pitt took it. His surprise increased as he read. It was an IOU, clumsily worded in pseudo-legal phraseology, admitting the debt of one thousand pounds to John Henry Connaught. And it was signed by James Latimer.

The Inspector pulled thoughtfully at his rather prominent nose and handed the paper to the Sergeant.

'Interesting,' he said slowly. 'Most interesting. I see it is dated October the twenty-first — the day before Mr Connaught was found drowned.'

'So that's why he called on J.C. that evening. I told you we'd seen him, didn't I?' And as Pitt nodded Colin went on. 'The part that interests *me* is that bit at the end, where he promises to transfer shares in the school if the debt is not repaid within the year.'

'Is Redways a limited company?' asked Maddox.

'It's a company of some sort, and the Latimers own all the shares. And if the old man had known that his precious son was contemplating the transfer of some of them — and to J.C. of all people — there might well have been another sudden death in the school.'

'Whose? Mr Latimer's? Or his son's?'

'Either. Joseph's from apoplexy or James's by murder.'

'It probably isn't legal,' said Pitt. 'I doubt if it could be enforced.'

'Legal or not, it — Here!' For Pitt had taken the paper from the Sergeant, folded it, and slipped it into his pocket. 'You can't keep that, damn it! I promised Cramp I'd give it to James.'

'Sorry, Mr Russell — I'll do it for you. Don't worry; I won't tell him how it came into my possession.'

'You don't have to. Cramp will. Next time he bumps into James he'll ask him if he got the paper, and then the fat will be properly in the fire.'

Pitt was unmoved. 'Tell him I snatched it out of your hand,' he said serenely. 'Tell him anything you like — I won't contradict you.' He turned away. 'I'd like a word with Mr James now. If you're not keen on giving him that message yourself perhaps you would ask someone else to do so?'

In the library Maddox said, 'This doesn't really concern us, does it? It's interesting, of course — but it can't have anything to do with Moull.'

'No.'

'Then why bother with it?'

'Because I'm still not convinced that Moull's our man. That's why.'

Maddox opened his mouth to protest, thought better of it, stuck his hands in his pockets, and walked over to the window. Bags of evidence, the chap does a bunk, and he's still not convinced, he thought angrily. What's he waiting for? A confession?

Pitt guessed something of what the Sergeant was thinking. 'You think I'm crazy, don't you?' he said. 'But Moull isn't the only one of this bunch whose behaviour hasn't been according to the book. Granted he's spun a few lies; but so have most of the others if you ask me — including our friend Russell. They all seem to have a skeleton in their own particular cupboard; but who's to say which skeleton is a corpse and which a dose of cyanide? True, Moull has decamped. You say that implies guilt. Well, maybe it does; but, alternatively, it might merely imply a thinner skin than the others. He may have killed Connaught and he may have tried to poison Russell. I'm not saying he didn't. But, until we know, I'm not going to ignore the opportunity to find out if someone else *did*.'

It was a long and, for the Inspector, an almost impassioned speech. Maddox, impressed, grinned at him genially. 'I'm with you, sir,' he said.

James Latimer seemed aware that something serious was toward; perhaps Russell, stricken by conscience, had warned him what to expect. He exhibited none of his former cynicism, but politely inquired the reason for his being summoned.

Pitt showed him the IOU.

'It explains itself doesn't it?' James said. 'What more do you want to know?'

'I see the document is dated October the twenty-first, sir, the day before Mr Connaught was drowned. Did he give you the money that evening?'

'He gave me a cheque, yes.'

'Have you cashed it?'

'Yes. I handed it in to my bank the next morning. There was no difficulty; Mr Connaught also banked there, and he had warned the manager that it would be presented. I can assure you, Inspector, that there is nothing sinister about this loan. It just happens to appear so because it was made at that particular time.'

'And why *was* it made at that particular time, Mr Latimer?'

'Because I was hard up, and Mr Connaught agreed to help me out. Since he had known me all my life, that isn't very surprising, is it?'

'No. But the wording of the document *is* rather surprising, don't you think?'

James Latimer frowned. 'You mean about the shares, eh?' he said. 'Yes, that surprised me too. When J.C. and I first discussed the loan some weeks ago there was no mention of any proviso such as that. He sprang that on me when he gave me the cheque. I knew what he was after, of course; he had always hankered after a share in the school. It was probably also meant as a slap in the face for my father, whom he heartily disliked. But beggars can't be choosers, Inspector, and I needed that money badly. So I signed.' He smiled faintly. 'Between ourselves, it did occur to me that the document might not be legally binding if the worst came to the worst.'

I'm sure it did, thought Pitt. 'May I ask why you needed this money so urgently?' he said.

'You know, Inspector, I rather fancy that's *my* business, not yours.' James spoke politely, but with a hint of annoyance. 'I don't wish to be rude or obstructive, but — well, it is, isn't it?'

'As you wish,' Pitt said tranquilly. 'I presume you left this document with Mr Connaught?'

'Of course.'

'Then how does it come to be in your possession after his death?' The other flushed and Pitt went on, 'Before you answer it is only fair to warn you that — '

'Be damned to you and your warnings!' All pretence of politeness had vanished. 'I know what you're thinking. Why don't you ask straight out if I killed the old man?'

'And did you?' Pitt asked obediently.

'No. Nor did I burgle his house afterwards. I haven't been near the place since he died.'

'Then what about this?' said Pitt, indicating the IOU.

'I don't know.' Nothing the incredulous expression on the detective's face, he added, 'Oh, I can tell you how I *got* it. It came by post a few days later. But who sent it, or why — well, your guess is as good as mine.'

'There was no covering letter?'

'No. And the address was typewritten. And, since I had no premonition that I should shortly have to explain to the police, I didn't keep the envelope.' There was bravado in the words, but he looked worried, even frightened. 'My immediate reaction was that Miss Connaught was responsible. I thought she had found it in the old man's desk and had returned it to me anonymously to spare my blushes. A generous gesture, I thought.' His brow puckered. 'But now — no, I don't think it was her. I don't know who it was.'

'Did you ask her?'

'Not in so many words. But I hinted at it, and she obviously hadn't a clue.'

Pitt subjected the man to another of his long and impersonal scrutinies, reviewing in his mind the evidence that seemed to be piling up against him. Connaught's death and the recovery of his IOU had virtually turned the loan into a gift and had prevented what might later have become a very nasty situation. No one had a stronger motive for wishing to dispose of Russell. And the maid had said —

'Will you recognize me next time?' James asked irritably.

Pitt's eyes did not waver. 'You have already told us you were away on the night of the twenty-first, Mr Latimer,' he said. 'What time did you return the next morning?'

'Goodness knows. You must credit me with a damned good memory, Inspector, if you expect me to give the exact time of something that happened over a fortnight ago.'

'I don't. But was it before or after seven?'

'Before. Somewhere around 3 a.m.'

The Inspector pulled thoughtfully at his chin.

'And you left the Lodge at around ten o'clock the evening before. 'Away for the night' was somewhat misleading, wasn't it? Why was it necessary for Miss Connaught to take your prep that morning?'

'Because I didn't expect to be home until much later, that's why. Aha!' James raised a warning finger as Pitt was about to speak. 'Don't waste your breath, Inspector. I told you before that where I went is my own business. Well, it still is.'

Pitt shrugged his shoulders. 'We may decide to make it ours.' He held up the IOU. 'I'll keep this for the present if you don't mind.'

'As far as I'm concerned you can keep it for ever, so long as my father doesn't set eyes on it.' Relief was evident in his relaxed bearing, in the bantering note that had crept back into his voice. 'And don't be too sure that I'm the answer to a policeman's prayer. A thousand quid is nothing to what I might have had if J.C. had lived. He was all in favour of my marrying his granddaughter, you know — a happy event which, without his support, is now unlikely to take place, I fear. I'm not such a fool as to kill the goose that was all set to lay me a beautiful golden egg.'

'I am becoming allergic to Latimers,' Pitt said to Maddox, as James, his good spirits restored, walked jauntily from the room.

There was still no news of Moull when, for a brief period, the two detectives stood talking on the terrace after lunch. The sun was warm after the heavy rain of the previous night. On the playing-fields a few boys were kicking a football about, and behind them the trees rose up out of the valley, partially obscuring the farther view. In the far distance was the blue haze of a line of hills.

'I wonder what it costs to send a boy to a place like this,' the Sergeant pondered aloud.

'Couple of hundred a year, I dare say.

Why? Thinking of sending yours?'

Maddox grinned. 'On my pay? No ruddy fear.'

A bell rang loudly inside the building. Pitt looked at his watch. 'Twenty-past two,' he said. 'What could that be for?'

Slowly the boys drifted in from the field. They seemed in no hurry, kicking a ball along the paths between the bushes, chasing each other and wrestling. They cast frankly curious glances at the two policemen as they passed. Dicken and Rodgers, bolder than most, came up to them, followed at a distance by three smaller boys.

'What's the bell for?' asked the Inspector.

'Scripture,' said Dicken. 'We have a lesson at half-past two. It's a beastly swiz, having to work on a Sunday.'

'Have you caught the Mule yet?' asked Rodgers.

'Who?'

'The Mule. Mr Moull.'

'Oh! No, not yet.'

'What'll happen when you *do* catch him?'

'We'll just ask him a few questions. Oughtn't you boys to be getting in?'

'There's bags of time yet,' said Dicken. 'Have you caught lots of criminals?'

'Quite a few. But a detective's life isn't always as exciting as I dare say you boys think it is. Much of the time it's just honest-to-goodness hard work — and pretty dull at that. I don't think you'd fancy it.'

'I bet I would. And I bet it isn't *really* dull; not like swotting at lessons or working in an office.' He sighed. 'This has been a wizard term. I almost wish we weren't going home tomorrow.'

The three smaller boys, emboldened by the friendly reception accorded to their elders, had crept closer. One of them ventured to join in the conversation.

'I'm going home today,' he said. 'My mother's coming for me in the car.'

'And where do you live?' asked Maddox.

'At Tanbury. It's only six miles away, so I can easily ride over here on my bicycle. I shall, too. Then p'raps I'll see you catch the murderer.'

Pitt frowned. 'You boys are letting your imagination run away with you,' he said. 'There isn't any murderer that I know of.'

'Mr Russell said there was. I heard him talking to Miss Connaught.'

'Do all you boys live near here?' asked the Sergeant. He disapproved of the way the conversation was going.

'Gosh, no!' said Dicken. 'I live in High Wycombe, and Rodgers lives in Colchester. Lots of us have to go even farther than that. There's one boy comes from Scotland.'

'I live in London,' volunteered another small boy. 'In Kensington.'

'That's nothing,' said Trent, the third small boy. He had the most upturned nose that Pitt had ever seen, with startlingly blue eyes set in a face smothered with freckles. 'I live in Bradford. That's in Yorkshire. I'm going home this afternoon too.'

'You certainly spread yourselves around,' said the Inspector. 'But I suppose a change of environment is a good thing.'

'What's that?' asked the first small boy.

'Environment? Well — surroundings,

308

really. A change of environment means a change of air, different scenery, fresh faces. It means you won't be meeting the same people in the holidays that you meet at school.'

'I do,' said Trent. 'Layman lives in the same street as us. I see him every day.'

'Well, that's only one. He can't do you much harm.'

'And last hols Miss Connaught came to stay with us,' the small boy continued imperturbably. 'And Mr Connaught. He's the man who was drowned. He was a friend of Daddy's, he used to teach Daddy when he was here. We saw Mr James too. And once we spent a week at Scarborough in the same hotel as Oakes.'

'And where did you see Mr James?' asked Pitt, refraining from referring to a small world. 'In Bradford?'

'Oh, no. We had a bungalow by the sea, near Whitby. Mummy and I had gone into the town to do some shopping with Mr Connaught, and Mr James was coming out of a hotel, but he went back when he saw us. Mummy said there was a ginger horse,' he added inconsequently.

'A ginger horse!' exclaimed the astonished Inspector.

'Yes, that's what she said. I didn't see it, but Mr Connaught did. He said he'd seen it the last time, too. He looked quite cross.'

'I expect Mrs Trent meant a roan,' Rodgers suggested. 'My father's got a roan. I ride it sometimes, but I'm having a pony for Christmas.'

'A roan doesn't seem to make any more sense than a ginger horse,' said Pitt. 'Not under those circumstances. Where *was* this horse, young feller-me-lad?'

'I don't know,' said Trent. 'I told you, I didn't see it.'

A male voice shouted imperatively from the school. With hurried farewells to their new friends the boys ran off, Trent and another waving energetically until they disappeared from sight.

'Nice kids,' said the Inspector. 'A pity they had to get mixed up in all this.' The two men walked round the east side of the building towards the front door. As they turned on to the gravel the Sergeant gave a throaty chuckle.

'What's the joke?'

'I was thinking of what those kids said. First a Mule (nice way to describe a teacher, eh?) and then all that talk about a ginger horse.' He laughed again. 'I wouldn't mind betting his ma never mentioned a horse at all, let alone a ginger one.'

'No,' Pitt said thoughtfully, 'I don't suppose she did.'

In the hall Joseph Latimer and Diana Farling were talking to a parent, who eyed the two detectives with interest. Diana smiled; Mr Latimer ignored them. Pitt wondered how he would explain their presence. Were they being palmed off as parents — of new boys, perhaps — or did they look too much like what they were?

As soon as he could he drew the headmaster into the library.

'You have a small boy named Trent here, sir, and I want a word with his mother. The boy tells me she is collecting him this afternoon. Is that correct?'

Latimer was startled. 'Yes. But what can you possibly have to discuss with Mrs Trent, Inspector?'

'I can't tell you that, sir. But I should be obliged if you would let me know when she arrives.'

Mr Latimer did not hesitate. 'No,' he said firmly, 'I most certainly will not. I have no wish to defeat the ends of justice; but since Mrs Trent — or any other parent, for that matter — can know nothing of the reason for your presence here, I will not have her pestered by the police.' He leaned forward, staring hard at Pitt. 'Did Russell put you up to this?'

'That is a most improper question, sir,' Pitt said sternly.

'Yes, I suppose it is. I apologize. But I regret that I cannot accede to your request.'

'In that case, sir, I shall station a constable at the front door with orders to establish the identity of every visitor until Mrs Trent is found.'

The headmaster winced, licked his dry lips, and decided, much against his inclination, to plead his cause.

'You are putting me in a very difficult position. I assure you, Inspector, that if Mrs Trent discovers why you are here it will jeopardize the whole future of the school.' He paused hopefully. But Pitt made no comment, and he went on, 'The Trent family has been connected with the school for years. Mr Trent was here, and his eldest son left last term. There is another boy to come, and it was through the Trents' recommendation that other parents — the Laymans, Mrs Fisher, the Brownwells, to name only a few — have sent or entered their boys here. So you see the importance of the connection. Yet at the beginning of this term Mrs Trent hinted that she might be severing this connection; I cannot think why, for our relations have hitherto been most friendly. I had hoped to talk to her this afternoon; I am sure that if anything has upset her it can easily be rectified. But if she is confronted by a policeman on her arrival . . . if she is questioned . . . ' The headmaster shuddered at the prospect. 'You see why I have to refuse your request, Inspector?'

Pitt shook his head. 'I'm sorry, sir, but I must speak to the lady. I won't tell her anything she doesn't need to know. But if you won't produce her — well, the constable will.'

Mr Latimer capitulated. Pitt, much as he disliked the man, felt sorry for him. 'It's a hell of a position he's in,' he said to Maddox. 'I don't blame him for trying to hush it up, but he's a fool to think he can. Here! What's biting you?'

Sergeant Maddox was staring hard at the closed library door. Now he turned to face the Inspector, his eyes troubled.

'I've just thought of something, sir.'

'What?'

'You remember yesterday evening, when I was telling you about how Moull had been seen on his bicycle? Well, when I went to fetch Doris I had a feeling something was wrong; but I couldn't place it, and I thought I must be imagining things. You know how it is. Sometimes a job gets on your nerves so that you scent a mystery in the most ordinary occurrence. I thought it must be like that with me.'

'I didn't know you had any nerves,' said Pitt. 'But cut out the philosophy. What are you trying to tell me?'

'That the door wasn't properly shut when I left the room. Yet I'm sure I shut it when I came in.'

'And you think Moull may have overheard our conversation, and decided to go while the going was good?'

'Yes. Either that, or someone listened in on his behalf. There was no one in the hall when I left to fetch Doris, but both Miss Farling and James Latimer were there when I arrived. I thought they were having a bit of an argument. Latimer cleared off when he saw me, but the girl didn't.'

'Miss Farling, eh? Yes, that's possible. Even if she isn't sweet on Moull she may feel sorry for him. If she suspected you were on to something' — Sergeant Maddox fidgeted, remembering his conversation with the girl — 'she may have decided to find out what it was. And perhaps her little natter with Prettyman last night was to distract his attention while Moull made his escape.' The Inspector paused. 'No, that won't do. Not if we are to believe Russell's story of hearing Moull at 3 a.m. Oh, damn these meddling idiots! You can't trust a soul in this place. Not one. A fine bunch to be in charge of the young! If I were a parent . . . '

Maddox said, grinning, 'You're supposed to get married first.'

But Pitt was not listening. As so often happened a spoken phrase — from his own lips this time — had sent his thoughts dancing away at a tangent.

'Now wait a minute!' he said, his eyes gleaming. And then the gleam was gone, to be replaced by concern. For if he followed his thoughts to their natural conclusion . . .

A light tap sounded on the door. The Sergeant opened it to reveal the tall figure of the headmaster.

'Mrs Trent is here, Inspector.'

The slight quiver in his voice, the mute appeal in his eyes, were wasted. Pitt, lost in a conflicting whirl of evidence and suspicion, neither heard nor saw them.

\* \* \*

It was dark by the time the Inspector was ready to leave. As he went into the hall from the library Diana Farling, a scarf tied over her hair and under her chin, was struggling into a coat.

Pitt helped her. 'Going anywhere in particular?' he asked. 'Can I give you a lift?'

'No, thanks. I'm only going for a short walk before dinner, in search of an appetite.'

'Not afraid of the dark, eh?'

'No. Nor of things that go bump in the night.' She smiled at him. 'I'm not even afraid of policemen.'

Pitt believed her. 'If that's an invitation I'll accept it,' he said. 'I could do with some exercise. *And* an appetite. Mind if I accompany you?'

'Not at all,' she answered politely, but with no show of enthusiasm.

'Fresh air might help me to some clear thinking,' he said, putting on his coat. 'And I certainly need it. For the past two hours I've been sitting in that room with my mind going round in circles and getting nowhere.'

It was a fine night with a touch of frost in the air, and the grass was crisp under their feet as they crossed the lawn to the main gates. The day's sun had dried up most of the previous night's rain, but by the side of the road small pools of water glinted in the beam of Diana's torch. They walked for a while in silence, the man's steel-tipped shoes striking occasional sparks from the flinty surface, the girl padding beside him like an animal in her rubber-soled shoes.

It was she who broached the subject that was in both their minds.

'I don't intend going far, Inspector,' she said. 'You had better say your piece, and then we'll turn back.'

Feeling rather foolish at the ease with which she had sized up his intentions, Pitt began to protest. But she cut him short.

'I imagine that police officers don't normally go strolling in the moonlight with young women when they're on duty,' she said serenely. 'Not without a motive, anyway. You came out to pump me, didn't you? Of course, if you've changed your mind that's all right with me. But don't try to make me out a fool.'

Pitt grunted. He disliked being trapped.

'I admit the charge, miss. But I never under-estimated your intelligence.'

'You may cut out the compliments. I presume this isn't that kind of walk. What is it you want from me, Inspector?'

'I want to ask you an embarrassing and personal question, Miss Farling. Are you in love with Mr Moull?'

He could not see her face, but he heard the quick intake of breath.

'No,' she said.

'Is he in love with you?'

'I haven't the faintest idea.'

'I have always understood that it was practically impossible for a man to be in love with a woman without her becoming aware of it,' Pitt said. 'Women's intuition, I believe they call it. But then most of my knowledge of romance is obtained from books. Perhaps it isn't altogether reliable.'

The girl made no comment.

'However, reliable or not,' the Inspector continued, 'I fancied it must be love — either yours or his — which prompted you to tell Mr Moull what you overheard Sergeant Maddox and myself discussing in the library last night.'

This time there was no mistaking her agitation. 'You — you know that?' she gasped.

'Yes. So it was obvious when Mr Moull disappeared that he had been warned by you.'

She made no answer to the charge, and they walked on steadily. Pitt decided not to press her. She'll talk sooner or later, he thought.

'So I'm not so clever after all, eh?' she said at last, her voice once more under control. 'You're right; Chris was in love with me, and I knew it. Unfortunately, I didn't feel the same way about him; and that's something that makes a girl feel guilty. I don't know why it should, but it does. You wouldn't understand that, being a man.'

'It seems to make some sort of sense,' he said.

'It also made me — well, more *aware* of him, if you can understand that too,' she went on. 'As soon as all this started I knew there was something worrying Chris. I tried to find out what it was, but he wouldn't tell me. And yet he must have known I wouldn't give him away.'

'I should have thought it was fairly obvious,' said Pitt.

'Not if you knew Chris. It was difficult to believe anything bad of him. But I did begin to suspect, of course; one couldn't help it. And yesterday — well, Sergeant Maddox has a very expressive face, Inspector; I guessed he was on to something. And if it was to do with Chris I had to know about it. So I listened. Despicable of me, wasn't it?'

'Very,' he agreed.

'Thanks.' She laughed, but there was no mirth in her laughter. 'My eavesdropping may have helped Chris, but it didn't help me. I'm no wiser now than I was before.'

'He didn't explain?'

'No. He thanked me very nicely for telling him, and said he was going away and would I help him. So I did.'

'How?'

'There was a policeman in the hall. I took him a cup of tea and distracted his attention while Chris left by the door next to the common room. He thought the policeman might stop him if he saw him. Would he have done?'

'Yes. What time did Mr Moull leave the building?'

'About eleven-thirty.'

Either she or Russell must be lying, thought Pitt. But why? Why did it matter what time Moull had left?

He was still pondering this when the girl said, 'May we turn back now, please? There isn't anything else, is there?'

'I suppose I don't have to tell you that you have laid yourself open to a very serious charge, Miss Farling,' he said, obeying her request. 'If Mr Moull were to be convicted of murder your own penalty might be anything up to imprisonment for life.'

'But I didn't really *do* anything,' she protested. 'He could probably have dodged the constable on his own. I only made it easier for him. Anyway, why *should* he be convicted of murder? Colin Russell is still very much alive.'

'I was thinking of Mr Connaught.'

'Oh.' There was a pause. 'Yes, of course. I had forgotten about J.C.'

'Did Mr Moull spend that Friday night
— the night before Mr Connaught was
drowned — at your cottage?'

She hesitated. 'Since I'm confessing, I
may as well confess fully,' she said
eventually. 'Yes, he did. He arrived rather
late, and quite unexpectedly. It seemed a
bit mean to send him back, so I let him
sleep on the couch downstairs. I don't
know what time he left the next morning;
he had gone when I got up. That was at
nine o'clock — and Chris had to be in
school by then, of course.'

'What reason did he give for his visit?'

'He didn't give any. Just said he wanted
to see me. But he didn't talk much. In
fact, he seemed unusually quiet, even for
Chris.'

'Do you believe now that he killed John
Connaught?' Pitt asked bluntly.

'I told you before, Inspector, I don't
think J.C. *was* murdered. It may look that
way to you — I dare say it does — but *I*
don't believe it.'

'You could be wrong, miss. Why did
someone try to poison Mr Russell, do you
think? And if Mr Moull has a clear

conscience, why has he run away?'

'I don't know. Yes, if I'm wrong about J.C., then I suppose — oh, I don't know *what* I think,' she said passionately. 'And what does it matter? It's what *you* think that counts, isn't it?'

'What I can prove — not what I think,' he told her. 'Were you the only person who knew that Mr Moull intended to leave last night?'

'I should think so. I don't suppose he went round broadcasting the news, do you?'

'Did he mention the poison?'

'I told you, he didn't mention or explain *anything*. He just said he was going and would I help him, and I did and — oh, for Heaven's sake stop asking me questions, can't you? I've had just about as much as I can stand.'

The outburst surprised him. He had not expected such a display of emotion from the calm Miss Farling.

They walked the rest of the way in silence. It was not until he said goodnight to her at the school that he put his final question.

'What was Mr Moull wearing when he left? His duffel-coat is missing, and we mentioned that in the description we circulated. But what else?'

'A grey suit, I think. Or perhaps grey flannels and a sports jacket. I can't be sure about the jacket; he had his coat on.'

When Pitt reached the police station Maddox had gone; the Sergeant in charge thought he had returned to the Forester's Arms for a meal. And there was still no news of Moull.

Pitt was not ready to eat yet; he was not hungry, and he had found in the past that his brain was more nimble when his stomach was empty. Nor did he particularly long for Maddox's company. So he stayed on at the neat brick villa that was the local police station, and tried to bring some semblance of order into the chaos of his thoughts.

On the face of it any of them — the Latimers, Smelton, Moull, Miss Farling, even Russell or Miss Connaught — could have murdered the old man. So, he supposed, could Mrs Smelton. Any of them, Miss Farling and Mrs Smelton excepted, could have made the attempt on Russell's life. But motive and opportunity were of little avail, since they were more or less common to all; and the evidence against each was conflicting. Most of it pointed to Moull — but how much of it was reliable? How many witnesses had doctored their statements — not necessarily with any intentional bias against Moull — to suit their own ends? And why was it, wondered Pitt, that the few tiny scraps of evidence in Moull's favour seemed to him to outweigh the more solid evidence against the man?

Well, at least he knew the answer to that. He was not now building up a case with which to convince a jury; he was trying to convince himself. Most of the evidence made a pattern in which he himself did not believe. He had his own pattern; he had had it since early that afternoon (for Diana Farling had told him little that he had not known or guessed); but a pattern was useless unless you had the material with which to complete it. If he could find that . . .

Moull was involved — he could not be

entirely blameless; despite the contradictions there was too much positive evidence against him for that. But there was someone else . . . there might even be two . . .

With a sigh he began to wade once more through Russell's statement and his own copious notes.

★   ★   ★

It was after ten o'clock when Sergeant Maddox, intrigued rather than worried by Pitt's non-appearance, eventually disturbed him. 'They told me you were here and that you didn't need me,' he said; 'but I was thinking you must be feeling a bit peckish. There's some sandwiches for you over at the pub when you're ready.'

Pitt had put away his papers and was gazing into the dying fire. He nodded and stood up. 'Now you come to mention it I'm starving,' he said. 'And I could do with a pint of beer.'

As they walked through the quiet village to the Forester's Arms Maddox said, 'I hope they pick Moull up soon.

This is my part of the country, but I don't like this village and I don't like the folks up at the school. The women and kids are all right, but the men give me the willies.'

'We'll find him tomorrow,' Pitt promised.

'Well, that's a . . . Eh? Did you say *we'll* find him?'

'Yes.'

'Go stick a pin in me old Aunt Lucy!' exclaimed the Sergeant piously. 'You mean to say you know where he is?'

'I don't know *where*,' Pitt said, 'but I think I know how. I think he's dead.'

# 11

## One More Body

There were no lessons that Monday morning. Text and exercise books had been stored away; the desks were empty. But since the boys were dressed in their best suits they could not be left to their own devices. Mr Latimer knew that he was due for several unpleasant interviews before the day was over; he did not wish to add to the unpleasantness by confronting an already displeased parent with a grubby and untidy son.

About a third of the school had already left early for London by train under the care of Mrs Latimer — a journey which that lady had welcomed, since it took her away from school at a time when visitors would be there in plenty. The remainder of the boys sat in their classrooms, occupying themselves as the masters or mistress in charge saw fit. The top form, full of an indignation which they dared not express, were translating a piece of Latin prose written on the blackboard by Smelton; their indignation was stretched to almost mutinous lengths as they listened to the laughter of the two middle forms playing paper games with Mr Russell. The Fourth Form either drew or read or played with cotton-reels converted, by means of elastic bands and a piece of candle end, into army tanks. They could do what they liked, James Latimer had told them as he spread his newspaper on the desk, provided they were silent and did not disturb him.

Anne was reading aloud to the bottom form. 'Being read to' was something they loved, the only tried and trusted method of keeping them still and quiet. Even with the exciting prospect of meeting fathers and mothers and of a long holiday stretching blissfully ahead, the magic still worked.

But not, on this occasion, for long. At first there was only a soft whisper, instantly stilled at her command. Then the whispering started again. Heads were turned to peer out of the far window; one or two of the smallest boys were standing up and pointing excitedly.

'Sit down,' Anne said sharply. 'What's the matter with you all?'

'Please, Miss Connaught, there's a man.'

Her eyes followed the pointing fingers. 'There's no one there,' she said. 'Don't be so silly.'

'Yes, there is, Miss Connaught. He's in the bushes. Look! You can see his legs.'

Horror filled her as she thought of Chris. Had he too been murdered? She hurried to the open window. Yes, they were right — there *was* someone lying in the bushes.

The boys left their desks and came crowding round her, their shrill voices arguing excitedly. Anne was about to shoo them away, to go for help, when the legs moved and horror was turned to astonishment. The legs wriggled slowly backward, turning from side to side; and presently a man's body appeared, and he stood up, dusting the soil from his clothing.

It was Inspector Pitt.

Anne began to laugh — a low giggle which developed into a shrill peal. She could not help it. The relief had been so great that it had left her weak and slightly hysterical. The boys, taking their cue from her, joined in the laughter.

Inspector Pitt turned and saw them. At first he frowned. Then the frown changed to a smile, and he walked across the terrace to the window.

'I'm glad you found it funny,' he said, shaking a fist at the boys in mock severity. 'I didn't.'

'But what were you doing,' asked Anne, 'rummaging about in the shrubbery with that stick?'

He still held it in his hand; now he looked down at it. 'That? I was just searching for something.'

'Did you find it?'

'Yes, thanks.' He looked at the now silent boys and then at the girl. 'Can you leave them for a few minutes, miss? I want a word with you in private.'

'I ought not to,' she protested. 'They'll get up to mischief.'

'You can keep an eye on them from

here.' He turned to the boys. 'Go and sit down, the lot of you. Any larking about and I'll put handcuffs on you,' he said sternly.

He put one hand in his pocket and rattled an imaginary handcuff. They boys laughed delightedly.

'You don't know how to handle them,' Anne told him. 'Now they'll be as naughty as they can. There's nothing they'd like better than a pair of handcuffs.'

She restored such order as she could and hurried out to the terrace. 'I can't leave them for long,' she said. 'What was it you wanted?'

'It's about that bottle, miss; the one you found. Remember you told me there was an M embossed on the base? What kind of an M was it?'

Anne was puzzled. 'Just an ordinary M. A block capital, with the two uprights spread out a little at the feet.'

Pitt handed her notebook and pencil. 'Draw it, please.'

She obeyed. He took the notebook from her, looked at it from several angles, and nodded. Anne thought he looked pleased.

'Thank you, miss. Now, just one thing more. Did your grandfather receive many letters?'

She was surprised at the sudden switch.

'No, not many. I was his only relative, and he had few friends. Most of his correspondence was with bookmakers and football pool firms. He betted a lot.'

'Mr Russell was telling me about an occasion last April when your grandfather accused you of spying because you interrupted him when he was reading a letter.'

'Yes, that's right. But whatever — '

'Would you recognize that letter now?'

'No. I never saw it. Only the envelope. And I didn't see the writing on that, either. J.C. was standing some distance away, and I only just glanced at him casually. I wasn't really interested, you see.'

'How far away was he?'

She looked round. 'About from here to the wall, I should say.'

Pitt walked to the wall, followed by the

curious eyes of Form One. They had abandoned all pretence at obedience and were once more crowded round the window. But they were reasonably quiet, and Anne let them be.

The Inspector took something from his pocket and held it up. 'Was it anything like that?' he asked.

'That' was an envelope. Anne screwed up her eyes and craned forward.

'Yes, it was. It was the same shape and colour, certainly — but I think there was a white edging to the blue. And it had that blue stamp, whatever it is.'

'There's a white edging to this also,' he said, replacing the envelope in his pocket. 'Maybe it doesn't show up in this light, but it's there.'

'Where did you get it?' she asked, completely mystified. 'And why is it important?'

'I got if from Mr Connaught's executors; they had found it stuffed away at the back of his desk. I don't suppose he meant to keep it, so it's lucky that they did.' Pitt hesitated, and then said slowly. 'Unless I am greatly mistaken its importance lies in the fact that, indirectly, it killed your grandfather.'

She gasped. 'An envelope? But how?'

'Because it should never have come into his possession.' He spoke more briskly. 'Thank you, miss — I won't detain you any longer; those kids sound as though they need you in there.' He jerked his thumb at the open window, no longer crowded with faces. Form One had lost interest in the police and were chasing each other round the classroom. 'But I'd be glad if you would keep this to yourself — and from Mr Russell in particular. That fiancé of yours has an infinite capacity for meddling in police affairs — with unfortunate results. Better to leave him uninformed, or he might be tempted to interfere again.'

Anne was puzzled. Why an 'infinite' capacity? Surely Colin had interfered only once?

'I'm all for keeping him out of it, Inspector,' she assured him. 'I won't tell a soul.'

In the hall Pitt was waylaid by an indignant headmaster.

'This is disgraceful, Inspector. The grounds are full of policemen — '

'Three, sir. All they could spare me.'

' — and on the very day the boys are leaving,' Mr Latimer went on, unheeding. 'The effect on parents will be disastrous. I am told they are looking for something. Well, whatever it is, I must ask you to call off the search *at once*. It must wait until tomorrow, or at least until after the boys have gone.'

'No, sir, that's impossible,' Pitt said firmly.

'But why, man, why?' He was pleading now, not commanding. 'Do you want to ruin me? What is it you expect to find?'

'A corpse, Mr Latimer.'

Instantly Pitt regretted his bluntness. It was not the tactful and considerate reply which the question deserved. He pulled a chair forward and watched the head-master's long length collapse on to it.

'I'm sorry, sir. I should have broken the news more gently. But you see now why the search must go on?'

'Yes. Yes, of course.' Mr Latimer looked a broken man. All the fight had gone out

337

of him. 'But — whose?'

'Mr Moull's.'

The other nodded as though expecting this reply. 'Suicide, do you think?'

'Possibly. We'll know better when we find him.'

On the gravel outside a car drew up, a door slammed. The headmaster shook himself and stood up, wriggling his long neck as if the collar were throttling him. 'More parents,' he muttered, with a pleading look at the Inspector.

Pitt took the hint and went into the library. He was beginning to feel sorry for Mr Latimer. The man was autocratic and domineering, completely selfish in his lack of co-operation. But it was never pleasant to see a purposeful character deteriorate into the helpless, bewildered creature he had just left. If only . . .

Then he smiled. There were voices in the hall, and dominating them came that of the headmaster. Mr Latimer was talking pleasantly but forcefully, giving his visitor no chance to utter the expected complaint. The deterioration, Pitt decided, had been very temporary.

He was about to send for Smelton when the telephone rang. 'Pitt speaking,' he said into the mouthpiece, and listened attentively to the voice at the other end of the wire. When it had finished he replaced the receiver slowly, wrote 'pot cy — Trynn, King's Road, Chelsea — June 22,' in his notebook, and stood for a moment gazing thoughtfully at the closed library door, on the other side of which Mr Latimer's heavy voice could still be heard. Then he shrugged. It was, after all, only what he had expected. Yet the man had been clever. He had only inferred the lie, he had not spoken it.

Smelton seemed more irritated than perturbed by the Inspector's summons. He marched into the library, slammed the door behind him, and curtly demanded to be told what the police thought they were playing at. 'You may have a job to do, Inspector, but so have I. Moull's disappearance has left us short-handed, and until this afternoon is over the boys still have to be supervised. What is it you want now?'

Pitt looked at him. He disliked Joseph

Latimer and he disliked Smelton. But, whereas Latimer had character, this little man had nothing but his bombast.

'I wanted to ask if you slept well on the night of October the twenty-first,' he said.

Smelton fairly bristled. 'What sort of a joke is this?'

'No joke, sir. That was the night, you remember, before Mr Connaught was drowned. I believe you spent it in the cells at Tanbury Police Station, didn't you?'

The little man seemed suddenly to shrink still further in stature. School-teachers wilt easily, Pitt thought; first Latimer, now this chap. Maybe small boys have that ultimate effect; a gradual erosion, as it were, of one's moral strength until suddenly it flops completely. Or — remembering Joseph Latimer — until at least it sags.

'How did you know?' asked Smelton, his voice a whisper of its former self.

'We policemen tell each other things,' Pitt said cheerfully. 'Drunk and incapable, wasn't it?'

He rallied at that. 'No, certainly not,' he said indignantly. 'There was no charge;

340

they merely gave me a bed for the night.'

'But you were drunk, if not incapable?'

Not drunk, said Smelton. Certainly he had had a few drinks; but he wasn't drunk — there hadn't been time. And when the constable spoke to him he had already spent the little money he had had on him when he rushed out of the house; so he couldn't go to a hotel and he couldn't hire a taxi. And he thought it unwise to tell the constable about the car parked on the square; he knew that to be drunk in charge of a car was a serious offence, and that one could be charged with it even if one was not actually in the car. And at the police station the Sergeant had said —

'All right. How did you get your head wet?'

'Eh?' Smelton, cut short in his flow of rhetoric, was left floundering. 'Head wet? I don't understand.'

'I'm told that when you arrived at the school next morning your head was dripping with water. As though you had been in the river. Had you?'

'Certainly not. But I'm not used to

heavy drinking, Inspector, and I felt very muzzy the next morning. I stopped the car at the bridge on the way here, and went down to the river to sluice my head. There was no time to go home for a bath and a change, and I thought the cold water might brace me up.' Smelton hesitated. 'Is it necessary for this to go any further, Inspector? My reputation — one has to be so careful in this profession; and Mr Latimer is — '

'I didn't get much co-operation from you, Mr Smelton.' Pitt stared at the little man for a moment and then relented. 'All right, sir; I won't mention this to your headmaster unless I find it necessary.' He picked up the stick that Anne had seen him with earlier and regarded it thoughtfully. 'I want a word with young Locking. He hasn't left yet, has he?'

'No, he's still here. I'll send him along. And thank you, Inspector. I — er — I had thought of sending a small donation to the Tanbury police.' Smelton summoned a rather watery smile. 'Payment, as it were, for a night's lodging. Do you think that would be misinterpreted as a bribe?'

'Probably,' said Pitt. 'But send it to the Standing Joint Committee, and you won't have any trouble.'

★　★　★

It was Colin who drew the attention of the police to the smashed handrail on the bridge. 'I'm not going to hang around the school to be pestered by inquisitive parents,' he had told Anne after lunch. 'I'll go and help them look for Chris. I'll be down by the stream if I'm wanted.' And when she had pointed out that the police were not by the stream, but in the woods, he had grinned and said, 'I know. But somehow I don't feel comfortable with a lot of coppers around me. I'd rather be on my own.'

'Look at that,' he said to Sergeant Maddox, pointing to where the handrail on the downstream side of the bridge had been broken away. 'It wasn't like that on Saturday afternoon when I was down here with the boys.'

Maddox walked gingerly on to the bridge and peered down at the sharp rocks over which the water now tumbled in a sullen swirl. 'He wouldn't have much of a chance if he fell in there,' he said. 'It's quite a drop. If he cracked his head on those rocks he'd be out cold.'

They made their way slowly down the side of the stream. The banks were high and thickly wooded; the water was muddy and still moving fairly fast. It was impossible to see the bottom. But gradually the banks became less steep, the ground levelled out, and the stream widened into a small lake some hundred yards before it joined the Tan. And it was there they found Chris Moull. He had drifted out of the main stream to the side of the lake, where he lay in shallow water face downward among the reeds.

The Sergeant blew his whistle. Colin turned away when the others arrived and they began to pull the body out of the water. He had been fond of Chris; he could not bear to look at him now.

Maddox came over and put a hand on his shoulder.

'Nasty business this, sir,' he said sympathetically. 'Would you mind going

ahead to warn them up at the school?
We'll be taking the body up there for the
present, and it would be best to get the
boys out of the way first.'

Colin nodded and set off up the slope.
He was thinking fast, for he knew that if
he was to act at all he must act now. At
any moment the police might pounce
— and then it would be too late. There
was no time now to balance pros and
cons. Now he must decide — and act.

★   ★   ★

'That's what killed him, Inspector,' said
the doctor, pointing to a deep wound at
the base of the skull. 'And if he fell head
first on to a jagged piece of rock that
would account for it. The lacerations on
the rest of the body were probably
incurred as it was carried downstream by
the current.'

The body lay on a trestle-table in the
gymnasium, whence it had been brought
while the boys were assembled in the
study. The windows were too high for a
boy to peer through, and the only

precaution necessary after that had been the posting of a constable at the door. Pitt had promised the headmaster that the body would not be moved from the gymnasium until the last boy had left that afternoon.

He went out into the corridor with Maddox. A few boys were wandering aimlessly about, cap in one hand, raincoat trailing from the other. They showed little interest in the two detectives. Familiarity had bred acceptance of their presence in the school, and the boys' minds were now concentrated on the holidays.

'Any luck with Records, sir?' asked Maddox.

'Yes. Amazing, isn't it? There might have been any of a dozen reasons, and by pure chance we hit the jackpot first go.'

'What was it?'

'Twelve months for embezzlement.'

'Does that mean we can go ahead?'

'I think we'll have to. There's a lot to do before the case is sewn up, but I daren't wait for that.' Pitt sighed. 'Get Russell, will you? I'll be in the library.'

But Colin Russell was not to be found. When a search of the building proved unavailing Pitt extended it to the grounds, and gave orders for the entire staff to be rounded up and assembled under police guard in the common room.

'I'm not taking any chances,' he said grimly to Maddox.

Then he sent for Anne.

She looked pale; her eyes were swollen with crying. 'I don't know where he is, Inspector,' she said. 'But when he came to tell me that they'd found Chris he looked — well, odd. He talked oddly too. Of course, I know he was upset, but . . . '

She began to cry softly in a tired, helpless manner. Pitt realised how near to breaking point the girl must be. But he had to find Russell.

He handed her a glass of water — why, he did not know — and she sipped it slowly, the tears still rolling down her cheeks.

'I'm sorry to badger you, miss, but I must find Mr Russell. He — '

Anne interrupted him. 'There's nothing else wrong, is there? He's not in any danger?' she asked, alarm overcoming her distress.

'No,' he said slowly. 'No, it's not Mr Russell that's in danger, I fancy.'

Relief at his assurance obscured from her mind the full meaning of his answer, and she relaxed against the back of the chair.

'You say he talked oddly, miss. How?'

'It was in the common room,' said Anne. 'We were alone, and after he'd told me about Chris he began walking up and down, not taking any notice of me, but talking to himself about having made a mess of something or other and whether he ought to take a chance. It didn't make sense to me, and he wouldn't explain, and . . . ' A look in the Inspector's eye stopped her. 'Do *you* understand what he meant?'

Pitt nodded. 'I think so. Go on.'

'What was it?'

'Never mind that now,' he said impatiently. 'Go on, please.'

'Well, suddenly he came up to me and caught hold of my shoulders. I was frightened; I'd never seen him look like that before. He said if I discovered that he'd done something wrong — something for which the law could punish him — what would I do?'

'And what did you tell him?'

'I said I'd stick by him no matter what happened, because I love him. And so I do, Inspector. Besides, I know Colin; he's inclined to make mountains out of molehills; he takes things so intensely. I knew he couldn't have done anything really *wrong*. It just isn't in him.'

'What happened then?'

'I was just going to ask him to explain when Diana — Miss Farling — came in to tell me that Mrs Dickson wanted to speak to me. I had to go, of course; and when I got back to the common room Colin wasn't there.'

'Didn't Miss Farling know where he'd gone?'

'She wasn't there either.'

Pitt, more worried now than he wished the girl to realize, was anxious to be rid of her; he thanked her briefly and signalled her dismissal by opening the door. As she went out of the room there came the sound of voices from the hall, and he was about to close the door again when a shrill feminine voice made him pause.

'Miss Connaught! Oh, I'm so glad I didn't go without seeing you. I hear congratulations are in order. Miss Webber has just been telling me of your engagement to that nice Mr Russell.'

Anne uttered a low word of thanks.

'Of course, I only met him once,' the shrill voice went on, 'but he's terribly attractive in a *manly* way, isn't he? I do think you're frightfully trusting to let him go wandering around the country like that. She's not as pretty as you, of course; but still — well, you know what men are.'

Pitt's hand tightened on the door-knob as Anne said quietly, 'I'm afraid I don't understand, Mrs Spellman.'

'Oh, dear, I hope I haven't put my foot in it,' said the voice. 'But we passed them up the lane just now. Of course, I didn't know then that you — oh!'

Mrs Spellman's terrified shriek was echoed by Miss Webber as the Inspector almost leapt at them from the library. 'Where did you see Mr Russell?' he asked, grasping the woman by the arm and all but shaking her in his urgency.

Mrs Spellman, quickly recovering from her initial fright, freed her arm imperiously and looked sternly at her attacker.

'Really!' she exclaimed. 'By what right — '

Pitt controlled his temper.

'I'm a police officer, ma'am. Mr Russell is urgently wanted for questioning. Where did you see him?'

'Why, down the lane, as I said. They were getting over a stile this side of the fork. If you'd asked me — '

'The chalk pits!' exclaimed Anne.

Pitt wheeled swiftly. 'You know the place?'

Anne nodded, too frightened to speak. The Inspector's unease had communicated itself to her, and the vision of Colin climbing up the hillside to the chalk pits had somehow revived her former fears. But she was given no time to dwell on them. Pitt whisked her out of the hall and into the back seat of the waiting police car. He turned to her for instructions, and she pointed dumbly. With deceptive smoothness the car gathered speed, turned swiftly out of the gates, and sped off down the lane.

The short journey enabled Anne to recover her wits. As the fork came in sight she tapped the Inspector on the shoulder.

'Stop just this side of the fork,' she said. 'There's a stile on the right. The chalk pits are up there, on the other side of the hill.'

Pitt nodded, and spoke to the driver. As the car pulled up, so suddenly that Anne slid to the floor, he was out on the road and making for the stile. Anne and the driver followed. They were both young and fit, and gradually gained on the older man in front; but all three were panting heavily as they crested the slope and paused involuntarily.

On the lip of a deep chalk pit cut into the side of the hill a man and a woman were struggling, in front of them a thirty foot drop. Although the three watchers were less than fifty yards distant, they were powerless to intervene, for the pit lay between them and the struggling figures. For a few moments they stood motionless; then, with a loud shout, the Inspector was clambering down the near side of the pit and racing towards the cliff, the driver after him. Anne tried to follow, but her legs, her whole body seemed numb. She could only watch, hands tightly clasped, an unconscious prayer in her heart.

The policemen were half-way across the floor of the pit when one of the struggling figures reeled back, away from the cliff. For a moment the other teetered, arms flailing desperately. Then, with a cry that Anne was to remember for many days to come, it toppled over the edge and fell, a whirling octopus of arms and legs, down the white face of the cliff.

★　★　★

Anne recovered consciousness to find Colin kneeling beside her, an arm about her shoulders. Her relief at knowing he was safe caused her to burst into tears.

'It's all right, darling,' he said. 'It's all right.'

She put her arms round his neck and pulled herself up to kiss him. Colin held her close while he drew a handkerchief from his pocket and wiped the tears from her eyes.

'I'm an awful cry-baby,' she said, smiling faintly. And then, remembering, 'Was it Diana?'

'Yes.'

She shuddered. 'Colin, it was horrible! I couldn't do anything but watch. I couldn't even shout — not that shouting would have helped you, I suppose. And when she fell I couldn't see properly; I thought it was you. That's why I fainted.'

'You'd better get up,' Colin said. 'The grass is damp.'

This practical suggestion struck Anne as being very funny indeed. But she knew that if she gave way to laughter she would become hysterical, and obediently she scrambled to her feet. As she did so she gave a quick glance behind her and then looked questioningly at Colin.

'Yes,' he said, understanding, 'she's still there. The Inspector is with her. He sent the constable for an ambulance.'

'She's not dead?'

'I don't know. I didn't go down. The

Inspector shouted at me to look after you.'

They began walking slowly down the hillside to the lane, their arms linked. 'Shall we walk back to the school?' asked Colin. 'Or would you rather wait for the car? It won't be long.'

'Let's walk.' The fog had cleared from her brain, and she was beginning to think again. 'Don't be cross with me, Colin — I've got to know. Did you — did you kill her?'

'No.' He helped her carefully over the stile. 'But I meant to. I wanted to get even with her for Chris, I wanted to make sure she didn't escape.' He laughed shortly. 'I guess I'm not cut out for an executioner. My nerve failed me.'

Anne pressed his hand. 'Tell me,' she said.

'After you left the common room I asked her to go for a walk. I said I wanted to get away from the place, I didn't want to be button-holed by inquisitive parents. She seemed a bit surprised, but I don't think she suspected anything; I suppose I must have looked and sounded quite normal, although I didn't *feel* normal. I felt as though there were several volcanoes erupting inside my head. *And* in my stomach.

'I can't remember what we talked about on the way here. Chris, I expect. I hadn't made any definite plans, but I knew I had to get well away from the school or the police might interfere. When we came to the stile I remembered the chalk pits, and it seemed the ideal spot. But I waited until we were up there before I told her.'

'What did she say?'

'Nothing. Not a word. When I accused her of having murdered Chris and J.C. she neither denied nor admitted it. She just stood there looking at me in a funny sort of way. Even when I'd worked myself into a frenzy and told her I was going to throw her over the cliff she didn't bat an eyelid.'

Anne shuddered. 'Colin, how dreadful! Didn't she try to run away?'

'No. She walked to the cliff-edge and then turned round and dared me to do it. But I couldn't. It wasn't that I was afraid,

Anne. I just couldn't do it.'

She pressed his hand. 'I'm glad, darling. But what happened? Why were you struggling with her?'

'She grabbed me as I turned away. I suppose she thought that if she could get rid of me the way she had got rid of Chris she would still have a chance. The police didn't seem to suspect her, and no one knew we'd gone up there together; and even if they did she could have said it was an accident. She fought like a fury; and catching me off my guard like that gave her an initial advantage. She nearly had us both over a couple of times.'

'Did you push her?'

'No. She let go suddenly and pushed *me*. I was off balance and fell back — on to the grass luckily. She'd probably lost her sense of direction by then — didn't realize that the cliff was behind *her*, not me. I heard her cry out, and then — well, she just disappeared.'

'How did you know it was Diana who killed Chris?' Anne asked, after they had walked a little way in silence.

'I didn't. I just guessed. I reckoned that

Chris was killed because he knew too much; there couldn't be any other reason. That meant he was shielding someone — and who could that be but Diana? He wouldn't have lied to the police to save Smelton or the Latimers; he didn't like any of them.'

'But, Colin — suppose you were wrong?'

'I wasn't wrong. If you'd seen her up there you'd know that.'

As they neared the school gates the police car went past followed by an ambulance. Anne shivered.

'I'll be glad when we're away from here,' she said. 'It seems a horrible place now. And once I'm away I'll never come back. Never.'

# 12

## A Chronicle of Crime

It was two days before Inspector Pitt came again to Redways, and meanwhile the staff were tied to the school. Some of them were called to the police station for further questioning and to sign statements. There was the inquest on Chris Moull to attend, and later his funeral; at his parents' request he was buried in the local cemetery. And between these spasms of activity they filled the dawdling hours with open surmise and (in some cases) secret dread of what the trial of Diana Farling might reveal. For Diana had not died of her fall — though there were some who thought it might have been better if she had. She lay in hospital, her body broken and mutilated and in constant pain. Her conscious moments were monopolized by the police, apart from whom her mother was her only visitor.

Pitt was alone. He stood with his back to the fireplace, a stern, forbidding figure, greeting the staff with an impersonal nod as they assembled in the library at his request. Only James Latimer was absent. James, said his father, had felt unwell after lunch and had retired to bed.

'Very wise of him,' was the Inspector's comment. 'He wouldn't derive much pleasure from what I have to say.'

Mr Latimer frowned. 'Will any of us? Why single James out?'

Pitt's expression did not alter. Much of his sternness was adopted as a shield against moments such as this. To cause pain, even to someone he disliked as much as he disliked Joseph Latimer, was distasteful to him.

He said slowly, 'Your son has not told you, then, that he was engaged to Miss Farling?'

The headmaster gripped the arms of his chair, rose slightly, and then sank back. His face was grey.

'I don't believe it,' he said harshly; and

then again, his voice firmer this time, 'I don't believe it.'

Pitt looked at the others. Their faces showed that they too did not believe it. He moved away from the fireplace and sat down.

'It's true,' he said, his voice warmer, less brittle. Now that he had flung his first bombshell he felt less need of his shield; he could afford to relax. 'Young Trent hinted at it; his mother confirmed it. Or she had reason to suppose it, anyway.'

Joseph Latimer, immersed in unhappy thought, was barely listening. But one word came to him clearly.

'Trent? How can Trent know anything of this?'

'He doesn't, sir. Not consciously. He was merely telling me about his summer holidays. He mentioned seeing your son; and since at that time Mr James' — unconsciously Pitt adopted the term of reference to James Latimer commonly used by the boys — 'was under suspicion of having been connected with the murder of John Connaught — '

'John Connaught's death was an

accident. The coroner said so.'

'No, sir; he was murdered. There was also reason to suppose that your son might have attempted to poison Mr Russell.' Here the Inspector glanced sharply at Colin, who grinned back self-consciously. 'So any item of news concerning him interested me. And when the boy told me this extraordinary story about a ginger horse at the hotel — '

This time it was not the headmaster alone who interrupted. 'A ginger horse!' they echoed in incredulous unison.

Pitt sighed.

'We're not getting along very rapidly, are we? I'm a busy man, Mr Latimer; I came here for my own satisfaction, not yours. However, I'm prepared to relate the facts if I'm allowed to do so without all these interruptions.'

The headmaster glared at him. The man was adopting far too dictatorial a tone for a public servant, he thought. But his curiosity was whetted . . . and there was this extraordinary suggestion that James . . .

He contented himself with a brief nod.

'Thank you,' said Pitt.

He told them the odd little tale he had heard from Trent. 'If there had been a horse he must have seen it; so obviously he had misinterpreted what was said. But how? Why did Mr James seek to avoid them? And why should the sight of this horse — or whatever it was — have angered Mr Connaught?' He paused, recalling the knot that this particular problem had tied in his brain. And no one spoke. 'It was the 'horse' that intrigued me; 'ginger' seemed less important. I was puzzling over it when we came into the hall — and the first thing I noticed was Miss Farling's red hair! And then, quite simply, 'horse' became 'horsey,' and 'horsey' 'hussy.' The ginger hussy.'

There was a gasp from Anne, instantly suppressed.

Colin wondered whether 'hussy' was indeed the word Mrs Trent had used; he could think of another more easily mistaken for 'horse.' Had Mrs Trent substituted out of delicacy the milder term of opprobrium? Or was it the Inspector who was being delicate?

'Mrs Trent confirmed the details later. She and Mr Connaught had seen the girl behind Mr James, but the boy had not. And at that I might have lost interest in Miss Farling; her association with Mr James was no concern of mine, however shocked Mrs Trent might be. But although I could appreciate Mr Connaught's annoyance — I had been told that he hoped Mr James would marry Miss Connaught' — here Joseph Latimer glanced swiftly at the flustered Anne — 'I couldn't understand how he could say with such certainty, 'I'll see this is the last time *this* happens.' As he did, apparently.'

'Didn't he explain to Mrs Trent?' asked Colin.

'No, unfortunately. It would have made my task a lot easier if he had.'

Mr Latimer was not interested in J.C. The bitter realization had come to him that it was James who had been behind Mrs Trent's threat to remove her son — a threat which had since become a reality. 'When did this disgraceful association begin?' he asked.

'Between Miss Farling and your son?

Shortly after she came here, I believe. But they were both anxious to keep it a secret. That was why he bought the cottage at Chaim.'

'You mean James *paid* for it?'

'Certainly. It was in her name, but he put down the cash. Otherwise she would have had to return to Ireland for her holidays. That wouldn't have suited either of them.'

Mr Latimer, Anne thought with pity, looked a beaten man. And with what James and Diana had done between them he was probably also a ruined man. She wondered what would become of him if he had to leave Redways.

'A few days after the end of the Easter term, when Miss Farling had left Abbey Lodge for the cottage, a letter for her arrived at the Lodge from her mother in Ireland.' Pitt looked at Anne. 'That was the letter you saw your grandfather reading, Miss Connaught. The one with the blue stamp.'

'But he wouldn't open someone else's letter,' she protested.

'The envelope wasn't properly sealed.

And there are people who cannot resist reading the correspondence of others. Perhaps he was one of them. Anyway, he *did* read it.'

'He would,' growled the headmaster, relieved at this deviation, however temporary, from his own burdens. 'What good did it do him?'

'None, ultimately. But from it he learned that Miss Farling hoped to marry your son. He also learned that three years previously she had been sentenced to twelve months' imprisonment for embezzling money belonging to a London firm of contractors by whom she was then employed.'

'Good God!' ejaculated Mr Latimer. 'A gaolbird!'

The realization that he had actually employed such a person obviously appalled him. Miss Dove, who caught only a fraction of what was being said and showed little interest in the rest, continued to knit busily. The others were as shocked as their headmaster, although Smelton appeared somewhat embarrassed at this reference to gaol.

'If the facts weren't all in the letter there were enough for him to ferret out the rest when he made inquiries in London,' Pitt went on. 'And he then told Miss Farling that unless she broke off her engagement he would expose her. I gather there was a lot of tearful pleading from her — but she had to agree. Or pretend to agree.'

Perhaps that was why J.C. left her the money, thought Anne, ashamed. Conscience money.

'She didn't give James up, then?' she said. It was more a prayer than a question. At that moment it seemed vitally important to her that J.C. should not have succeeded in his blackmail.

'No. She merely insisted that they must take greater precautions against being found out — without, of course, telling Mr James the reason.'

'I bet that suited James down to the ground,' Colin said angrily, voicing his thoughts regardless of the hurt it might cause Mr Latimer. 'It gave him a chance to have a crack at Anne and her money without blotting his copybook with

Diana, the skunk.'

Anne flushed; Miss Webber looked happily scandalized. Pitt expected another outburst from the headmaster, but none came. He did not even look at Colin, but sat slumped in his chair, his eyes fixed on the detective's face, his thin lips pressed tightly together. Friend James is going to find life rather trying after this, thought Pitt, if that expression bodes what I think it does.

'Mr Russell has put it rather crudely, but he may not be far off the mark,' he said. 'Miss Farling believed Mr James when he assured her that his purpose in paying attention to Miss Connaught was to conceal their own liaison. His true purpose, however, is known only to Mr James himself. So far he has not been at all informative.'

Again he glanced at the headmaster. Mr Latimer's eyes narrowed a little, his breathing had grown heavier; but still he did not speak.

'It was at the end of August that Mr Connaught saw Miss Farling and Mr James at Whitby,' Pitt went on; 'and on his return he told the girl that she was to give notice at half-term and leave in December. Either that, or he would let every one know that she was an ex-convict; she was having no second chance to doublecross him. Again Miss Farling had to pretend to agree. But this time she could see no way out — until, as the weeks passed and she became more and more desperate, she decided to kill him.'

'But how do you know all this?' Colin asked.

Pitt found himself welcoming the question. He was no longer in haste to be done. Although not conceited, he considered he had done well to unravel so much from so little. There was no reason why others should not be given an opportunity to think the same.

'After my talk with Mrs Trent I asked Mr Connaught's executors if they had found his papers any correspondence concerning the girl or Mr James; I was looking for tangible proof that he had some hold on one or the other of them. All they could produce was this blue envelope — and that at least was something. The Dublin police were asked to make inquiries there, and in the meantime I got in touch with Scotland Yard. There was nothing to suggest that Miss Farling had a criminal record; it was merely one of numerous possibilities that occurred to me. It was also the easiest to check; so I checked it. And I got what I needed — a strong motive for murder.'

'She might have changed her name since,' Colin said.

'She might, but she didn't. And finger-prints are more reliable than names,' Pitt told him. 'Of course, all this only hinted at the bare facts — the skeleton, as it were. Miss Farling added the flesh later when I saw her in hospital.'

'She confessed, then?'

'She made a statement,' Pitt said cautiously.

'And how did she kill J.C.?' asked Smelton, now recovered from his embarrassment.

But Pitt was not as yet prepared to explain that. He knew that Colin, and possibly others, had distrusted his handling of the case, had suspected that the denouement had come as a surprise to him. So he told them first how the evidence had piled up against Christopher Moull, making it appear almost certain that he was the murderer of John Connaught. Let them get that into their heads first, he thought, and then maybe they'll appreciate better what we were up against.

'But there was just enough contradiction in the evidence to make me doubt,' he said. 'I hadn't then seen the envelope, so I knew nothing of Miss Farling's past; but from what Mrs Trent had told me I guessed that she or Mr James had a reason for wanting Connaught out of the way — whereas Moull had not. He had made no attempt to hide when Bain met him on the towpath; and what was he doing there, anyway? If he had just committed a murder one would expect him to vanish from the river. But most decisive of all was the milkman's insistence that the cyclist he had seen was wearing brown trousers. Moull, you see, possessed no brown trousers. Neither does Mr James.'

'But what about the beret and the duffel-coat?' asked Colin. 'And who was the chap seen by the gardener the night before?'

'James, no doubt,' Mr Latimer said grimly.

'That's right, sir. Mr James had cycled over with the intention of staying the night at the cottage; but that didn't suit Miss Farling, and at some time after midnight she sent him packing. The beret was one of Moull's that he had left there some time ago; she wore it to conceal her red hair, hoping, if seen, to be mistaken for a man. The duffel-coat was her own, bought earlier that month. None of you could tell me about it, since she had never worn it before or since. But neither beret nor coat was chosen to implicate Moull. That happy idea came later.'

'And did the actual murder happen as I thought?' asked Colin.

'It did, sir.' Pitt smiled faintly. 'I've no doubt you have already told the others.'

'Yes, but what about the identity-disc?'

asked Smelton. 'How did that get there?'

'I don't know, and neither does she. Probably the string became entangled in the ring she was wearing — it had a very large stone — and fell off as she put her hands on the bank to hoist herself out of the water. That was just before young Cuttle arrived on the scene. When she heard him coming she slipped back into the water — and then remembered that she needed Connaught's keys. She had to get into the Lodge and retrieve that incriminating letter before anyone else read it. So after Cuttle had gone she swam across to the other bank, took the keys, and swam back. She had dressed and was cycling home along the towpath when she met Moull.'

'That must have shaken her,' said Colin.

'It did. Moull, you see, was the jealous lover; he knew there was something between her and James. He suspected that James had spent the night at the cottage' — so that, thought Anne, was why Chris wouldn't take James's prep; he wasn't going to make it easy for him

— 'and that Miss Farling had cycled back to the school with him that morning and was now on her way home. To appease him she told him she had spent the night with Mrs Bain; Bain was on night duty, and the old lady was nervous of being alone at night. But she also said Mrs Bain didn't want anyone to know that; if her husband found out he would worry about her, and if the school knew they might tell Bain and repeat their suggestion that one of the male staff should sleep there. And Mrs Bain didn't want that either, she said; her daughter comes home for occasional weekends, and the daughter is attractive. She is also promiscuous, I'm told.'

'And Moull swallowed that?' Mr Latimer asked incredulously.

'Why not? Much of it he knew to be true. And Miss Farling was about to go on her way, having rescued herself from a very tricky situation, when she heard Bain's auto-cycle. So she thrust her bicycle at Moull and dived into the bushes, telling him she did not want anyone to see her dressed in that fashion.'

'But didn't Bain notice that it was a woman's bike?' asked Colin. 'Didn't he mention that when you spoke to him?'

'No. In fact, when I asked him outright on Monday morning he said it was a man's.' Pitt smiled. 'At one time, Mr Russell, you held the clue to that problem in your own hands.'

'*I* did?'

'Yes. Remember those two boys fighting with sticks? One of them, Locking, had part of a broom-handle painted black. He told me on Monday that he had picked it up by the river when on a walk.' He smiled at Anne. 'I was fishing for it, not with it, Miss Connaught, when you saw me in the bushes. I remembered that Mr Russell had thrown it there.'

'She rigged it up as a cross-bar, eh?' said Colin.

'That's right. It was enough to deceive the casual observer, but naturally Moull spotted it when he was holding the machine. Miss Farling explained that she had been nervous of cycling over from Chaim the previous evening and had wanted to deceive any would-be molester into mistaking her for a man. Then she took the bar off and threw it away. And Locking found it.'

Anne remembered how puzzled Chris had looked the next day when Diana had said she was not afraid of cycling home alone in the dark. Well, after two such contradictory statements he had a right to be puzzled, she thought.

'Moull seems to have been a most foolishly credulous young man,' said the headmaster. Now that he had recovered from the first shock of his son's behaviour he looked more himself.

'Perhaps. But he was also in love,' said Pitt, and wondered if that had any meaning for Joseph Latimer. 'And he didn't stay credulous.

'The next afternoon, the Sunday, Miss Farling cycled back to the school; ostensibly to offer sympathy and help, but in reality to ensure that the Lodge was unoccupied. Finding that it was, she waited until dusk and then, on her way home, used Mr Connaught's keys to let herself in and take the letter from his desk. It wasn't in the envelope, so she presumed the envelope had been destroyed; and it was while searching for the letter that she came across Mr James's IOU.'

Joseph Latimer came to life with a bang.

'IOU? You mean James had borrowed money from J.C.?' He stressed the last initials.

'I'm afraid so. Buying that cottage had left him short of cash.' Pitt decided to omit the details; Latimer, he thought, had been harassed enough. 'Realizing that it might incriminate him, she took that also, and later sent it to him anonymously. No doubt she would have liked to let him know that she was his benefactress; but she could not do that without proclaiming herself a murderess.'

Was that what James was trying to thank me for last Thursday? Anne wondered. Did he think *I* had returned his IOU? No wonder he said I was sporting!

Pitt turned to the headmaster. 'It was after lunch on the following Saturday, wasn't it, that you told Miss Farling you had arranged for Moull to lodge with the

Bains?' he asked. But Mr Latimer's mind was too full to recall trivialities. 'It was after the inquest,' he said. 'That's all I can tell you.'

'Well, it put her in a spot,' Pitt said. 'Moull was still suspicious of her and Mr James. With Mrs Bain's acceptance of a lodger Moull would say there was no further need for secrecy, and in no time at all he would find out from the old lady that she had lied about where she had spent that night. She went down at once to persuade Mrs Bain to reverse her decision — and found no one there. Wandering round the cottage, she came to the shed, saw the lamps and the tin of petrol, and decided that in them lay her escape. She emptied the paraffin out of the biggest lamp and partly refilled it with petrol, hoping that the explosion, when it came, would cause sufficient damage to upset the arrangement for Moull to lodge there. Of course, when she walked down the hill with Moull later she couldn't anticipate that the explosion would come while she was actually there. But I imagine she considered the result highly satisfactory, if not quite as expected.'

'But Mrs Bain!' Miss Webber exclaimed, aghast. 'Didn't Diana consider what might happen to *her*?'

'I doubt it. Miss Farling seems to be a very single-minded young woman,' Pitt said drily. 'She was determined to marry Mr James, and nothing or nobody was going to stop her.'

'But you couldn't *know* all this,' Anne protested, horrified that one of her sex could be so callous.

He looked at her gravely. 'About the lamp, you mean? No, I didn't know. Not until she told me.'

'And Chris didn't suspect?'

'Why should he? Did anyone? But when Mr Russell told him the next day that he thought Connaught had been murdered he *did* begin to wonder whether it might have been murder, and not Mr James, that had been responsible for her presence on the towpath that Saturday morning. The poison in Mr Russell's milk had him really worried. Unfortunately, at the time I questioned him he had not yet decided where his loyalties lay.'

So that was why Chris and Diana were arguing on the front drive that afternoon, thought Anne. *And I imagined romance and a lovers' quarrel!*

'But Miss Farling knew which way his loyalties were heading,' Pitt said, his voice grave. 'And when she overheard Sergeant Maddox and myself discussing the evidence against him she knew he would crack under our questioning. To her mind, therefore, there was only one solution — murder.' He sighed. 'I suppose that after one has committed a singularly cold-blooded murder there can be nothing very horrifying about another.'

Miss Webber shivered. She had often felt that hers was a colourless life. Now there was too much colour — but of the wrong hue. It was the aura of romance she had craved, not that of death.

'When you heard that Chris had disappeared did you *know* she had killed him?' Colin asked doubtfully.

'Not until that evening.' Pitt told them of the walk he had taken with Diana. 'When I gave her the opening she leapt at it. Yes, Moull had spent the night before

Connaught died at her cottage, she said; he had left early the next morning. But I knew it hadn't been Moull who had nearly collided with the milkman, and it seemed unlikely that there had been two separate cyclists in duffel-coats and berets. So I decided she was lying. And that was when I knew Moull was dead.'

'How did she kill him?'

'She arranged to meet him by the bridge (that was a favourite meeting place of theirs) at midnight on Saturday, and distracted the constable's attention while Moull left by a side door. After Mr James had locked up she locked the common-room door, climbed out through the window, and went down to the bridge. And if she still had any hopes of winning him back he wrecked them at once by telling her that he had already written and signed a true statement which he intended to give me in the morning. At that she lost her temper and went for him; he backed away, the handrail broke — and over he went.' Pitt shook his head doubtfully. 'That, at any rate, is her version of what happened. And it was not until some hours later she remembered the statement. He might have had it on him, or it might be in his room. Well, it was in his room; it was Miss Farling, not Moull, whom you heard at 3 a.m., Mr Russell.'

He paused, and for a moment sat staring at Colin, who fidgeted under his gaze. And as the silence lengthened there were others who fidgeted. It was Mr Latimer who eventually put the question that was in most of their minds.

'Why did Miss Farling attempt to poison Russell?'

Pitt continued to stare at Colin. 'She didn't,' he said laconically.

'Then who did?'

'No one. Mr Russell added the poison himself.'

Pitt waited for the storm to break, but none came. For a moment they stared at him in disbelief, then all eyes were focused on the red-faced Colin. All except Anne's. She sat gazing down at her lap, a slight frown on her pretty face. I suppose he has already told her, thought Pitt.

'Mr Russell might like to explain that

himself,' he said.

Colin, looking very foolish, explained.

'I was merely trying to speed things up,' he said, carefully avoiding the beetle-browed glare of the headmaster. 'My first effort was a flop; nobody panicked when I said I knew who had killed J.C.; and that afternoon, while I was talking to my friend at Wisselbury in the lab (it's a private lab; she does a lot of research work), I got the idea that if I could pretend that someone had tried to poison me — well, I might get a bit of co-operation for a change,' he said defiantly. 'So when she was called to the phone I picked up an empty bottle, poured a little of the cyanide into it, and shoved it in my pocket.'

'Well, of all the — ' began Mr Latimer. But Colin did not let him finish.

'I was late home on purpose, so that the milk would be in my room long enough for J.C.'s murderer not to have an alibi,' he went on hurriedly. 'I poured the cyanide into the milk, put the glass on the floor (I didn't want to drink it by mistake!), and wrote a letter. And when I looked under the bed for my slippers there was the cat — dead.'

'Crystallizing your point very neatly for you, eh?' said Pitt.

'It did, didn't it? Well, I went downstairs to tell Mr Latimer, and on my way I hid the empty bottle in a boxing-glove in the gym and shoved it under the vaulting-horse. I meant to retrieve it later and bury it, but whenever I tried to do so there was always someone around. And then Anne found it.'

'So you took it from her and got rid of it, eh? And then told me that cock-and-bull story about its having been filched from your raincoat pocket. Not very helpful,' said Pitt.

'I know. I'm very sorry. But at least it worked,' said Colin. 'I was right about J.C. being murdered, and if I'd taken no action at all Diana would have got away with it.'

'And Moull would still be alive,' said Latimer.

There was a shocked silence. Colin went very white. Anne took his hand and gripped it tightly.

'Why did you ask me about the M on the bottle, Inspector?' she asked, hoping to lessen the tension in the room.

'Because when I realized it was Mr Russell who had added the poison I guessed he must have got it on his visit to Wisselbury. So the letter had to be a W, not an M; and your drawing confirmed that. You had looked at it upside down. But I should have guessed it before — from Mr Russell's unconcern (as though he were daily accustomed to escaping death by a miracle!), from the fact that no one but he went out that afternoon, and from his remark to you when you told him you had put the milk in his room yourself. He mentioned cyanide then; yet at that time only the poisoner could know that cyanide had been used.' He shook his head. 'You had me thoroughly confused, Mr Russell. Miss Farling was one of the two people who could *not* have tried to poison you, so that I tended to ignore her in connection with the other crime.'

'I'm sorry,' Colin said again. It was inadequate, he knew, but he could think of nothing better.

'And so you should be.' Mr Latimer stood up, his eyebrows working overtime. 'You lied to me, you lied to the police you . . . you . . . well, don't ask me for a testimonial, young man, because you won't get one. I never liked you; I knew you for a damned interfering young fool who was doing his best to ruin me. But at least I thought you were honest.'

He strode angrily to the door.

'Just one moment, Mr Latimer.' Pitt's voice was ominously smooth. 'Talking of lies — what did you do with the potassium cyanide you bought in the King's Road, Chelsea, on June the twenty-second?'

The tall figure stiffened and turned slowly.

'I threw it away,' he said, voice and face expressionless. 'I threw it away because I knew that if you found it you would, like most of your kind, cease to look further. I did not lie to you. I told you that there was no cyanide in my darkroom, and that was the truth.'

'But not, perhaps, a very honest truth,'

Pitt suggested. 'Almost bordering on a lie, don't you think? Personally, I prefer Mr Russell's intention to yours.'

Joseph Latimer stared at him bleakly and then walked out of the room.

'Well! Well!' said Miss Webber. 'This has been quite an afternoon, I *must* say.'

'You remember I told you Moull wasn't in his room on Thursday evening when I went up to borrow a book,' said Smelton. 'Did you ever find out where he'd got to?'

'Yes, sir. He was in Miss Farling's room. Mr Russell's assertion that he knew who had killed John Connaught had shaken him badly, and he wanted to talk to her about it. When Miss Farling found him there, shortly after eleven o'clock, she was furious and got rid of him as soon as she could.' Pitt turned to Colin. 'You didn't hear him go back to his room, did you?'

'No. But perhaps that was after I'd gone downstairs.'

Anne went over to the Inspector.

'What will happen to Colin?' she asked anxiously. 'Will he get into trouble?'

'I don't know, miss. I hope not, for your

sake. I think it would be a matter for the Director of Public Prosecutions to decide.' He looked at her, his head a little on one side. 'What would be the charge? Attempted suicide? No, I think not. Obstructing the police? Well, he hoodwinked us properly, and he certainly took the law into his own hands at the end, didn't he? But then he was also largely instrumental in bringing a criminal to justice. That should count in his favour.'

'You think he might get off, then?' Anne said, swaying slightly as Colin came up and put an arm round her waist.

Pitt smiled at them both.

'He might. But I'm in agreement with Mr Latimer on one point.'

'What's that?' asked Colin, surprised. He had begun to like the Inspector.

'If you ever think of joining the police force, Mr Russell, don't come to me for a testimonial — because you won't get one!'

We do hope that you have enjoyed reading this large print book.

Did you know that all of our titles are available for purchase?

We publish a wide range of high quality large print books including:
**Romances, Mysteries, Classics**
**General Fiction**
**Non Fiction and Westerns**

Special interest titles available in large print are:
**The Little Oxford Dictionary**
**Music Book, Song Book**
**Hymn Book, Service Book**

Also available from us courtesy of Oxford University Press:
**Young Readers' Dictionary**
**(large print edition)**
**Young Readers' Thesaurus**
**(large print edition)**

For further information or a free brochure, please contact us at:
**Ulverscroft Large Print Books Ltd.,**
**The Green, Bradgate Road, Anstey,**
**Leicester, LE7 7FU, England.**
**Tel:** (00 44) **0116 236 4325**
**Fax:** (00 44) **0116 234 0205**

*Other titles in the*
*Linford Mystery Library:*

# DRAGNET

## Sydney J. Bounds

Johnny Fortune meets Ava Gray at the races, and learns that her sister Gail has become involved with a crooked bookmaker, Harvey Chandos. When Johnny helps her to bring Gail home, he's soon up against Nugent, a giant of a man, and Madame Popocopolis, the brain behind Chandos. Popocopolis's plan, to kidnap millionaire's son Roy Belknap for ransom money is thwarted when she finds herself at the centre of a police dragnet — wanted for murder . . .

# ONE REMAINED SEATED

## John Russell Fearn

Maria Black, M.A., Principal of Roseway College for Young Ladies, is faced with murder in the cinema when a stranger seated in Number 11 on Row A is found to be dead. Assuming her role of detective, she becomes Black Maria — the crime solutionist. Working with Inspector Morgan, the local police chief, they go behind the scenes of a cinema, into the homes of those workers who'd maintained the entertainment industry — and into the recesses of a killer's mind . . .

# RAT RUN

## Frederick Nolan

Her Majesty's Secret Service agent Garrett, investigating a series of suicides by scientific researchers, discovers the parameters of a cataclysmic terrorist strike. The fanatical André Dur puts his unholy scenario into operation over the geological fault called the 'Rat Run', where nuclear submarines stalk each other in the dark depths. Helplessly the world looks on as the minutes tick away. Garrett's desperate mission is to neutralise Dur's deadly countdown — the ultimate ecological disaster, Chernobyl on the high seas.

# THE SECRET AGENT

## Rafe McGregor

Two days after September 11, 2001, an intelligence officer from the South African Secret Service arrived in Washington, D.C. Three months later he was responsible for the arrest of Richard Reid, the notorious British *al-Qaeda* operative ... A series of short stories follow secret agent Jackson from Boston to Oxford, Quebec City, the Italian Alps, and his final and most deadly mission four months after his premature retirement.

# THE PRICE OF FREEDOM

## E. C. Tubb

When his wife is murdered, the victim of an assassin's bullet, businessman Dell Weston soon finds his life is falling apart. Betrayed by his partner, he loses control of his company, and descends into the lower strata of a dog-eat-dog society. Somehow, Dell manages to survive long enough to question the very fabric of civilisation — and the role played by the mysterious figures in grey — the Arbitrators . . .